THE BARN

Rachel McLean writes thrillers that make your pulse race and your brain tick. Originally a self-publishing sensation, she has sold millions of copies digitally, with massive success in the UK, and a growing reach internationally too. She is the author of the Dorset Crime novels, the Zoe Finch novels and the spin-off McBride & Tanner series. She is also the co-author of the Cumbria Crime series and the London Cosy series. In 2021, she won the Kindle Storyteller Award with *The Corfe Castle Murders* and her last five books have all hit No1 in the Bookstat ebook chart on launch.

Joel Hames is a Lancashire-based writer of crime fiction, and the editor of million-selling books across multiple genres. Joel's own works include the Dead North series featuring lawyer Sam Williams, and the psychological thriller *The Lies I Tell*. Most recently, he has been working with titan of crime fiction Rachel McLean on the hugely successful Cumbria Crime series.

ALSO BY RACHEL MCLEAN AND JOEL HAMES

RACHEL McLEAN
JOEL HAMES

CUMBRIA CRIME BOOK 4

THE BARN

ACKROYD PUBLISHING

Ackroyd Publishing

ackroydpublishing.com

Printed and bound in the UK by CPI Group (Uk) Ltd, Croydon CR0 4YY

CHAPTER ONE

AT LEAST THEY'D been lucky with the weather.

For the last three months, Pat hadn't shut up about the forecast. Half a dozen different websites and apps, historic rainfall levels, the effect of global bloody warming. When she'd finally declared that late September was their best bet for a dry night, Carly hadn't believed her.

There was no science to it. They were in Cumbria, and the only thing you could be sure of was that if it wasn't raining now, it would be raining later. Late September was nothing more than a guess.

But the thing about guesses was that sometimes they were right. They'd been hiking by moonlight for three hours, from Thackthwaite, right over Fellbarrow. Apart from fifteen minutes of light drizzle at the start, it had been a dry night after all.

Ambling more than hiking, really, and ambling in the wrong direction mostly. But Pat wasn't the only one who took her abilities more seriously than they deserved. Joanne was on maps, and Joanne would have struggled to find her way out of a paper bag.

Which was why Carly had suggested a shortcut, even if it wasn't a marked route. Cut west over some private farmland, and soon enough they'd be on the road and just a short trot from where she'd left her car.

Except there was light in the sky ahead of them. Dawn wouldn't come for hours, and they were heading west, so it wasn't that. But whatever it was, it was stronger than streetlights, which shouldn't have been ahead of them any more than the rising sun. Stronger than anything you'd expect to see around here.

Heading west shouldn't have been much of a challenge, even for Joanne. But Joanne had fucked up again.

"This can't be right," said Pat, stopping a dozen yards ahead of them. Pat was faster than Joanne or Carly, her long legs making easy work of the uneven ground. The full moon was better than nothing, but it hadn't stopped a few stumbles from Carly and a lot of complaining from Joanne, who'd hardly looked up from the map for the last half hour. It was no wonder she kept falling.

"It is," insisted Joanne, catching up. Carly reached them a moment later. "I promise you, this is west. Just over that hill there's a barn, and half a mile past the barn we'll find the road."

The road was one of those tiny routes without a name, winding between farms until it ended in either a lake or a bigger road. If Joanne was right, this one would lead them to Mosser, where Carly's car was waiting for them.

If Joanne was right.

Carly looked up past her friends. The moon was to her left now, huge and cold, but the light ahead was warmer.

And it was flickering.

"Guys," she said.

Pat was already talking. "Give me that map."

"No." Joanne took a step back and folded her arms defensively over the poorly-folded paper.

"Guys," Carly repeated, a little louder.

"Seriously," said Pat. "Show me where you think we are. Because there shouldn't be anything that bright round here."

"Machinery," replied Joanne. "It's just a bunch of tractors, isn't it?"

"Can you hear any tractors?" countered Pat.

They fell silent, joining the silence of the countryside around them, a silence of no tractors, but a silence broken by a noise of a different sort, the sound of wind punctuated by bangs and cracks.

"Guys," said Carly, a third time. "I think it's a fire."

She strode ahead, the others following, until she reached the top of the hill.

And then she started running.

She could hear them behind her, their footsteps pounding the ground. Pat had almost caught up already, while Joanne was breathing heavily and lumbering behind but still pushing on.

Joanne and Pat were a pair of bloody idiots, but they were her friends, and they were the sort of people who'd see her running towards a burning building – *a barn*, Carly corrected herself, glancing over to see that confirmed by a sign on a wooden fence – and run after her.

"Slow down," panted Joanne.

Carly ignored her.

Because she wasn't running towards a burning building.

She was running towards the figure she'd seen just a few yards from the burning building.

Without breaking stride, she turned her head back in Joanne's direction and shouted.

"Call an ambulance!"

When she looked back, the figure was raising itself onto its elbows. Looking in her direction, possibly startled by her call.

It's the shadows. The shadows from the fire, and the moonlight.

A face couldn't look like that.

She reached the figure a moment later, just ahead of Pat, and bent down, to see that she was wrong.

A face *could* look like that after all.

It was so many different colours. White and black and brown and pink. That must have been from the burns. The man's clothes – it was a man, she thought, but couldn't be sure – were smouldering rags. She could see skin the same colours as his face in the places where it had burned away entirely.

And there was something else, too.

She edged closer. The man was shaking his head. But it didn't look like a voluntary movement. It looked like...

No.

She could hear Joanne behind her, talking on the phone, relaying their location. *Fell Barn*, the sign had said.

The shaking grew more intense. Carly could see the blood, could feel drops of it land on her own skin as he shook. She sensed Pat, crouching beside her, looking on in silence.

But her attention was entirely on the man.

There was so much blood. From a few feet away, she'd been too appalled by the burns to see anything else.

But this man hadn't just been burned.

He'd been cut.

She was watching a man in the act of dying.

The shaking subsided, suddenly. Carly reached forward and placed her hands around the man's hand. She watched his face, hoping against hope that she wasn't too late, that he was alive, that in the moment before he died, he'd feel something, know that he wasn't alone at the end.

His face went slack. She looked back as Joanne finally caught up with them, talking on her phone, then falling silent.

"Jo," she said, without looking around.

"Yes?"

"Tell them they'll want to bring the police with them. Whatever this was, it wasn't just a fire."

CHAPTER TWO

"THAT WAS THE MORTGAGE BROKER," Carl said, putting down the phone.

Zoe raised her eyebrows in surprise. She couldn't say anything – her mouth was still full of pizza – but Carl knew her well enough by now to hear the implied question.

How come a mortgage broker's working at this time of night?

"He's on commission," he said. "He'll work long hours until everything's signed, and then he'll probably disappear. But that's OK."

Zoe nodded and swallowed.

"So?" she asked, her hand dropping. Her cat, Yoda, was curled up beside her, mewing gently.

He smiled. "Turns out experienced police officers with decades of service between them are seen as a good risk."

He took a sip from his beer. She returned the smile and stroked the cat, trying to ignore the thoughts racing through her head.

It was all good. They were looking into buying a house

together, finally, here in Cumbria. Zoe liked her team, liked the job, didn't hate the politics as much as she'd feared. Even her boss, Detective Superintendent Fiona Kendrick, wasn't all that bad.

And then there was Carl. She loved Carl.

Of course she loved Carl. If she didn't love Carl, she wouldn't have moved up here with him in the first place. She certainly wouldn't be contemplating moving out of the perfectly comfortable rented property in which they'd been living for the last year, and into something else, something that would mean putting down roots.

But she loved Carl. And the fact that they were still arguing about Kay, the civilian who'd been seconded to Zoe's team and then questioned and thrown out of the police by Carl's team, well, that was to be expected. Carl's job was to investigate the police and the people who worked with them. It brought the two of them into conflict from time to time. Just because Zoe thought Kay was innocent, or mostly innocent, just because she'd been frozen out, not just by the official investigation, but by her own partner... It was a professional disagreement. That was all.

And things were going well. For more than a month they'd played host to Elena, a woman who'd been trafficked to the area and needed somewhere safe to recover. But now Elena was staying with Nina, a DC on Zoe's team. And then Nicholas had turned up with his new 'person.'

Zoe smiled as she recalled the few days the couple had spent with them, most of it in Nicholas's tiny room, but emerging every now and then for food and sometimes even conversation. Fox had been shy, but pleasant, and definitely intelligent. And they seemed to make her son happy, which was the most important thing.

"So what d'you think?" Carl was frowning at her. She realised he'd asked her twice, and she still didn't know what he was talking about.

"About what?"

"About the house." He shook his head. "The one I sent you earlier?"

Zoe nodded and shrugged at the same time. "Sorry. I haven't had a chance to—"

"That's OK." He reached across, encircling her waist. "Plenty of time for all that. Trouble at work, then?"

Zoe shook her head. "Not really. Still trying to get approval for the forensic accountant, but Fiona says she'll have an answer soon enough."

"You're sure this isn't something you can do yourself?"

Zoe laughed. "That's what Fiona said. Apparently I have a reputation as a numbers woman."

"You've done it before," he pointed out.

"That was different."

And it was. She'd cracked the Canary case back in Birmingham, because the financial side of it had involved three companies and half a dozen people, and she'd not been a DI at the time. She'd not had the responsibility of running a team.

The empire she was looking into now was different. Myron Carter's business was a sprawling mess. Every time she looked at it, there were more people and more companies involved. Given time, maybe she'd crack it by herself.

But unless every criminal in Cumbria decided to go clean for a month or two, she wasn't getting that time. And besides, a forensic accountant would spot things she couldn't. She had a knack for that sort of work, but it wasn't her job.

Zoe felt a nibble on her finger and looked down. Yoda was staring up at her, disappointment written across her face.

She'd been neglecting her stroking duties. She shook her head and got back to work just as Carl spoke.

"Here." He was pointing at his phone, a photo of a house. A white terrace, the sun shining on the paintwork.

It certainly looked pretty. She watched as he scrolled through more photos. Interiors. Bedrooms. A huge, art deco bathroom that had her mouth falling open in surprise. A tiny back yard dominated by a hot tub.

"It's different," she said, when the slide show had finished.

"Different good?"

"Yes." She leaned towards him. Just as she decided she could risk ignoring the cat for a while, she heard her phone ring, from the kitchen table.

She'd come so close to being relaxed. She'd managed not to think about David Randle for almost the whole evening, but all it took was one phone call, which wouldn't be from Randle anyway. Now there he was, front and centre, dominating everything. Just like he'd done when he'd been her boss.

Randle had been exposed as corrupt, had gone into the Protected Persons programme, or more informally, witness protection. He'd disappeared from her life so completely he might never have been in it, if not for the memories.

But then he'd started calling her. Leaving messages. He'd told her he knew where she was.

It was ridiculous, all of it. Carl had heard those early messages and insisted she report Randle for breaking the conditions of his witness deal and for what had sounded very much like a threat.

But she'd talked him round. And then Randle had gone silent, and that had been the end of it, as far as Carl was concerned.

Because Zoe hadn't told him about the more recent calls. The calls in which Randle mentioned Myron Carter. The calls in which he even offered advice.

Would this be him again, now? Would she have to lie again? Pretend she was talking to her DS, Aaron? Or Lesley, her old DCI?

She forced herself to stand and walk to the kitchen, feeling Carl's gaze boring into her back. In the kitchen, she made herself turn to face him as she answered the phone. *Unknown number*.

"DI Finch?" She heard a female voice.

She sighed with relief. "Yes?"

"There's been a report of a murder. Up near Mosser."

Zoe swallowed.

"It's near Loweswater, Ma'am. About half an hour from the Hub. Uniform are on their way, but I thought, if it is what it sounds like..."

If it *was* what it sounded like, then Zoe would want her people on the scene before anyone else made a mess of it. Forensics, too. She took down the details, thanked the woman, and returned to Carl.

"Don't wait up," she said. "I've got a feeling this is going to be a late one."

CHAPTER THREE

It wasn't difficult to find the place; she just had to follow the orange light in the distance and the beams of blue and white light from the patrol cars. But by the time Zoe parked, a hundred yards from what must once have been a barn, the fire was mostly out. The crew from Frizington Fire Station was split into one group dousing the remaining flames, and another checking the structure.

DS Aaron Keyes was waiting as she got out of the car and donned her forensic suit. Aaron was the slowest, most cautious driver she'd ever come across. How had he got here before her?

"I was in the area, boss." He led her across a patch of short grass to where two other people were standing.

Zoe raised an eyebrow.

"Finally made it, have you?"

"Good to see you too, Stella. Caroline."

Stella Berry was Crime Scene Manager for the Cumberland area of Cumbria Police. She stood beside her subordinate, Caroline Deane, the two of them staring out towards the firefighters. In the light from the dwindling flames, Stella's peroxide-blonde hair shone even brighter than usual.

"What have you got?" Zoe asked.

"We're waiting till these guys tell us it's safe," Stella replied. "But they've already told us there was accelerant."

"So not an accident," Aaron pointed out.

Stella turned towards him, shaking her head. "If you'd seen the dead guy, Aaron, you wouldn't be talking about accidents." She jerked her thumb to the side, where a body was being loaded onto a gurney. They'd called Zoe as she drove and asked for permission to move it before she arrived. It was that, or nothing more than a pile of ashes for the post-mortem.

"I didn't mean—" Aaron began, but Zoe stopped him and led him away.

"Don't worry about it. You know Stella likes to wind people up. What have we got?"

"Chris Robertson's with the body," he told her. Dr Robertson was the area pathologist, one of the increasingly rare breed who insisted on viewing bodies at the crime scene. "Uniform are with the witnesses, but I've had a quick chat with them already."

Zoe could see them in the flickering light: two women sitting on the ground and a third standing and talking to a uniformed officer. Over all four loomed a huge shadow, complete with arms and legs and even a squat round head.

Zoe smiled. PC Roddy Chen was back on duty, then.

Chen had been badly injured just a few months earlier. If Zoe was pleased to see him back on duty, she was doubly pleased to see him paired up with Harriett Barnes. PC Barnes had been devastated by Roddy's injury. She might have broken the heart of one of Zoe's team, DC Tom

Willis, but she seemed like a good person and an excellent officer.

Zoe had been informed about the witnesses as she drove to the scene. Night hikers, apparently. People who walked the fells in the dark, when they couldn't see the majesty of the landscape, which was supposed to be the whole point of walking around here.

And they'd stumbled across a fire and a dead man. How likely was that?

"Does anything they say add up?" she asked.

Aaron nodded. "All of it, boss. I've taken preliminary statements, but I've also seen their photos."

"Photos? Of the dead man?"

"Of their walk. Shots from when they left, the trees, the fell, all of it. Times on the photos tally with their statements."

"They took photos?"

He nodded.

"Of what? The darkness?"

"Pretty much, boss. It's a thing round here. People do it. And, well, at least there's a full moon."

Over the previous year, Zoe had grown to grudgingly appreciate the Cumbrian views. She'd never be a true lover of nature, the way Carl was, but she could just about see how other people might be. But doing those same walks by night sounded ridiculous.

"You're sure?" she said.

"Sure as I can be, boss." They'd reached the ambulance. Zoe peered past Dr Robertson at the body he was leaning over.

She took a step back.

In her years as a police officer, Zoe Finch had seen a lot of dead bodies, in varying states of injury or decomposition.

She hadn't seen many to rival this one. There were what looked like stab wounds around the face, but the burns were the worst of it. She could see where the skin had peeled and blistered.

Whoever this man was, she hoped he'd died quickly.

She waited as Dr Robertson raised himself from a crouching position with a grunt. Perhaps the years were finally catching up with him. She listened as he told his assistant how to load the body into the ambulance, and found herself smiling underneath her mask, in spite of the circumstances, as he answered her questions with patience and encouragement.

In public, Chris Robertson had a reputation: a man who treated his assistants with contempt, who never remembered their names, who referred to them interchangeably as his "lad," regardless of age or gender.

She reckoned a lot of that was an act.

He turned and noticed her. She dropped the smile.

"Nasty one, this, Zoe," he told her. "PMs going to be a bugger, but we'll get what we can. Here's what I can tell you now, though. The fire didn't kill him. It might have done, but it was the stab wounds that did for this poor fellow. If I had to guess, he was driven out of this barn by the smoke, then stabbed and left to bleed out."

"How confident are you?" asked Zoe.

The pathologist shrugged. "We'll know more later. When Stella's had a poke around. Oh, and there's nothing on the body. No ID. Nothing."

"Is it possible," asked Aaron, standing behind Zoe, using her body to shield himself from the sight of the corpse, "that we're looking at the arsonist?"

Zoe turned.

"What do you mean?" asked Dr Robertson.

"Could he have set the fire, then somehow got trapped inside?"

The pathologist grunted. "I see your point. And I suppose then he stabbed himself just in case he wasn't feeling rough enough." He walked away, shaking his head.

"I understood what you meant, Aaron," Zoe said. "And I'm sure Chris did too. Yes, he might have lit the fire. And then someone else might have stabbed him. It's a good theory. No worse than anything else we've got, at least."

"Clear!" Zoe heard from behind her. She turned again, to see the last of the flames gone and two firefighters walking back from the remains of the structure, approaching Stella and Caroline with their palms out.

It's all yours.

Something about all this didn't add up. The barn had been a derelict building before it was a smouldering husk. There shouldn't have been anyone there. No one to stab, no one to get stabbed. No one to light a fire.

Zoe hadn't seen a car, or cars. Whoever this person was, how had they got here?

Hopefully the CSIs would find something. In the meantime, Zoe had some night hikers to meet.

CHAPTER FOUR

IT WAS NEARLY four by the time Aaron turned his key in the door. Dawn wouldn't come for hours, but he thought he could see the sky lightening over the fells.

Probably just the memory of the flames.

He pushed open the door and headed straight for the kitchen. He filled a glass with water, tasted it, and ran the tap again until it was cold enough.

There was a noise from upstairs. He stopped, the glass halfway to his lips, and waited until it came again.

A child's cough. Annabel, again.

Had he woken her? He'd been back all of two minutes, clattering around with a glass. He hadn't even bothered to shut the kitchen door. Or had he done it on purpose, without knowing it, hoping to take out his anger on Serge?

But Serge was still asleep, by the sound of it. And there was no more coughing. Annabel was asleep, too.

Aaron stripped off his clothes and entered the living room. The duvet was arranged neatly on the sofa. Maybe he'd grab a couple of hours' sleep before work.

More likely he'd lie there, turning from front to side to back again, wondering where his life had gone wrong and whether it was too late to put it all back together again.

Aaron wasn't sleeping on the sofa because he'd been out late, working, and didn't want to wake his husband and daughter when he got back.

He was sleeping on the sofa because Serge and he couldn't spend more than five minutes in the same room without breaking into the same old arguments. And even when those arguments weren't happening, they were still running through Aaron's head.

Just that evening, when they'd been running Annabel's bath. Earlier the same day, when Aaron had got back from work to find Serge and Annabel sitting in front of a cartoon he'd never seen, laughing together about something he didn't understand. That morning, in the kitchen, when Aaron had gulped down a coffee and prepared to rush out just as Serge walked in, his face buried in the technical specifications for his latest piece of hardware.

Was that where it had all started?

Earlier in the year, Serge had lost his biggest client and decided to try something new. Drones. He'd buy a pair of state-of-the-art drones and set up a video business. Aaron had made encouraging noises, until he'd found out just how much a pair of state-of-the-art drones would cost. And then he'd tried to carry on making encouraging noises, ignoring the cost and the fear that built up inside him.

Possibly he'd been too convincing, because Serge had decided to 'surprise' him with a family holiday in Provence.

As usual, Serge didn't do things by halves. The holiday would have cost even more than the drones, which he'd been playing with for weeks by then, without a single paying customer and without any clear sign of one, either.

The fear had won out in the end. Aaron had insisted Serge cancel the holiday, insisted he *grow up, get a grip, remember he was responsible for a family now*.

The arguments had been compelling. They were running through money like water.

If he'd not said anything, they'd be in Provence now, basking in the sunshine. Annabel would be running through fields of lavender. Serge would be smiling as he drained a bottle of local wine. Aaron would be watching the euros flying from his wallet and trying not to say anything about it.

He shook his head, trying to banish the image, and sank onto the sofa. It wasn't that uncomfortable.

The least he deserved.

Two days after the holiday had been cancelled, Serge's first client had turned up. A week later, his second. By the end of the month the business was thriving, and now, just a few months after flying his first drone, Serge was making more money than he ever had as a web designer and was talking about taking someone on to help manage the work he was having to turn down.

Aaron pulled the duvet up over his head, squeezed his eyes shut, tried to think of something else, but he couldn't. Just Annabel in that field of lavender and Serge with that bottle of wine.

Serge had succeeded. He'd done what he'd set out to do, what he'd assured Aaron he'd be able to do, and all Aaron could think of was the way his husband had risked their family, their future, their stability.

That, and the fact that Serge had been right.

CHAPTER FIVE

Emma shivered.

She didn't know if it was cold, fear, or tiredness, or something more serious. Could it be the smoke? Had she been in there long enough to inhale enough of the stuff to make her ill?

She hadn't coughed for an hour. Maybe longer. She didn't know how long she'd been out here, staggering through the woods. She'd heard the sirens, seen the blue lights cut through the darkness, but she'd been miles away by then.

And then she'd lost her bearings. For all she knew, she was back where she'd started.

Still, at least she hadn't coughed for a while. And if she felt one coming on, she'd stifle it.

Because it didn't matter if she felt like shit. It didn't matter if she was cold or scared or tired or even if she'd burnt her lungs, not really.

The only thing that mattered was keeping quiet.

Staying invisible.

Making sure what had happened to Neil didn't happen to her.

She stopped and looked around. Trees to her right, open fields to the left. Full moon, still. She didn't have to use her torch or her phone. She clutched her battery pack. Save it for when she needed it.

But the full moon meant he'd be able to see her. And in open fields, he'd see her all the easier.

She headed right, into the trees. Had she seen these trees before?

Maybe he'd gone. The police had been, and the fire crew, and the ambulance people. Surely he'd gone when he'd heard them coming?

But she couldn't risk it. And what was the point? They'd have found the body by now.

Neil. They'd have found Neil by now.

She stopped, leaning against an oak. She screwed her eyes shut and saw it again: one man on the ground, the other squatting over him, plunging down with a knife.

She couldn't have done anything. She was sure of that. Neil was dead, or as good as, and had been since before she'd decided to run. Going back to check on him wouldn't have helped him or her. It would just have meant she'd be dead too.

Had the killer looked up while she'd watched him murder Neil? Had he seen her?

The darkness seemed thicker. She flicked on the torch, just for a moment, grateful that she always brought one to these things. Torch and phone and a fully charged battery pack.

But she hadn't been prepared for this. For the smoke. The flames. The screams. For Theo, staring at her, at Neil, as they tried to put the fire out, then turning and running. For the sound of the engine as he took the car and fled, leaving her and Neil to...

To die, in Neil's case. To die.

Moving on again, she stopped.

Was that a noise?

She waited. It came again, a crack, the sound of pressure on wood.

Of feet on sticks.

She focused on her breathing. Slow. Quiet. She waited.

There it was, again.

She ran blindly, the torch useless in her hand, the light of the moon filtering through to the ground in sharp, narrow fingers, in daggers, in knives, leaving blood on the earth, on the...

She stumbled, felt something fall, righted herself, kept running. It didn't matter. Nothing mattered except getting away.

She ran on, into the woods, or out of them, she didn't know which, until her breaths were coming so fast and so loud she felt sure the killer would hear her. She stopped, finally, and flicked the torch on and off again. She held her breath.

There was nothing. No sound but the gentle breeze through the trees above her, and her own breathing. Nothing to see but darkness, and in front of her, something solid.

Another barn? Something smaller. Not much more than a shed.

But there was a doorway. Another abandoned building. Only this one wasn't on fire.

She stepped inside, keeping the torch low, her fingers over the beam so that it illuminated just the patch of ground in front of her. She moved it upwards. Walls. A ceiling. It was basic.

But it would do.

She sank to the ground, and before she could figure out whether sleeping here would be a good idea, she felt her eyes falling shut and the decision was no longer hers to make.

CHAPTER SIX

ZOE WALKED into the team room. It wasn't yet eight, but they were in already, all three of them.

Tom stood as she entered. Aaron was a second slower. Was it her imagination, or did he look pale?

Nina was staring at her screen and didn't notice anything for a moment, not until Aaron cleared his throat and said, "Boss."

She swivelled her chair to face Zoe and gave a nod.

"Boss," repeated Aaron. "I've briefed Nina and Tom on everything from last night."

"That's good." Zoe nodded and went to sit at the spare desk. She'd fallen asleep within minutes of getting home last night, and she'd slept deeply, but not for long enough. "I'm still waiting to hear from the pathologist and the fire crew, but as Aaron will have told you, we're looking at accelerants for the fire and stab wounds for the death, so any notions you've got about bad luck and accidents, you can chuck them out the window."

Her right hand, which was moving idly across the desk,

made contact with something. A scrap of card. What was it doing there?

"I've been through the CCTV, boss," said Tom.

Zoe squinted. "What CCTV? It was a derelict barn."

"A derelict barn on the edge of an actual working farm," he corrected. "If you're heading to the barn, you've got to come off the main road by the farm, and the rest of the buildings, and they've got CCTV there. Usual reasons."

Usual reasons meant rural crime: opportunists stealing machinery, quad bikes, sometimes fuel. Zoe's hand closed on the scrap of card.

"Find anything?" she asked.

"I started from a few hours before the fire was reported, and I've already got a hit."

"Go on."

"Two cars. Plates are visible. They both head past the main farm building just under five hours before the call came in from the hikers."

"Where else could they have gone? Other than the barn, I mean?"

"Nowhere, boss. I mean, they could have stopped in the middle of nowhere. Could have gone on past the barn, a quarter mile or so, but there's nothing. Nothing there at all except fields and that barn. And no other way out. It's a dead end."

"I didn't see any cars there," Aaron pointed out. "Just the ones we know. The pathologist's, Stella's van, the ambulance, a patrol car, and a fire engine."

"I jumped forward," said Tom, "to see if I could spot anything heading back. It's not that clear, coming the other way, but I've found one of them. Heads back about an hour before the call from the hikers. No sign of the other one. I'll get back to it, though. Might have missed something."

Zoe nodded. "Have you run it through the PNC?"

"Next job on the list," Tom replied, as Nina's phone rang.

The DC looked down at the display and answered with the speakers on, mouthing the word 'Stella.'

"DC Kapoor," came the familiar voice.

"Stella. I'm here with the team. DI Finch, DS Keyes, DC Willis."

"Great," grunted Stella. "The whole Addams Family. Well, we've managed to recover some samples from the fire. Not a lot. The fire crew wouldn't let us over the whole site, so we'll have to return later to see what else we can get. But I've got some initial findings for you from what we do have, and it's interesting."

"What is it?" asked Nina, and Zoe nodded. Over the last few months, Nina had increasingly taken the lead on liaison with the CSIs. Nina and Stella seemed to rub each other up the wrong way, but Stella rubbed most people up the wrong way – and it was Nina she'd chosen to call, without being told to.

"Drugs, Nina. Traces of cocaine and cannabis. And by 'traces' I mean shitloads. If that poor bastard had stuck around in the building instead of heading outside to get himself stabbed, he'd probably have overdosed before he choked to death."

Zoe leaned forward. "He was stabbed outside, then? You're sure of that?"

"Blood on the ground says yes, Zoe."

Zoe saw movement in the corner of her eye. Tom had

stepped forward, a gleam in his eyes, his hands shifting in excitement.

"Stella, that fire, the other one," he said. "You know, the one at Cawter Hough, cocaine, burnt-out barn, it's—"

"Tell your puppy to calm down, Zoe," Stella shouted from the other end of the phone.

Zoe looked at Tom, eyebrows raised.

"Sorry, boss," he muttered.

Stella sighed. "We're aware that you were looking into a barn fire earlier this year. We're aware that the investigation wasn't a priority. We're aware that there are similarities. We might not be strutting around the Hub locking up murderers, but we're not idiots, Tom. Caroline's already retrieving the material from your old fire. I'll call you when we have anything else."

The phone went dead. Zoe looked up at Tom.

"Back in May," he explained. "There was another barn fire. Cawter Hough. Derelict, not that interesting, only there were traces of cocaine there, too. Didn't think much of it at the time. But now..."

Zoe nodded. Now things were different.

She glanced down at the scrap of card in her hand, deciphering the edge of a letter, forming them, in her head, into the logo of a well-known brand of cigarettes.

For a short while, this hadn't been a spare desk. It had been Kay's desk.

And Kay was one of the tiny minority who smoked real cigarettes.

Even now, months after she'd been fired, Kay was making her presence felt.

CHAPTER SEVEN

"So, no leads, then, is that right?"

Detective Superintendent Fiona Kendrick, Zoe's boss, looked at her through narrowed eyes, her head tilted to one side. Everything about the question, from the words to the tone of voice, should have set alarm bells ringing.

But it had been a year. Zoe was used to Fiona's little tricks.

"No leads *yet*," replied Zoe. "I'm confident my team will unearth something."

There was no criminal so smart they wouldn't leave a clue. If there was physical evidence, Stella would find it and analyse it and her team would figure out what it meant. If they didn't leave a physical clue, Nina and Tom would find something else: CCTV, a phone record, something about the victim that would lead back to the person who'd killed him.

"Good." Fiona nodded, smiling. "That's not what I called you up here for, though."

"No?" Zoe had been summoned to the super's office

upstairs within seconds of reaching her own desk. She'd
assumed Fiona wanted an update on the investigation.

"I've got news for you. Your forensic accountant."

Zoe sat forward and waited.

"The request has been approved."

"Thank you, Fiona. Who knows about it?" Zoe knew
better now than to call Fiona by anything other than her first
name.

"Nobody. Well, you, me, and the Chief Constable, if
she's bothered to read the memo before signing it. Even
Finance doesn't know what they've just granted the budget
for. And there's no reason for anyone else to find out. A lot of
secrecy, Zoe."

"Thank you," Zoe repeated. "And as for the secrecy, well,
that's the thing about organised crime. The better organised
it is, the more links it has with the police. I can't risk—"

"Yes, yes, I understand. You can't risk your colleagues
finding out until you know for certain which of those
colleagues you can trust. But it's funny you mentioning
organised crime, Zoe. Ralph Streeting would probably want
to know about this."

Zoe found herself staring at her boss, conscious of her
heartbeat.

Ralph Streeting probably *would* want to know all about
it. Partly because, as a DI in Specialist Crime and Intel,
organised crime was his territory. But mostly, Zoe was
convinced, because he was passing information onto Myron
Carter, the businessman who seemed to be running the
whole show.

"Are you planning on telling him?" Zoe asked after a
moment's silence.

She'd seen enough corruption in Birmingham to know it

would be up here, too, however green the hills, however clean the air. And Streeting had failed almost every test she'd set for him. She'd implied she had evidence off-site connecting Carter with the murder of his employee, Victor Parlick. That location had gone up in flames overnight. Fiona didn't know about that, but she did know about Streeting's more recent attempt to muscle in on Zoe's investigation into the murder of a local fell runner and amateur accountant. Zoe hadn't realised why Streeting was interested at the time, but it turned out the killer had been stuffing his so-called hair salons with women trafficked through the local port.

A port controlled by Myron Carter.

The killer in question, Dean Somerville, had made payments through a web of companies in the UK and the Cayman Islands, coming to rest in another local business. Jenson & Marley Offshore Services. Which was also owned by Myron Carter.

All of which explained not only why Zoe needed a forensic accountant, but, more importantly, why no one could know about it.

Least of all Ralph Streeting.

"No," said Fiona, finally. She had been watching Zoe carefully, in silence, for nearly a minute. "No. But I'll expect you to keep me up to date on your progress."

"Of course."

"And I hope Alistair's still being helpful."

Zoe resisted a smile. She didn't know what the relationship was between her boss and Alistair Freeburn, but whatever it was, it had worked to Zoe's advantage.

When she'd first come across Freeburn, he'd been a typically obstructive lawyer. Unsurprisingly, he'd worked for a number of clients who interested Zoe. More surprisingly, following the intervention of Fiona Kendrick, he'd been both able and willing to help her. It had been Freeburn who'd given her a link between Dean Somerville's hairdressing business and Myron Carter's company.

"I'll need to speak to him," she told Fiona. "Hopefully, he'll be prepared to work with the forensic accountant."

"Just let me know if he isn't," Fiona replied, then nodded. *You're dismissed.*

CHAPTER EIGHT

"That's odd," said Tom.

He ran the check again. Same result.

"Have you seen this?"

The sarge was staring at his screen and gave no sign of having heard. Nina sighed and stood up from her desk. "Struggling with the computer again, are you?" she asked. "Come on then, what's got that gigantic brain all confused?"

"It's these cars," he said. "Just surprising, really. Here are the registered owners."

He pointed at his screen, to two names. Theo Georgiou and Neil Colvin. Two driving licence photos alongside them. Theo was dark-haired, the hint of a smirk playing across his lips. He was good-looking, by driving licence photo standards, at least. Neil was sandy-haired, his face rounder, wearing the fixed stare of someone who'd been told to look serious.

"Theo's from Nottingham," he explained. "But the address for Neil Colvin comes up as Burnley. Both twenty years old."

"And you find that surprising?"

"Just seems unusual. Them being from two different places, then showing up here. What are the odds?"

Nina smiled at him.

"What?" he asked.

"Don't you know?"

"If I knew, I wouldn't have asked."

She nodded. "OK. Here's the deal. They're both students. Right age for it. And what you've got there are the home addresses. Not where they're studying."

"OK," Tom replied. "That makes sense. But you've got more, haven't you?"

"A bet."

And there it was. A bet. And there was only ever one stake. The antimacassar. The hideous piece of cloth Nina's mum had created, with a motif supposedly representing a gull eating a mackerel, which looked like something a disturbed child might have nightmares about. It was currently draped across the back of Nina's chair, but anyone in the team who took on a bet knew what they were risking: the loser had the antimacassar until they managed to win another bet.

But backing down wasn't good form, even when you didn't know what the bet was.

"Go on, then," Tom said.

"I bet you I know what they're studying."

He shook his head. "I'll buy the possibility that they're students. That makes sense. But how can you know what they're studying?"

"Try me. Look them up."

He turned back to his computer as she walked over to her

desk. He heard her typing quickly, and she returned as he heard the ping of an email hitting his inbox.

"Right," he said. "Neil Colvin, Lancaster University. Theo Georgiou at UCLAN in Preston. And they're both studying Chemistry."

He clicked on Nina's email.

It read, 'Chemistry, loser.'

"How did you know?"

"What did Stella say this morning?"

"Apart from when she called me a puppy?"

Nina laughed. "Yeah."

"Cocaine," Tom replied. "Cannabis. Oh."

Suddenly, it was all clear.

"Chemistry students," he said. "They're the ones who know their drugs. So Neil and Theo weren't just getting high last night."

"Long way to come for a fix. No. Whoever these lads are, they're involved on the supply side."

Tom stood and made his way to Nina's chair. He lifted the antimacassar and draped it over his shoulders as he returned to his own desk, where he removed it and dropped it over the back of his chair.

The sarge had turned, finally, and was watching as he did this, but didn't seem to find the whole thing funny. He was frowning.

"Everything OK, Sarge?" asked Tom.

No reply. Not even a twitch.

"Sarge?" he repeated.

DS Keyes blinked and offered a weak smile. "Yeah, yeah, all fine, Tom. All fine."

CHAPTER NINE

ANOTHER STUPID BET, then.

Aaron had been wondering for a while when the boss would put a stop to it, and had been surprised when she'd joined in. That hideous piece of cloth had adorned DI Finch's office chair for weeks before she'd got rid of it. Meanwhile, the DCs were clowning around, leaving him to do the real work.

Which was fine. Doing the real work meant he didn't have time to think about anything else. About Serge, and whether he owed his husband an apology. About Annabel, and whether the mood he'd been carrying around with him had turned him into a bad father.

Had he ever been anything other than a bad father?

He turned back to his screen, where he wouldn't find the answer to that question, but might find something else. Within thirty seconds, he had.

There was another car. No. Two more cars.

"Tom," he called. The DC stood and approached, Nina a step behind.

"What's up, Sarge?" asked Tom.

"Why did you stop looking at the CCTV?" Aaron asked.

"Sorry?"

"When you found those two cars. Yes, that was good work, but you said you'd spotted one heading back."

"I skipped to the point where the fire engine showed up and worked backward until I found Theo Georgiou's car heading back again."

"So you've got a name, then."

"Yeah. Both of them. Chemistry students. But the CCTV..."

Aaron rubbed his eyes. "Yes, Tom. Look, both of you. It's good that you've found something. But you don't just stop and head off. You keep looking. There're other vehicles on the footage. You find them, too. Make a note of which one went in which direction, and when. And then figure out which ones you need to track first. It's about priorities."

Tom was looking at the floor. Nina met Aaron's gaze.

"Yes, Sarge," said Tom. Nina nodded, but Aaron couldn't miss the fraction of an eyeroll.

He deserved that.

"Anyway, look. I've got two more vehicles. We've got a flash little one. Maybe an Audi TT. Drives past the camera not long after your two. Then heads back half an hour later." He enlarged the image, frozen on his screen, so the registration plate was clearly visible. "Nina. See what you can find on that one."

"Got it, Sarge," she said, and returned to her desk.

"The second one looks like a Land Rover. Look." He brought up the vehicle and enlarged the image.

"I think it's a Defender, Sarge," said Tom.

Aaron nodded. "Maybe. Anyway, this one's very close to

the TT, but unlike the TT, it doesn't seem to come back. Disappears the same way your..."

"Oh, yeah. Neil Colvin."

"Right. Disappears the same way Neil Colvin's did. Maybe these two are involved in something together. See what you can find out about the Land Rover, anyway."

Tom hadn't even made it back to his desk when Nina started swearing.

"Fuck's sake, Sarge. Look at this."

Sighing, Aaron got to his feet, feeling cracks in joints he'd never felt before.

He wasn't yet forty. He'd always been fit. His nights on the sofa weren't doing anyone any good.

He peered over Nina's shoulder at her screen. There was the request, the TT's plates, Nina's warrant number underneath it.

Below it was a message he hadn't seen before.

Unable to complete search request. Please try again later.

"Let me have a go." He leaned over and typed in his own number.

Same result.

But there was something else. He returned to his desk, brought up the image of the TT, enlarged it again, and stared at it.

Had he seen that car before?

"Have you seen this error message before?" he asked Nina, without looking round.

"No, Sarge. But I've seen plenty like it. System's fucked. Too much data, not enough security, so every now and then it gets a bit above itself and locks everyone out."

"Not me," said Tom.

"Eh?" asked Aaron, still staring at the image of the Audi, wondering where he'd come across it, or if he'd just imagined it.

"This one, Sarge. The Land Rover. Defender. It's stolen."

CHAPTER TEN

THE GOOD MOOD the meeting with Fiona had put Zoe in lasted precisely one minute and thirty-eight seconds, which was the amount of time that elapsed between her closing the super's door behind her, and turning a corner on the way to the team room downstairs and walking straight into Alan Markin.

DI Markin was short and bald, with a habit of wearing tight-fitting clothes that revealed more of his pasty stomach than Zoe cared to see, but it wasn't his appearance or his dress sense that bothered her. She'd never been entirely sure of the man's competence. Lately, she was worried about more than that.

"Sorry," said Markin, stepping aside with exaggerated courtesy, but slowly, like a man struggling with his limbs. Zoe didn't know his age, but she had the feeling it was a lot less than the sixty-plus he looked.

"You OK, Alan?"

"Yeah."

She could see the veins in his nose, the dryness of his lips. He didn't seem keen to elaborate or return the question.

"I've been meaning to ask you," she continued. "Did you ever find out about that woman?"

"What woman?"

"Vicky Speares. The one who attacked Roddy Chen. Did anyone ever work out how she died?"

Markin frowned. It hadn't been that long ago. Months. He couldn't have forgotten already, could he? After a moment, his expression cleared.

"Yeah," he said. "That one. Choked on her own vomit."

Zoe nodded, slowly.

"Classic junkie," added Markin, then turned and walked away.

In the team room, she listened patiently while Aaron complained about the glitch in the system that was preventing them from identifying the sports car. She tried her own authorisation code and was presented with the same message: *Unable to complete search request. Please try again later*.

The fact that the Land Rover had been stolen came as little surprise, but now there were two cars that had driven up that farm track and not come back down it. Zoe wasn't an expert on cars, but if there was one thing she knew about them, it was that they didn't just disappear. And when they looked like they had, it was usually because someone was trying to hide them.

"We'll need to find those vehicles," she said. "Nina, can you..."

She stopped, her attention snagged by the images she'd just spotted on Tom's screen.

"Who's this?" she asked.

"The drivers of the first two vehicles," Tom replied. "Theo Georgiou." He pointed to the slender, dark-haired one. "And Neil Colvin," he continued, indicating the other. "Both chemistry students."

Zoe stepped closer, examining the photograph of Neil Colvin.

"Aaron," she said. "Does this man look familiar?"

"I'm not sure," Aaron replied, stepping closer. "Oh."

The image was of a healthy young man, in the prime of life, a photograph taken in the security of a well-lit room with a roof and walls. Very different from the last time they'd seen him.

But still. Zoe was surprised Aaron hadn't recognised him. Her DS had been off his game lately.

"Neil Colvin," she said, turning to face her team, "is our victim."

There was a moment's silence, followed by the sound of typing.

"Right," Nina announced. "Neil's on the system. Intent to supply. Late last year. Slap on the wrist, four hundred quid fine. No record for Theo, though."

"There was coke and cannabis at the scene," Zoe said. "And you say Neil was a chemistry student?"

Tom nodded. "Both of them. Neil's studying – sorry, *was* studying – at Lancaster University. Family home's in Burnley. And Theo's a student at UCLAN in Preston."

Zoe checked her watch. It would be a long drive, there and back. But it might be worth it.

"OK. Tom, I'm heading down there."

"There?"

"Burnley. Get onto Lancashire Constabulary, let them know what's happened, tell them I want to see the family.

They'll want an FLO and whatever else they use down there. They can break the news before I get there. Nina."

"Yes, boss?"

"The other one. Theo Georgiou. Track him down and tell him to come in."

"When you say 'tell him,' you mean a voluntary interview, right?"

"Yes. But under caution."

Nina nodded.

"He probably already knows his mate's dead," Zoe continued, "but if he doesn't mention it, don't tell him until he's in the room with you. I don't want him disappearing before he's had the chance to tell us everything he knows."

CHAPTER ELEVEN

"Is this Theo?"

There was silence on the end of the line, before a male voice gave an uncertain, "Yes?"

Theo Georgiou hadn't been hard to track down. Nina had thought she'd have to use police resources to find him, or at least make some delicate enquiries at the university, but no: thirty seconds online and she had access to his phone number and address, three different emails, and more photos than most people had taken in a lifetime. Maybe it was a generational thing, not that Theo was too many years younger than Nina herself.

Or maybe Theo just had no sense of privacy.

What he did have were nerves. A whole truckload of them. Just that one word, 'Yes,' with its rising intonation, was saturated with them. She'd have to tread carefully.

"Theo, my name's Nina Kapoor, and I'm a detective constable with Cumbria CID."

She waited. She could hear him breathing, fast, then slow

again, like he was trying to steady himself. But he said nothing.

"We're looking into an incident that took place at a barn near Fellbarrow last night, and I understand that you were in the area."

"Fellbarrow?"

"It's a hill, Theo. Between Mosser and Thackthwaite. Either of those names ring any bells?"

"Erm..."

"Listen, Theo. I'm a police officer and I'm asking you to come and talk to me. Now, it's entirely up to you whether you're going to do that or not, but for now, this is all voluntary."

Silence.

"For now," she repeated.

"OK," said Theo Georgiou, with what sounded like fear poorly disguised as bored resignation. She gave him the address, and he told her he'd drive straight over.

Ending the call, she looked over at Tom, who was still on the phone with Lancashire Constabulary. Behind him, the sarge was staring at his screen again, frowning, muttering to himself. She couldn't hear what he was saying, and she'd never been much of a lip reader. But whatever it was, it was the same word, over and over again.

The sarge hadn't been himself lately. Maybe a drink would sort that out. A drink sorted most things out.

Her next call would have been to the fire station to ask about the two missing vehicles, only they called her first, to say they'd found them.

"Found them?"

"Old Defender, even older Astra?"

Nina checked the team inbox. Neil Colvin had been

driving a Vauxhall Astra, light blue, 57 plate. Even older than the Fiesta she drove.

"Where were they?"

"In the woods a few minutes' walk from the barn. Badly burnt, both of them. If your forensics people want 'em, they can have 'em, but not sure there's gonna be much to look at."

"Any sign of occupants?"

"No trace of anything. Sorry. No people, no other cars."

Nina thanked the woman and ended the call.

Two vehicles abandoned in the middle of nowhere. The Astra driver they knew about. Neil Colvin was dead. What about the Land Rover driver? Whoever they were, they might have left with the little TT, the one they still couldn't trace. Or maybe Theo had given them a lift back. She'd ask him when he turned up.

Or maybe the Land Rover driver had shared Neil Colvin's fate. Just because the fire crew hadn't found another body yet, didn't mean there wasn't one.

Or maybe...

It was always possible the Land Rover driver had walked to the main road and got transport from there. A friend. An accomplice. But you couldn't find a friend or an accomplice if you didn't know who the person was.

A cab, then.

There was a list of cab companies, both the licenced operators and the less formal ones, on the system. Nina picked up her phone again and dialled the first number.

CHAPTER TWELVE

Zoe drove through the Lakes, the sun high enough not to blind her.

She could do this. She could put aside the rest of it – Kay Holinshed, David Randle – and just enjoy things.

Couldn't she?

Her phone rang. No number. Which meant it could quite easily be Randle. Or it could be someone trying to sell her a boiler.

It turned out to be neither.

"DI Finch."

"Olivia. How've you been?"

"Still alive. If you can call it living."

Olivia Bagsby had been in hiding for almost a year now. She'd been an artist – still was, as far as Zoe knew. She took photographs of scenes, to capture the moment, before recreating them on canvas. She'd been in Workington, painting landscapes around the port. And as bad luck would have it, she'd taken the wrong photograph of the wrong moment.

Olivia had got out before Myron Carter's people could

get to her, and she'd been one step ahead of them ever since. One step ahead of Zoe, too, who wanted to keep her safe, and wanted whatever it was she'd captured on her camera. If Carter was so keen to get hold of it, it would be valuable. Incriminating.

But to Olivia Bagsby, it was just dangerous. And Zoe's promises to keep her safe weren't worth a thing. Because Olivia knew about Ahmed Hosseini, the man Zoe had previously known as Ahmed Iqbal. The man who'd gone into witness protection, but still been tracked down and killed by the same people looking for Olivia now.

"Listen, Olivia—"

"No, Zoe. It's your turn to listen. Can you do that?"

"Yes."

"I've had enough."

Zoe bit back her words, which would just have been more of the same: *come back, we'll keep you safe, at least let me see the photographs.*

There were a few seconds of silence as the road curved around a sheer rock face. Zoe worried she'd been cut off, but then Olivia spoke again.

"I can't live like this. I want to be able to sell my work. To move about like I used to. I used to be a free spirit, Zoe. Now I'm wrapped in chains."

Zoe was surprised by the tone. She'd known Olivia to be an artist. Maybe the misery of life in hiding was turning her into a poet, too.

"Then come back," Zoe told her. "Come to Cumbria. I know—"

"There's no point either of us pretending you can keep me safe. You want me there so you can get Carter locked up, but I won't be safe until he *is* locked up. Something of a catch-22, isn't it?"

Zoe couldn't argue with that.

"So yes, I want to break Carter. But I won't come to Cumbria. You're going to have to figure out some way that I can, Zoe. Because I can't go on like this. You nearly found me. If you can, he can. Eventually, I'll slip."

"So come—"

"No, Zoe. You're good. I like your persistence. I like the way you think, but no. That's not why I've called. I've called to say that yes, I'm willing to help you. But not if it means putting myself in danger. It's up to you to figure out a way to keep us both happy. That's all."

"Olivia, I—"

Zoe stopped. The line was dead.

Not far to the motorway, now. She could drive in silence, digest what Olivia had just told her. She could talk to Aaron about it, because Aaron was the only other person who knew about Olivia, and it had been him more than anyone who'd almost found her.

But Aaron wasn't himself. Not at the moment. And what Olivia needed, it wasn't possible, was it? If she had evidence on her camera, then she'd need to be on the spot to present it. Photos were useless without the testimony of the person who'd taken them, all the more so in the age of digital image manipulation.

Zoe sighed and pulled over. There were other people she knew who'd come up against Myron Carter and lived to tell the tale. Two of them, in fact. And she had phone numbers for both.

But Ryan Tobin's phone just rang out. And Fatima

Coutts-Brennand had disappeared. The number was no longer recognised.

Zoe started the car again and drove on, towards Burnley and a family who'd be hearing, even as she joined the motorway, that their son was dead. She focused on the traffic, and the problem Olivia had posed. She tried to convince herself that 'no longer recognised' didn't mean anything, that it was just a change of number, nothing more sinister than that.

She wasn't so sure.

CHAPTER THIRTEEN

EMMA OPENED ONE EYE, saw more light than she'd expected, and shut it again. Her mouth felt like someone had sanded it. Where had she been last night? What had she been drinking?

She gave herself a moment, lying there on her back with her eyes closed, gradually feeling the shape of the world around her.

Had she crashed on someone's floor? Where the hell had she been?

She opened an eye again. Saw the brown of wood and the green of tree and grass. Where the hell—

Fuck.

It came back in a rush, from the first sniff of smoke to the desperate run through the trees. She didn't know how long she'd been here, sleeping, but she'd woken several times to the sound of rain, animal noises, things that had her jumping up and then falling back into sleep before she could do anything about them.

And that had just been the real things. Owls and the fucking rain. The things that weren't real, the nightmares, the flashbacks— How she'd gone back to sleep with all that running through her head, she had no idea.

Fucking Theo, though.

He shouldn't even have been there. Some boyfriend he'd turned out to be. When she got hold of him...

She felt in the pocket of her jeans, found nothing, looked to the side and located her phone.

One bar of 3G. Enough, even if the battery was down to 12%. She waited for him to answer.

Voicemail.

"Pick up the fucking phone, Theo," she said. "We need to talk."

Her voice sounded scratchy. Had the smoke caused any permanent damage?

Beside her phone was the torch. Beside the torch, purse with keys, and—

No keys. The purse was empty, just a few coins. She'd left her handbag in the barn, and she doubted there was any of the barn left. But at least she had the battery pack in her pocket.

She checked her pocket again.

Nothing.

She remembered stumbling, feeling something fall, not stopping.

Fuck. She'd lost it. She grabbed her phone, turned it off, laid back down.

She could call her contact. He'd know what to do. He'd been there, like always, to hand over the product and run through the procedure, like she hadn't done this a dozen times, like she didn't know it back to front. Her and Neil.

Just her, now.

Only, was her contact safe? Had he known this would happen? If she called him, would he stick a knife in her the way the other man had stuck his knife in Neil?

Fucking Theo, though. What a waste of space. He wouldn't have been there if she hadn't needed his car when hers wouldn't start. He'd been on and on at her to get involved. Always hated being left out of anything.

At least he'd stayed in the car when they'd turned up. Waited for her contact to arrive, waited for him to leave. But talk about freaking out. The moment that first puff of smoke appeared, he was out of there like a shot. She was trying to put the fire out, Neil was trying to put the fire out, and Theo's legging it out to the car and driving away like the useless coward he was.

Safe to say that relationship had run its course.

Mind you, Theo had the right idea. He didn't have to see what happened to Neil.

She closed her eyes, tried not to remember. The two of them, Neil and Emma herself, fighting the flames. Trying, but what did they have? A couple of bottles of water. Some rags. The clothes they were wearing.

Eyes meeting from across the room, shouting.

It's not working.

Get out.

Neil at one end of the barn. Emma at the other. She emerged and there he was, looking around, and a moment later, there was someone else with him.

For half a second she'd thought, *Thank fuck, it's Theo, he's brought the car back.* But it wasn't. He hadn't.

She screwed her eyes shut, but it wouldn't stop.

Two men. Neil on the ground. The other man over him.

The knife.

The blood.

She opened her eyes, crawled to the doorway, and vomited.

CHAPTER FOURTEEN

HOWEVER MANY TIMES Zoe did this, it didn't get any easier.

At least she hadn't been the one to break the news, though.

Neil Colvin had left behind a mother, Pauline, a father, Barry, and a tiny little yappy dog that sat on Pauline's lap and interrupted every silence with a sharp bark that only Zoe seemed to notice or care about.

The Colvins lived in a neat end-of-terrace house on a side street between Burnley and the town of Padiham. Even inside, she could hear the faint rumble of trucks on the M65, when the dog wasn't drowning it out, at least.

"Would you like a cup of tea?" asked the Family Liaison Officer, a well-presented woman in her twenties who was nearly as tall as Zoe.

PC Ayton had been left behind once the news had been broken by a sergeant from the local station, and Zoe had the sense that she wasn't really there to find anything out, but rather to make sure the Colvins were OK.

Of course they weren't OK. Their only child had just been murdered. But it was nice that someone seemed to care.

"Not for me, thanks," Zoe replied, and turned back to Pauline and Barry.

Pauline was patting the dog, muttering to it. When Zoe had arrived twenty minutes earlier, Pauline had been standing in the hallway, her long, blonde hair a dishevelled mess, her mouth hanging open, the paths of her tears picked out in red and white on her cheeks. At one point, she'd disappeared and then come back no more than two minutes later, her hair and makeup returned to something like working order. Since then, she'd acted as if everything was normal. Sitting there, muttering to her dog.

Barry leaned over her, muttering his own platitudes. Every now and then he would turn to Zoe and say something like, "I don't believe it, Detective Inspector. I just don't believe it," and she'd have to smile understandingly, and nod, and act like this was just one of those everyday things.

Neil hadn't just been the golden child. He'd been the only child.

Now he was gone, and it didn't look like Pauline or Barry were in a position to help Zoe figure out why. Neil's friends were all away at university, except the ones who weren't, like Rick, who worked at the big Tesco, and Stevie, who'd landed a job at Turf Moor.

"Lucky bastard," muttered Barry. Zoe wasn't sure whether this was in reference to Stevie working at a football club or Stevie not being dead.

Neither of them knew much about Neil's university life.

"He'd been doing so well," Barry told Zoe, then stopped and frowned. "At least, I assumed he was. He never told us much, see?"

Zoe saw. She had her own son, Nicholas, away at university, telling her important things only when he remembered to. Which was usually months after they'd stopped being important.

She thanked the Colvins, and PC Ayton, and gave all three her card and told them to get in touch if they wanted anything.

They wouldn't. The Colvins wouldn't be identifying the body, given the state of it, so they had no reason to come up to Cumbria, and Zoe didn't think she'd have much reason to return to Burnley.

She'd keep in touch with Pauline and Barry Colvin. Regular contact was part of the job, and she knew how important it was to the victim's family. But they wouldn't have anything useful to tell her. She was all but certain of it.

CHAPTER FIFTEEN

THEO GEORGIOU WAS at the Hub less than two hours after Nina had called him, which meant either he hadn't been in Preston when they'd spoken earlier, or he'd broken the speed limit driving over.

Nina wasn't going to raise the issue.

As things turned out, she wouldn't have been able to anyway. Because Theo Georgiou, six foot three inches of dark, brooding prettiness, was all but shaking with fear from the moment Nina walked into the interview room. Along with the fear came the babbling.

"I didn't do it, I... It's not me, right," he said. This was before she introduced herself and well before she'd had the chance to sit down and caution him. They were in Interview Room Four, the comfortable one with the upholstered chairs. Probably a good thing. If they'd put him in Two or Three, he'd have fallen apart.

"Theo," Nina began, but the boy was still talking.

"Look, it's Emma you need to talk to. All this, it was her thing, not mine, I was just... I just gave her a lift."

There was a spaniel-like appeal in his eyes, a desperation that made Nina want to slap his nose and tell him to shut up, but then, she'd never had much patience with needy men. She couldn't slap him, of course.

"Theo," she said, louder this time. He fell silent, while she explained what was about to happen, cautioned him, and asked him if he minded providing his prints and a DNA sample.

"I... I don't know. Is that kind of thing normal?" he asked.

"It's normal in a murder investigation," Nina told him.

His eyes grew even wider. "A murder investigation?"

"Your car was at the scene of a murder last night, Theo. Why did you think you were here?"

"I... Well... I don't know," he said, shrugging, as if being summoned halfway across the country to talk to a police officer was the sort of thing that happened to him every day. "I... Was it... I," he continued.

Nina finally took pity on him. "Did you think it was about the drugs?"

He nodded. "The drugs."

"Right," Nina continued. "So can you tell me precisely—"

"No."

"I'm sorry?"

"I want a lawyer. You said I could have a lawyer, right?"

So he'd been listening. Sometimes she wondered if they heard a word of all that stuff at the beginning. But Theo Georgiou wasn't a police station regular. All this was new to him. Every word mattered.

"You can have a lawyer if you like, Theo, but as I mentioned at the start, you're not under arrest."

"I don't care."

He laid his palms flat on the table and stared at her.

Theo Georgiou had picked a hell of a time to grow a backbone. The boss wouldn't like it.

But at least he wasn't walking out and driving himself back to Preston, which he could have done if he'd wanted to. Nina left him sitting in Interview Room Four while she went off to organise a lawyer and took the opportunity to phone the boss.

She'd been right. DI Finch didn't like it.

"What did you say to him?"

"I'm sorry, boss. It was when I mentioned the murder. But I don't think I could have questioned him without him knowing what it was about. I reckon—"

"No. You're right. And at least he's there. He might give us something, even with a lawyer in the room. As long as it's not Basham."

Nina shuddered. Stan Basham was something of a regular at the Hub, and seemed to enjoy winding up the police a lot more than he enjoyed doing effective work for his clients. But it wouldn't be Basham. Basham hadn't been around for a while, now she came to think of it.

"Do me a favour, Nina," said the boss. "Get me a name and address for someone I can talk to at UCLAN. Theo's university. Tell them I'm heading over now. I can drop in on my way back from Burnley."

"Will do, boss."

"If Theo doesn't want to tell us anything, maybe someone else will be a little more forthcoming."

CHAPTER SIXTEEN

UNABLE TO COMPLETE SEARCH REQUEST. Please try again later.

Aaron had called IT and got the response he'd expected. Did he have the right credentials? Had he typed the plates correctly? Had he – and this one had him staring at the phone in fury – had he tried rebooting?

"Yes," he told them. "Yes, to all three."

"We'll look into it."

Which meant he was calling DI Finch with no news. But there was something else he wanted to talk to her about, and the more it preyed on his mind, the surer he was it couldn't wait.

"Aaron," she said. He could hear the rush of the wind, muffled then silenced as she closed her window. "Just hit the M65. What can I do for you?"

"Just wanted to update you, boss," he said, and went on to tell her they still couldn't trace the sports car and they didn't have any leads on the Land Rover driver.

"Right. So nothing new, then?"

DI Finch sounded irritated. Impatient. And she hadn't been forced to listen to someone suggesting she reboot.

Should he tell her the real reason for his call? He was sitting in her office, alone – this wasn't something he wanted Nina or Tom to hear. Would spelling out his fears just make him seem paranoid? Or was it something she needed to know?

"Boss," he said, swallowing. "There's something else."

"What is it, Aaron?" Her tone had changed to something like concern; she must have heard the change in his.

"It's... Well, I don't know if you're aware, but a few months before you arrived at the Hub, we had a murder case."

"Egremont Castle. I've read the reports."

Of course she had. She probably knew everything he was about to say. He wasn't just making himself look like a fool. He was wasting time.

He pressed on.

"That's right. Noah Cane. Local dealer. Or former dealer, really."

"Does the distinction matter?"

"Yes. That's the point, boss. Part of the investigation meant looking into the local drugs scene, picking up other dealers for a chat, finding out what they knew."

"That's what I'd expect."

"But they were gone, boss."

"Gone?"

"Half of them had disappeared or moved away. The ones that were still in the area had gone straight – and if I didn't believe them at the time, I do now, because they haven't shown up on our radar since."

"Sounds like," said the boss, then stopped. "Oh. They

won't have disappeared without being replaced. It's not like no one in Cumbria takes drugs."

"Exactly. And when we spoke to a couple of the former dealers, they didn't say much, but one thing they did say was that there had been supply-side issues."

"Supply-side issues?"

"That's why they stopped dealing. They shut up after that, wouldn't say anything else, but it's the sort of thing that sticks in the memory."

"Yes." There was a pause. "Why are you telling me this now?"

"Well, the barn. Cocaine and cannabis. I'm wondering if there's a link. If we've stumbled across that missing supply."

"That's not why you're calling me, Aaron. You could have told me that later. Could have gone through it with the DCs and then reported your discussion."

Aaron swallowed again.

"It's the super, boss. I went to tell her about all the missing dealers. Back then. All of it. There was no way it could just be the good news story everyone seemed to think it was."

"She'd have figured that out for herself. What did she say?"

"She said it was all in hand and not to worry about it."

"Right."

"And something else. She said DI Streeting was handling it."

The silence that followed his remark seemed heavier than all the ones that had preceded it.

The boss was taking it seriously. The missing dealers. The *supply-side issues*. The fact that Streeting, a man they both knew was working hand-in-glove with organised crime, was *handling it*.

"Let me ask you something, Aaron," said DI Finch. "Do you suspect the super? Do you think she's involved?"

For the second time in half an hour Aaron found himself staring at his phone, but this time it was in disbelief rather than fury.

The super? Was the boss really asking him if he suspected the super of being corrupt? He'd worried *he* was being paranoid, but he'd never gone that far.

"No," he said. "No, boss. I think she's straight. But I do wonder..." He hesitated. "I wonder if she's being played, boss."

"By Streeting?"

"By Streeting," he agreed. "And possibly by whoever killed Neil Colvin."

CHAPTER SEVENTEEN

MARYAN KHALIL WAS WAITING for Zoe outside an enormous glass-and-metal building that reminded her of the Hub. This place, though, was in the centre of a city and teeming with people, most of them so young Zoe kept having to remind herself these were adults, not children.

She hadn't realised UCLAN was so big, and certainly hadn't expected a place like this: a square surrounded by modern buildings and gardens and what looked like a Victorian church on one corner. She'd been forced to park nearly ten minutes' walk away and navigate by her phone, but that was the one part of this experience she had expected.

The sun was out, at least, and the walk gave her the opportunity to think about what Aaron had just told her.

Missing dealers. Hadn't Carl asked her something about that a few months back? He'd wanted to know what the situation was like, locally, in terms of dealers, but she hadn't been able to help him. She'd been so busy trying to keep ahead of Streeting, she hadn't really given it much thought.

And it had been that same night they'd picked up the

first message from David Randle. So it was hardly a surprise that Carl's question had slipped her mind.

But now Aaron had brought it all back again, and Zoe couldn't help wondering if Carl knew more about the local drugs scene than she did herself.

Zoe wouldn't have picked out Maryan from the crowds of students milling about – the woman didn't look much older than her charges, and was certainly no taller – but she didn't have to. She could hear her own name being called from halfway across the square.

"I thought perhaps we could talk outside," Maryan said, "given the weather. I don't know what it's like where you come from, but a little sunshine is a rare blessing here."

"I live in Cumbria these days," Zoe replied. Maryan tilted her head sympathetically and steered her towards a kiosk where the two women equipped themselves with coffees.

Maryan Khalil was a welfare officer, which meant she probably knew a lot more about the student body than most of the academic staff. She was short, with mid-length brown hair, and dressed in more browns and a little grey. She would have been entirely unprepossessing if it hadn't been for her smile, which she'd aimed in Zoe's direction as she called her name, and which might have lit up the square if it hadn't already been bathed in sunlight.

"Is it true, then?" asked Maryan. They'd found a bench, and although they might have been overheard, Zoe didn't think any of the students milling around them had the faintest interest in listening to the conversation.

"Is what true?"

"Theo's been arrested? There are rumours flying around."

"No," Zoe told her. "At least, he hadn't been arrested last time I spoke to my colleagues. He's been invited in to have a conversation, and he isn't proving willing to talk, so I thought I might see what I could learn here."

"And what makes you think I'd be willing to tell you anything, if Theo isn't?" Maryan asked, her tone still friendly but her gaze steely. "My role is to look after the students here, DI Finch. If Theo doesn't want to talk to you, then—"

"Someone died last night," Zoe said, and Maryan's smile fell away. "Someone was murdered. Right now, Theo isn't a suspect, but we know he was in the area at the time, and we know there are drugs involved. In your role, you'll have had plenty of dealings with the police. So you'll know I wouldn't even be telling you this much if it wasn't important."

Maryan nodded, sharply. "OK. What do you want to know?"

What Zoe wanted to know was what Theo was like, in general. Whether there had been any indication of drug use, or dealing, or any other cause for concern. Whether there was any connection between Theo Georgiou and Neil Colvin. And anything Maryan might know about Emma, the woman whose name Theo had spilled, before he'd gone quiet.

Maryan had never heard of Neil Colvin, but Zoe hadn't expected her to. But she had a wealth of information about Theo himself.

Theo was a troublemaker, but of the minor variety. "It's not that he gets in fights or gets thrown out of places, like some of them do," Maryan explained. "But when there are drugs found, he's often in the area. And he... Well, after you called, I had a word with one of his tutors. Theo's not what you'd call a stellar student. If you want someone bright, you'll want Emma Hudson."

"Emma?"

"His girlfriend. Also a chemistry student here. Very clever, apparently."

"Where will Emma be, now? Can you take me to see her?" Zoe asked.

Maryan frowned.

"This is a murder investigation," Zoe reminded her. "Theo mentioned Emma, before he went quiet, so it's likely she's involved in all this, which means she could be in danger. Neil Colvin was another chemistry student, from a different university, but not far from here. He's been killed. For all we know, Theo's also a target, but at least he's safe in our station. If you're interested in Emma's welfare, you'll want to help me find her."

Another sharp nod.

"No lectures at the moment," Maryan said. "But she might be at home, and I can get her address. Where's your car?"

CHAPTER EIGHTEEN

THE THIRST GOT to her before the smell did.

She'd got through the first hour without so much as looking at the little heap of her own vomit just outside the doorway. Her phone was almost dead, and the inside of the building wasn't enough to keep her attention.

Outside, there were fields and trees. Outside, there was Theo, somewhere, with his phone and his car and the fact that he'd left her in the middle of nowhere, in a barn, on fire, which meant he owed her big time.

Outside, though, were the police. Outside was the man who'd killed Neil. Who she hoped hadn't seen her. If he had, would he know who she was? Where she was from?

She should call Mer and Ali. But her phone was almost dead.

The sun rose more quickly than she'd expected. It penetrated the barn, shed, whatever, and the shadows shortened.

And it hit the little heap of vomit outside the doorway, warming it and wafting the stench inside. She went from thinking *How long's it been since I've eaten?* to *I'm never gonna eat again* in a matter of seconds.

So she could ignore the hunger. The fact that her throat was still sore made it easier. But she couldn't ignore the thirst. She'd been thirsty when she'd woken, and then she'd been sick, and it was warm, and she didn't know where she was...

She should check. She should risk a bit of phone battery.

Sandy Beck. Cleaty Gill. It meant nothing. But she was north. North of where she'd been. They couldn't be there still, could they?

Maybe they could. The police. But *he* couldn't be there. Surely.

The smell grew stronger, but she could take that. The thirst was something different.

The sun was already past the middle of the sky by the time she ventured outside. When she thought back on it later that day, she reckoned she couldn't have been out there for longer than two minutes.

She was wearing a bright red cardigan. Maybe that wasn't so bad, when you were standing beside a building that was on fire and the bloke you didn't want noticing you was otherwise engaged, stabbing someone to death.

But here, in the daytime, it wasn't ideal.

Ten seconds there, then. Another five seconds to get her bearings and see the field. No animals in it, thank Christ, just a big stone basin in the middle of it, and it had rained in the night, hadn't it?

The grass was still damp. She hadn't imagined that, at least.

No cover, though. A stone basin surrounded by a field, but now it felt like someone hadn't just sanded her mouth, but sanded her throat, until it was sore and bleeding, then chucked a load of salt down after...

She ran. She found herself standing by a stone basin, a long porcelain sink, a trough. *Animals* had been drinking from it. But it didn't matter. She dipped her hand in and the water was cool. She curled her hand, scooped the water to her mouth and squeezed her eyes shut.

She tried not to think about all the *animals* that had drunk from here, and what sort of diseases they had. Tried not to see the wool matted with shit. The taste of water was like honey.

One scoop. Two scoops. Three. She could have stayed there all day. It didn't matter if anyone saw her because if she didn't drink more, her throat would fall apart like a rusty exhaust pipe, which was the reason Theo had been there in the first place. *Don't think about Theo.*

Four scoops. Five. Six.

What was that?

A noise. Not the wind. Not the distant sound of cars – and where had that come from, anyway?

She froze, the water dripping from her right hand back into the trough. She tried to listen.

"I don't think," said a voice, then faded.

Drip.

"I know what you mean," said another. One male, the other female.

Drip.

She strained to hear more. I don't think *what?*

I don't think she's here, the girl we've been sent to kill? I don't think she'll have got far, all we have to do is wait and eventually she'll show up?

Who were they? What did they want?

Drip.

She couldn't see them. Couldn't hear them.

Couldn't risk it. She turned and ran, back in the shed, no more than two minutes after she'd left it.

She collapsed inside, her throat still stinging, but less than it had before. The shivering started, even as she huddled against the broken wall. They'd been walkers, that was it, almost certainly it. Two walkers. A sunny day in the Lake District.

Almost certainly.

CHAPTER NINETEEN

EMMA HUDSON's house was a little way outside the centre of town, on a series of roads which alternated terraced houses with takeaways, bars and convenience stores. As Zoe parked, the memory of her old house in Birmingham flooded back. She'd been surrounded by the buzz of student life, and for all its drawbacks, she'd loved it.

Maryan had insisted on accompanying her, and Zoe could understand why. But now they were visiting someone's home, the home of a possible suspect, and this wasn't Zoe's territory. So the welfare officer had been forced to wait while Zoe contacted Lancashire Constabulary, and then wait a little longer while the local CID decided they had no interest in a crime committed a long way north of their jurisdiction, but agreed to despatch Uniform to keep her company.

To keep an eye on me, more like. But local police would be welcome.

The PC was waiting for them on the pavement outside number eighty-three. He was a huge beanpole of a man, but so young he might have been one of the students. His face bore the scars of teenage acne, and his smile did little to cover his anxiety.

"I'm PC Harrison," he said, extending a hand, then pulled it back abruptly. "I mean, PC Harrison, Ma'am, reporting for... For duty?"

Zoe gave him a smile.

"I'm DI Finch," she said. "This is Maryan Khalil, student welfare officer. We're here to talk to Emma Hudson, whose boyfriend is currently being interviewed by my colleagues in Cumbria. His car was spotted in the vicinity of a crime scene last night."

PC Harrison nodded, and Zoe stepped up the path towards the front door.

"What sort of crime?" he asked.

She stepped back onto the pavement.

"Murder."

His eyes widened. Zoe stepped towards the door again.

A minute passed before the door was opened by a blonde girl wearing pink pyjamas emblazoned with what Zoe thought might be Disney characters, adorned with accessories that she suspected the Corporation wouldn't have approved of.

A tall, menacing-looking woman was smoking a long, fat joint. A group of dwarves were leaning over a table, snorting powder through a rolled-up banknote. As for Dumbo, the selection of pills being hoovered up his trunk would have had him seeing a lot more than pink elephants on parade.

"Yeah," said the girl, her gaze sliding over Zoe's face, to Maryan, and past her to the uniformed PC Harrison. "Oh," she said, rubbing her eyes and looking only marginally more awake.

Five minutes later, Zoe was sitting at a small square table in a kitchen littered with empty bottles and cups in which the remains of cigarettes and roll-ups floated on the surface of unidentifiable liquids. Maryan sat beside her, with PC Harrison standing behind, trying to look unobtrusive. Opposite them were the blonde girl, Meredith, and another girl, Aliyah, also in pyjamas, albeit more conventional ones.

The stench of cannabis had hit them as soon as they'd entered the house, but Zoe had shot PC Harrison a look, and he'd kept quiet, looking around, attempting to fade into the background. Difficult, at that height. The girls were able to talk, if a little slowly, and Zoe had the feeling they hadn't taken anything that morning. But whatever they'd taken or drunk the night before was still working its magic.

"She's not here," said Meredith, when Zoe asked where Emma was. Aliyah nodded.

"Do you know where she is?"

Shrugs.

"Probably been out partying," Meredith replied. "Could be anywhere."

"Or with Theo," Aliyah drawled. "Her boyfriend. Gorgeous Georgiou. You checked him out?"

She winked at Meredith. The blonde girl laughed, briefly, then saw Zoe's expression and fell silent.

"She's not with Theo Georgiou, no," Zoe said. "But are you sure she's not here? Have you been in her room today?"

The girls looked at one another, then back at Zoe, both shaking their heads.

"I think we'd better take a look." Zoe rose and turned to PC Harrison. "We have reasonable grounds to believe there are illegal drugs on the premises, but more importantly, I'm concerned for Emma's safety."

PC Harrison nodded. Maryan started to say something, and Zoe turned to her, but the welfare officer stopped before she'd managed a full word.

Zoe wasn't against following the rules. Particularly when it came to searching people's houses. But if Emma Hudson wasn't here, then where was she?

Emma didn't answer when they knocked on her first-floor door. Zoe turned the handle.

Locked.

"Got a key?" she asked.

"No," said Meredith. Aliyah just shrugged.

Zoe explained what was about to happen, why it was about to happen, and how she had reason to believe it was necessary. A moment later the door was open, and PC Harrison was trying to look cool while nursing what Zoe suspected was a bruised shoulder.

Inside, there was no Emma, but there was exactly what Zoe had expected: an unmade bed, clothes everywhere, small plastic bags, scales.

Some of the bags had product in them already.

"We don't know anything about this," said Aliyah, standing in the doorway.

"It doesn't matter," Zoe replied, kneeling to look behind the bed. "Do you have any idea where Emma might be?"

"You lot probably know as well as we do," Meredith said.

Zoe straightened and looked round at her. "What do you mean?"

"I mean, she spends half her time with the cops, doesn't she?"

"She does?"

Meredith turned to Aliyah, who gave another of those shrugs Zoe was becoming sick of, then back to Zoe.

"Work experience or something. Dunno the details."

Maryan, who'd been silent since they'd entered the room, already had her phone out.

"Do you know anything about this?" Zoe asked.

"No," replied the welfare officer. "But I'll find out."

CHAPTER TWENTY

Aaron stared at his screen. Again.

Unable to complete search request. Please try again later.

Aaron had seen that car before. He was sure of it. He picked up his phone and called IT.

"Sounds like a glitch," said the woman who answered.

He'd heard that before. "What are you doing about it?"

"Calm down, Sir."

He was calm. "It's only a murder investigation. Nothing important," he said, and ended the call.

His phone was ringing before he'd put it down. The boss.

"Aaron," she said. "I've been round to Emma Hudson's place."

"Emma Hudson?"

"Theo's girlfriend. Place is full of drugs. Dealer quantities. No one knows where she is, though. And according to her friends, she works with the police."

"With the police?"

"Stop repeating everything I say, Aaron."

He blinked. He'd never had to struggle to keep up before. Tiredness. He was exhausted. And the DI was still talking.

"Yes, with the police. No one seems to know the details. I've got a welfare officer looking into it, but the whole thing's looking more complicated."

"Still can't track the sports car, boss," he said.

"Put that on the back burner for now," she said, her voice tight. "From what we've seen, I'm starting to think Fell Barn was being used as a drugs lab."

"Yes."

"So we've got a bunch of chemistry students doing whatever they do up there, then taking the stuff back with them and selling it. I'm going to stop at Lancaster University on the way back, see if I can find anything out about Neil Colvin, whether he was dealing there. Nina set me up with the welfare officer at UCLAN. Get her to work her magic at Lancaster too. And Aaron, you can forget about cars for a minute."

"I can?"

"Yes. I want you to focus on Emma Hudson. Find her."

Emma Hudson. DI Finch ended the call and Aaron found himself rubbing his eyes, then his temples. There was a headache on its way, on top of everything else.

Emma Hudson. Theo Georgiou's girlfriend. Missing.

Time to set some wheels in motion.

CHAPTER TWENTY-ONE

Zoe had just hit the M6 heading north again when the phone rang. No number displayed, and a shiver hit her.

"Zoe. How are you?"

Shit. This time, it really was David Randle.

"The usual," she replied, trying to keep the distaste out of her voice. "Knee-deep in dead bodies." Something of an exaggeration.

"Trouble does seem to follow you around, DI Finch. Have you made any progress with our mutual friend?"

Our mutual friend, in this instance, was Myron Carter.

Randle was in the Protected Persons programme, supposedly. As Detective Superintendent, he'd been organised crime boss Trevor Hamm's most valuable asset in the West Midlands police. But when the tables had turned, it had been his testimony that had put Hamm away.

But Hamm wasn't the only person with a grudge against David Randle, and Protected Persons wasn't the six inches of solid lead it should have been. Ahmed Iqbal knew all about that.

Myron Carter's network had tracked down Iqbal, and they could do the same to Randle. Until Carter was neutralised, David Randle wouldn't be safe.

"I heard from Olivia Bagsby," she said.

Randle sucked in his breath. "That's good, isn't it? Manage to persuade her to come up and testify?"

"No. She doesn't think it's safe."

Zoe could hear voices in the background, the bark of a dog, children arguing, a mother telling them to shut up. Randle was out for a walk, like a normal person having a normal conversation.

"She's not stupid, your Olivia Bagsby," he said. Zoe realised he'd waited until he was out of earshot. Not that the mother and children would have been a threat, or the dog, for that matter.

But you never knew.

"So why did she call?" he asked.

"She's willing to help, she says. She's had enough of being in hiding. But it's a catch-22. We need her up here to put Carter away, but she doesn't think it's safe to come up until we *have* put him away. And I can't really argue with her. She's not stupid."

It was extraordinary, the way she could talk like this to a man she'd have happily seen drowned in a well. It wasn't like she had cause to trust him.

But it was OK, this time. She knew what the angle was. He couldn't surprise her.

"The photos," Randle said.

"What?"

"Olivia Bagsby's photos. Ask her to send them to you."

"They're no use without her there, telling a jury how she got them. If we just show up in court with a bunch of photos someone's sent us, Carter's lawyer will rip us to pieces. You know that."

"Zoe," he said, after a pause.

"What?"

"Why did you become a police officer?"

"To put the bad guys away."

"Right. Sometimes, that's about getting evidence you can use in court. But sometimes it isn't. Sometimes it's about finding clues. Getting information to steer an investigation."

This was how he'd been, back in Birmingham. Patronising. How he'd been when they were investigating ACC Jackson's death together. This was why she'd despised him even before she'd suspected him.

Jackson. Yet another bent cop. Jackson, Randle, Streeting. Ian Osman, too, back on her team in Birmingham. Never mind knee-deep in bodies, it felt like she was knee-deep in cops on the take.

"I don't—" she began.

"No, Zoe. You don't. You don't have to decide between one and the other, between evidence and clue. Sometimes you just have to take what's on offer."

"Listen," she said. "I don't have to listen to this."

"You don't have to listen to me at all, Zoe. You can block me. Cut me off. Report me. But you won't, will you?"

He was right, but she wasn't going to give him the pleasure of hearing her admit it.

"You won't," he said, "because you need me as much as I need you. Now, I'm going to send you a number. You can't trace it, but if you need to, you can reach me on it. When you decide you want to talk again."

Silence.

She hated David Randle. She hated everything about him.

But no one would understand how Carter worked, how he pulled Streeting's strings and made him dance, the way David Randle did.

He was right. She needed him as much as he needed her. Probably more.

CHAPTER TWENTY-TWO

IF THERE WAS one thing worse than Stan Basham in an interview room, it was Stan Basham in an interview room when you hadn't expected him.

Tom had agreed to sit in on Nina's interview with Theo Georgiou, not because he wanted to, but because he wasn't doing anything else except waiting.

Had he done something wrong? He'd missed the Land Rover and the sports car, first time round, and the sarge had made him feel bad enough about that already. Was he being punished for that?

Or was it just that they didn't have enough leads to go round?

And now he'd walked in with Nina and found Stan Basham sitting next to Theo Georgiou. And not just Stan Basham. Stan Basham wearing a smile.

Tom didn't think he'd ever seen Stan Basham smile.

And—was that a tan?

"Ah," said Basham. "I see we've got the B Team."

"I beg your—" began Nina.

"Apology accepted. I suppose you'll just have to do your best."

Smile and tan aside, Basham didn't seem to have changed.

"Haven't seen you for a while," Tom told him.

Basham ignored him.

"I've advised my client here that he can go home," Basham said, looking at Nina. Tom forced himself to breathe slowly.

He wasn't a good lawyer. But if he had any skill at all, it was in getting the police so wound up, they'd slip up. Say the wrong thing. Make a procedural error. Something that rendered the interview inadmissible, and, if Basham was lucky, something that could trash an entire investigation.

Tom wasn't going to rise to it.

Nina wasn't, either. Tom listened as she commenced recording, reminded Theo he was under caution, and ran through the rest of the formalities. By the time they were ready to start, the tiny smile he'd forced onto his own face didn't feel quite so uncomfortable.

"What precisely do you want with my client?" Basham asked. "Only, I'm just back from Tenerife, and if I'd known I'd be walking into this crap I'd probably have stayed at the airport."

"We'd like to know what he was doing last night at or around Fell Barn," Nina replied. "We'd like to know what he knows about the fire there, and about the death of Neil Colvin."

Basham turned to Theo. In what looked like a move they'd rehearsed, the two nodded to one another.

"No comment," said Theo.

"We haven't asked a specific question yet, Theo," Tom

pointed out. Basham didn't look at him. Tom waited for a moment. "Why were you in the vicinity of Fell Barn last night?" he said.

Theo smiled. "No comment."

"Did you witness the murder of Neil Colvin?"

At least Theo stopped smiling. But it was the same reply.

"No comment."

They were interrupted by a knock at the door. Nina stopped the recording, and the sarge entered, bent down, whispered to her, and left.

Tom hoped it would be good news. Another lead. Something he might be able to work on himself.

Nina recommenced the recording and addressed Theo.

"Theo, we suspect you've been involved in testing and distributing drugs. I'm sure you can see this is an extremely serious matter. You'll be aware that you're under caution, and that you haven't been arrested yet. You'll also be aware that as serious as these potential drugs charges are, it's the murder of Neil Colvin we're interested in. So I suggest you help us."

Stan Basham leaned forward. "Are you planning on asking my client a question at some point, or are you just enjoying the sound of your own voice?"

Nina ignored him.

"Theo, can you tell me where Emma Hudson is?"

There was a moment's silence.

"No comment."

"She's not in her flat. Her flatmates haven't seen her. She might have witnessed the murder of Neil Colvin. She might be another victim."

A flicker of fear crossed Theo Georgiou's face, a twitch of the lips.

"What's this Emma Hudson got to do with my client?" Basham asked.

Nina turned to him and spoke slowly. "Emma Hudson is your client's girlfriend. When he arrived earlier today, he made reference to her." She picked up a sheet of paper and read from it. "'Look, it's Emma you need to talk to. All this, it was her thing, not mine. I was just... I just gave her a lift.'"

Basham looked at Theo. Theo gave a tiny shake of his head, and said, "No comment," again.

Tom shook his head.

"Theo," he said. "The only reason you're not under arrest is that we're hoping you'll cooperate voluntarily. If you're not going to help us, well, things change. Do you understand?"

Theo turned to him and shrugged. "No comment."

CHAPTER TWENTY-THREE

STUART ETHERINGTON WAS as different from Maryan Khalil as it was possible to be. Imposingly tall, grey-haired, and wearing a bow-tie, he had the air of a man who considered himself better than those around him, which didn't strike Zoe as entirely appropriate for a student welfare officer.

What sort of person performed the role for Nicholas? Had he ever had cause to meet them?

Shouldn't she know this sort of thing?

But then she saw that the bow-tie, black from a distance, was adorned with tiny pink butterflies clearly visible at close range. If you looked like Stuart Etherington did, and you wanted to make your charges comfortable, you'd have to do something to soften your appearance, she supposed.

"Shocking," he said, shaking his head. "I don't know how we're all going to get through this."

"You don't?" Zoe asked.

"We've had problems before. Every university does. But this? It's so violent. And I know it shouldn't make any difference," he added, leaning towards her so she found herself enveloped in a cloud of citrus aftershave, "but Neil was popular. So many young people who will be personally affected by this tragedy."

Neil Colvin's flatmates had certainly been personally affected. Zoe had met with the local force, made entry into Neil's room, and found an array of drugs, bags, and scales almost identical to the collection she'd come across at Emma Hudson's. The other occupants had been dazed – not drugged, but shocked. They hadn't even remembered to deny anything, so now Zoe had confirmation that Neil had been a dealer, but not on the sort of scale that usually got dealers killed.

From what she'd seen in her room, Zoe had the same feeling about Emma Hudson.

"But we'll get through it," Stuart Etherington told her. The meeting was taking place in his office. It was comfortable enough, and there was a cat, who'd looked up from the sofa when Zoe had entered, and pointedly refused to vacate it.

Zoe had picked the armchair opposite instead, and the cat had returned to its inscrutable business.

"What was he like?" she asked.

"Very bright," Stuart replied. "Well-liked, as I've said. Something of a star. The faculty adored him, the other students, too. He was even in a band."

Zoe had seen the guitar in Neil's room, under the Jimi Hendrix posters, beside the record player and all the Hendrix albums, and a collection of vinyl that must have cost nearly as much as his tuition. But then, Neil had his own way of funding his little Jimi Hendrix shrine.

Stuart was still talking. "He wanted to work with you lot, you know?"

"Us lot?"

"The police. I think he'd got himself on some sort of work experience scheme, but I don't know the details, I'm afraid."

His flatmates had mentioned it, but they hadn't known the details either. Just like Meredith and Aliyah, at Emma's flat. And Maryan hadn't called back yet.

"If you could find anything," Zoe said, "I'd be grateful."

She thanked him, and five minutes later she was heading north again.

Her phone rang before she'd hit the motorway.

"Jake," she said, "how are you?"

"Same old. I hear you've got a fire and a dead body."

"I don't know how... No," she said. "Don't tell me."

Jake Frimpton was a journalist, and journalists had their ways of getting information that she'd never quite understood. But Jake was a good journalist, a man who seemed to care about the community he wrote about. He'd proven himself time and time again.

And he was a friend.

"How's your dad?" she asked.

Solomon Frimpton was in the grip of dementia, and from what Jake had told her, it was getting worse on a weekly basis.

"Not much change," he told her. "Still finalising the accommodation."

"It'll get easier, you know. And he needs to be looked after by professionals. You've done all you can."

"I keep thinking about what's it going to be like when he finally leaves this house. He's been here most of his life."

"Is he going to make it difficult?"

A sigh. "I'm not sure he's even going to notice, Zoe. I'd rather he screamed blue murder about it, but I think he'll be meek as a lamb, and that's... Enough about me. How's Carl?"

"Fine," she replied, without really thinking about it.

"Listen, want to meet up later?" he said. "Just a catch-up?"

Why not? Jake was good company, and sometimes he knew things she didn't.

"Sure. Usual place at eight?"

"See you then."

CHAPTER TWENTY-FOUR

AARON LOOKED at the photo of Emma Hudson, smiling at the camera. It was the sort of smile people wore when they were told to, but there was life enough in the eyes.

He added the photo to the description and looked through it again. It wasn't enough. The photo was good, but he needed more detail, and the lack of information on Emma's clothing was bothering him. He picked up his phone and dialled.

"Yeah?"

"Meredith Bawcombe?"

"Who is this?"

She sounded half asleep, still. It had only been a short while since she'd been informed her flatmate was missing. A little concern wouldn't have been out of place.

"This is Detective Sergeant Keyes, from Cumbria CID. We're trying to find Emma."

"Yeah?"

Aaron sighed. "I was wondering if you knew what she might have been wearing when she disappeared."

"Nah, sorry, mate. Bye."

"Wait." But the line was dead.

The other flatmate, Aliyah, didn't even answer her phone. Aaron read what he had, stared at the photo again, just in case there was some obvious detail he was missing, and hit submit. Every police force in the northwest would be on the lookout for Emma Hudson.

He'd been putting off calling her family, and he managed to delay it another thirty seconds by running the search for the little sports car, with the same result: *Unable to complete search request. Please try again later*.

He picked up his phone again.

"Hello, who's calling?"

The voice was solid, reassuring. Southern vowels, but Aaron wouldn't hold that against him.

"Is that Mr Hudson?"

"It is. Who's calling?" repeated James Hudson.

"This is Detective Sergeant Aaron Keyes, from Cumbria CID. I was—"

"Cumbria?" The voice was sharp now. "What's this about? Has something happened to Emma?"

Preston wasn't far from Cumbria. The connection was inevitable.

"Mr Hudson," he said. "We're not aware that Emma's come to any harm," he said. Reassurance was important, avoid panic. But you had to get the words right. Too much reassurance would just be a lie. "We think she might have witnessed an incident in Cumbria last night, but we can't get hold of her, and I was wondering whether you'd heard from her in the last twenty-four hours or so."

"Twenty-four hours? No. What sort of incident? Is Emma OK?"

Ten minutes of ineffective reassurance later, and Aaron was confident that Emma hadn't spoken to her parents since she'd disappeared. All he'd managed to do was to terrify them, both of them – Mrs Hudson had picked up the phone halfway through the call and repeated her husband's scared, staccato questions.

The Hudsons lived in Reading: it was possible Emma had made it away from Fellbarrow and jumped on a train south. Her car had been found where she'd left it, on a side street a few minutes' walk from her flat. Aaron added British Transport Police and Thames Valley to the distribution list for her description, and tried the sports car one more time.

Unable to complete search request. Please try again later.

CHAPTER TWENTY-FIVE

Zoe tried not to stare too hard at Aaron as he slumped in the chair opposite her desk.

He looked terrible.

He'd been ill, a couple of months back, one of those summer colds that turned into flu. He'd missed their last murder investigation entirely. But he'd recovered, physically, at least. Only now he was pale and clearly exhausted.

"Are you OK, Aaron?" she asked.

"Of course." He nodded and tried to smile, but it looked more like a grimace. "So we've arrested Theo Georgiou, anyway. Drugs charges. He wasn't saying anything, and I didn't want him disappearing."

At least Aaron's instincts were still intact. They had more than enough to charge Theo, and they hadn't even been through his car yet. A little time in a cell might change his mind.

"Good work. I take it Basham's been as helpful as ever."

"So Nina tells me, boss. I let her deal with it, for the most part. I've got alerts out for Emma Hudson, and we're still not getting anywhere with the sports car."

Zoe frowned. This was getting beyond a mere glitch.

"Thanks. Meanwhile, I've got both sets of welfare officers trying to find out what Neil and Emma's so-called work experience entailed. If we can find out who they've been talking to within the police, maybe we'll get a better idea of where Emma might be."

"Assuming they didn't just make the whole thing up, of course."

"What do you mean?" Zoe said.

"Well, it would be handy, wouldn't it? You're caught out in some random drugs test, assuming they still do that sort of thing, and you can say it must be contamination from all that work you do with the police. Won't help if they go through your room, but it might buy you a little grace."

Zoe nodded. She hadn't even considered that. It was unlikely, but it wasn't impossible.

"Good thinking. OK, I think we've got about as far as we can today. Hopefully we'll get more out of Theo in the morning, and maybe your glitch will have fixed itself. Have a good evening."

Aaron stood and shot her a pained smile. He didn't have the air of someone expecting to have a good evening. But Zoe had a call to make, and she wanted to be alone when she made it.

Zhang Chen, the forensic accountant, was already waiting for her on the secure video conference line that had been set up for their meeting. He was younger than she'd expected, not much more than thirty, wearing wire-framed glasses under an unruly mop of thick black hair and sitting close to his camera so that his round face filled most of the screen.

"Ah." He smiled when she switched on her own camera, the contrast with Aaron's grim smile inescapable. "DI Finch? It's a pleasure to meet you."

She couldn't help smiling back. It wasn't just the face. There was something else.

"You too," she said. "Is that a Birmingham accent?"

Zhang nodded. "Yup. I'm calling from Kings Heath. But what about you? I was expecting a proper northerner when they told me I was working with Cumbria CID, but you sound like someone I'd meet down the road."

Zoe spent the next minute explaining her background, and then Zhang went through his. He'd lived in Birmingham all his life, apart from three years at Bristol University. When Zoe glanced at the time what felt like moments later, twenty minutes had gone by, most of it spent talking about shared experiences in Birmingham.

"I used to go to Kings Heath Park all the time," Zoe said. "And York Road was the best. I miss it."

Zhang smiled. "I'm always at York Road, especially in the summer. It's still the best." York Road was a pedestrianised street in Kings Heath, lined with independent bars and restaurants.

Zoe enjoyed the reminiscence, but there was work to be done.

"So, have you received the documents?" she asked, when Zhang had stopped talking about the gigs he'd been to at The Hare and Hounds.

"Of course. I just wanted to nail down precisely what you're hoping to achieve here. As far as I understand it, you have a company – Hair by Dee, is that right?"

"Yes, that's it."

"Hair by Dee was effectively a brothel, yes?"

"Yes."

"And the company made a number of payments to Mills Allen Begbie Alliance. Mills Allen passed on all its earnings to its parent company, Dagon, River, Samuels, and Dagon paid fees to Jenson & Marley Offshore Services. We have all this, in black and white. What you want to do is see if we can connect all these payments and produce solid evidence that Jenson & Marley was receiving payments for women who had effectively been sold to Hair by Dee."

There was a matter-of-factness in the way Zhang said it that was both alarming and reassuring at the same time. It was sick, all of it, the very idea that people had been bought and sold just miles from where Zoe was sitting. But it was good that she didn't have to explain, that Zhang seemed to understand it all.

"That's it. You're treating all this as entirely confidential, yes?"

"Absolutely. No one else will see any of the results of my work. Not a soul. And I won't discuss the findings with colleagues or anyone else."

"Excellent. For background, then, Jenson & Marley is owned by a businessman named Myron Carter, who seems to be behind most of the organised crime in this area." She could see Zhang nodding to himself as he made notes. "Dean Somerville, the owner of Hair by Dee, is on remand awaiting trial for murder, and he's made it clear he won't talk to us. Much of the information you've already got came from a local lawyer with inside knowledge of a lot of these transactions. He might be willing to assist a little further."

"That would be excellent. If he'd be prepared to speak to me directly, that could save a lot of time."

Would Alistair Freeburn agree to talk to Zhang? It was always possible. Freeburn had surprised her lately. He was still as self-important as ever, but he was helpful. Sometimes, even friendly.

The call ended with an agreement to speak again soon. Zoe glanced at the time again, and stood. Jake would be waiting for her.

CHAPTER TWENTY-SIX

EMMA SIGHED and slipped her phone back in her pocket.

It had died hours ago, but since then she'd picked it up half a dozen times without thinking.

To check her messages, her socials, the time, the news.

Now it was just blank. And she was thirsty again, and hungry, and starting to get cold even in the shelter of the shed, even in the red cardigan.

It was nearly dark out.

She'd checked the news before her phone had died. But there had been nothing about the fire, Neil, or her.

Nothing about Theo, either, but that didn't mean anything. She screwed her eyes shut and pictured his face again, for something to project her fury against, but when it appeared, all she felt was tired. Sad.

And scared. Too scared to be angry.

Emma wanted her parents.

She'd been planning to call her contact. He'd have been able to help, she thought. But then she'd wondered whether he'd been behind it.

He'd known where they'd be, after all. He'd turned up, as usual, handed over the product, and disappeared before everything had gone to shit. Before the fire. Before Neil...

But he always disappeared early. Like he didn't want to be there.

She'd dithered about it too long, and then her phone had died, and now she was tired, and sad, and scared.

And she wanted her parents.

She crawled to the door and looked outside. There was enough light. She closed her eyes again and tried to conjure the image of the map.

Sandy Beck. Cleaty Gill.

Walk north. Mirk Lane. She could flag a car down. Half an hour's walk, maybe less.

But the man with the knife. He might be out there.

If he was, he probably wouldn't see her. Not in the dark. And if she stayed here any longer, she might never get out.

Fuck it.

She stood and started walking, not giving herself time to change her mind, heading across the field. She could see the trough, still. She walked straight past it, heading for the line of dark trees that cut into the sky.

Mirk Lane. Half an hour. She swallowed. Her throat was hurting worse than ever now. She could taste something metallic, like blood, but different.

She shook her head and kept going.

By the time she reached the trees, it was dark. No moon tonight – the clouds had begun to gather during the afternoon, and they hadn't stopped until the whole sky was gone. Her phone was dead, but she still had her torch. She turned it on and pointed it down, using its beam to avoid branches and roots and all the other shit that wanted to trip her up and leave her lying there for the insects and the wild animals and the man with the knife.

She could hear running water. Was that the beck? Or the gill? What was a gill, anyway? She stopped by a tree whose branches gleamed silver in the torchlight and tried to calm her breathing, to listen, but there was nothing except the water and the noises of the night.

No cars. Nothing with an engine.

She kept going. She tripped once, but got up immediately, brushing the dirt from her legs, pushing on in the same direction.

Only...

Only a few minutes later, when she paused for breath, suddenly exhausted, she could hear running water again. She gulped in air and lifted her torch, and a tree loomed out of the darkness, its branches silver.

Hadn't she been here already?

She turned around, a full circle, sweeping the darkness around her. The torchlight flickered and faded, but it was all just trees, just roots and branches and dirt. She didn't know where she was or where she should be going.

Did it matter?

If she put one foot in front of the other for long enough, she'd get somewhere. Eventually.

Putting one foot in front of the other was suddenly harder than it should have been. By the time she realised the trees were thinning out, she was gasping, and the light from her torch was just a faint stream, barely grazing the ground ahead of her.

But there was something ahead. Something different, something gleaming yellow-white in the darkness.

A light. There was a light.

She felt herself sway. She reached up, found nothing to hold on to, no trees, no branches. She could feel the earth rising around her, the air pushing her down.

But even as she fell, she heard something new.

The sound of an engine.

Her eyes snapped open.

An engine.

Everything went dark.

CHAPTER TWENTY-SEVEN

IT WAS BUSIER than usual at the Anchor Vaults, but in Zoe's experience of the place, anything more than a dozen people was busy. Jake was waiting at a small table by the bar in the main room, a glass full of clear liquid in front of him.

It would be lemonade. Jake didn't drink during the week, and rarely on weekends. She got herself a Diet Coke and sat down beside him.

"Sorry. Had a call that ran on, and I didn't notice the time."

He nodded, slowly, silently. For the second time that afternoon, Zoe found herself looking at a man she knew and seeing at once that there was something wrong with him.

"What is it? Is it your dad? Has something happened?"

"Not really. I... Look, I don't know if I should say this. Not out loud, at least."

"Say what?"

He laughed mirthlessly, and took a sip from his glass. He kept his gaze lowered, his gaze on the wooden table.

"I've had a call from the centre. He's not getting a place after all."

"Shit." Zoe touched his arm. "I'm sorry."

"I'm not sure anything else is going to come up. Not locally. And in the meantime, he's getting worse. Which is exactly what I expected. I just didn't realise it would all take so long."

"And you can feel your life slipping away?"

He looked up, surprised. "Yeah. Is it that obvious?"

"No. Reading people, that's part of my job."

"I didn't think it would go on like this. I thought something would happen. But it's all just so bloody slow. Nothing changes. He's still at home. Still in pretty decent shape, physically, most of the time. It feels like it's never going to end."

Zoe waited for a moment. As she'd just admitted, there was plenty about Jake that she didn't know, but there was one specific thing she'd avoided asking about.

Maybe now was the time.

"Do you mind if I ask you something?" she said. "Something personal?"

He shrugged. "I think this is a fairly personal conversation already."

"Your wedding ring," she said, and saw him glance down at his left hand, then back up again. "You were wearing it the first time we met. But then it disappeared. Is there a story behind that? You don't have to tell me if you don't want to. But it's... Well, I've wondered. That's all."

He nodded.

"Not a lot to it, really. Met her in Newcastle. While I was studying. She was the reason I stayed there, the reason I got a job there. But we got married too young."

"She's still there?"

He shook his head. "She went back to Australia. A more attractive prospect than coming to Whitehaven to help look after an ancient miner. She'd only planned on doing a year in England. And it was all fun, all a laugh, till Dad started to get sick. But look, I didn't come here tonight to wallow in misery. Tell me about your case."

Zoe told him what she could, which wasn't much. But there was something else she thought he'd be interested in.

"Remember Vicky Speares? The woman who attacked Roddy Chen?"

He nodded, his gaze still downwards. "The one your colleagues found conveniently dead?"

"That one." No need to go on the defensive with Jake. And he might be right.

"Well," she went on, "I gather she choked on her own vomit."

He frowned. "You gather?"

"That's what Alan Markin tells me."

"But it wasn't Markin's team that found her, was it?"

Zoe nodded.

He looked up. "It was Sergeant Cummings, wasn't it? The same Sergeant Cummings that ran away in the first place, leaving Roddy Chen to get beaten."

"What do you know about Tel Cummings, Jake?"

Zoe licked her lips while she waited for him to answer.

"Nothing concrete. But he's one of those that gets mentioned a lot. And not in a good way. Are you thinking there might be something more to this?"

She lifted her drink and took a long swig before replying.

"I don't know. I don't like Tel Cummings, but that's different from thinking he's a murderer. And it's not like there's anything for me to investigate, or anything you can base a story on. I just thought someone should know."

"And I was the lucky someone," said Jake, but he was smiling.

He got it, at least. If someone had to know, then it should at least be someone who was likely to care.

CHAPTER TWENTY-EIGHT

ZOE DROVE to work under a pale grey sky that reflected her mood.

At least she could talk to Nicholas as she drove. It felt like ages since they'd had a proper chat, and even this wasn't much of one, the signal fading in and out as she climbed out of one valley and descended into the next. But it was nice to hear his voice.

"When am I going to see you next?"

His last visit hadn't been more than a few weeks ago, but already it felt like months.

"I don't know, Mum. Bit hectic here at the moment."

She smiled. Nicholas had always been in control, on top of things. It would do him no harm to relax. He'd grown up having to look after himself more than other kids. At least it prepared him for uni.

A beep came through on the call.

Zoe glanced at the screen. "Sorry, Nicholas. Got to take this. Speak soon." She leaned forward to hit the answer button. "Kay?"

"DI Finch. Thanks for answering."

"That's OK. How are things?"

She'd almost reached the Hub. The journey had sunk into her skin, so that she didn't really think about it any more. Like the weather, like the way the people up here spoke. Like the way she'd recognised the number Kay was calling from, even though it was a payphone half a mile from Kay's house. Kay reckoned PSD were still monitoring her calls, and Zoe didn't know enough to say they weren't.

"They've finally told me what I'm supposed to have done."

Against the distant grey fells, the glass of the Hub came into view. There were mornings when the sun hit the windows, and Zoe had to shield her eyes.

This wasn't one of them.

"On top of the Davey Grant thing, you mean?"

"Yeah. I've told them that's fair. That was me."

Kay Holinshed had been seconded to Zoe's team for two investigations. She'd been worth her weight in gold, despite the frequent cigarette breaks. Zoe had been considering asking for her to be permanently assigned, until she'd been caught accessing police information for personal reasons, and kicked off the force.

And it was true. She'd looked up her daughter's new boyfriend, Davey Grant, because she'd seen him at the Hub a few times. All harmless enough, except it wasn't: looking him up was illegal, and had cost Kay her job and her pension.

Kay understood. She wasn't happy about it – nobody would be – but she'd known the rules, she'd broken them, and she'd been caught.

Only it hadn't stopped there. Carl and his colleagues had apparently decided Kay had been doing a lot worse with the data she had access to. Zoe had tried to find out what, and plead on Kay's behalf, but Carl refused to talk to her about it. Until now, Kay hadn't even known what it was she was being accused of, only that it involved organised crime.

"So what is it?" Zoe asked.

"They're saying I accessed other information. CCTV images, records, location data, case files. But mostly CCTV images. And apparently, I passed that on."

"To who?"

"I don't know. They wouldn't tell me."

"They?" asked Zoe, dreading the answer.

"Not Carl. DS Gaskill, this time. Just her."

Denise Gaskill was Carl's second-in-command. Zoe had only met the woman briefly. She hadn't formed the most positive impression of her, but PSD weren't supposed to be popular.

"What CCTV, then?"

"You remember Margaret Hooper?"

Zoe turned into the station car park and pulled up further from the building than usual. She didn't want to be interrupted. And that name rang a bell.

"The teacher, right?"

"Head teacher at Norris Academy. She was being black-mailed earlier this year. Someone had photos of her and her girlfriend."

Zoe nodded to herself. "Tom was looking into it. The woman didn't take it too seriously herself, but that didn't mean it wasn't a serious offence. But hang on, that's... That's not the sort of thing you'd be able to access anyway."

Kay had been a civilian worker at the Hub. She had certain clearances, which was how she'd looked up the information on Davey Grant. But random CCTV seemed a stretch.

"Exactly. They say I was using someone else's credentials."

Zoe swallowed. "Whose?"

"DS Oldman." Zoe relaxed. She'd been expecting to hear her own name, or someone in her team. DS Oldman wasn't someone she'd heard of.

"He retired a couple of years ago," Kay continued. "Never got to work at the Hub. And he'd have had the relevant clearances. But I promise you, DI Finch, I didn't—"

"I know, Kay. If you say you didn't do it, I believe you. And you don't work for me. So you can call me Zoe."

"That just doesn't feel right," Kay replied.

"Fine. In the meantime, I'll see what I can find out. Speak soon."

Zoe moved the car closer to the building before she parked and got out, on the phone now to Meredith Bawcombe, who sounded more asleep than awake when she finally answered, and had to be reminded twice who Zoe was.

"Nah," said the student. "No sign of her. She didn't come home yesterday."

"Can you check her room?" Zoe asked.

"I'm standing outside it now. No one there. Sorry."

The line went dead.

CHAPTER TWENTY-NINE

AARON WOKE on the sofa at four in the morning, his back screaming at him. He spent half an hour trying and failing to get back to sleep before giving up. He rose quietly, ate some toast, drank some coffee, and still felt like someone who'd woken on a sofa at four in the morning.

But at least he knew he wasn't going back to sleep.

He slipped upstairs and pushed Annabel's door open. He stood watching her, the way her hair fell across her face, the way it moved gently as she breathed.

He left the house, climbed into his Volvo, and drove to the Hub.

There was a note on his chair from Nina. She'd heard back from all the local cab companies, and no one recalled a pick-up from anywhere near Fell Barn.

Three questions.

Where was Emma Hudson?

Where had the Land Rover driver disappeared to?

And why had Nina left the note on his chair, instead of just messaging the team inbox?

He checked his messages and scanned the notice he'd sent out the previous day with Emma's details attached. No sign of her anywhere.

The Land Rover was history, but its actual history could be checked. Had it been spotted anywhere between its theft and its arrival at Fell Barn? Had it shown up on any ANPR or CCTV? He could have Tom look into that. Or Nina.

As for why Nina had left the note on his chair, he thought he knew the answer. If your boss looked like he did, and you were worried about them, you wouldn't want to send them yet another blank at the end of the working day.

On the subject of blanks, he ran the same search he'd spent half the previous day running, and got the same answer: *Unable to complete search request. Please try again later.*

He closed his eyes and sat back in his chair. He tried not to think about Serge, about the case, about anything at all.

He was startled by the sound of a throat clearing behind him. He opened his eyes and turned.

The boss.

"Are you OK, Aaron?"

He glanced past her at the clock on the team room wall. It was nearly nine.

He'd fallen asleep. He'd fallen asleep in his chair, and now his back was going to hate him even more.

"Aaron?" she asked.

He nodded. "All fine." At least he still sounded like a normal person. "The cab companies."

She frowned at him.

"Nina's been calling them."

"Why?"

He closed his eyes. There had been a reason, hadn't there? He opened them again.

"Aaron, are you sure you're OK?"

"Sorry, boss. We're trying to track Emma Hudson and the Land Rover driver. If they didn't drive away from Fell Barn, they must have walked, but it's pretty remote. So we wanted to see if anyone had taken a cab from anywhere nearby."

She nodded. "Good thinking."

"But they didn't. And that glitch on the sports car still won't go away."

"I don't know about you, but I'm starting to feel it isn't actually a glitch."

He nodded. They'd have fixed it by now.

Something, or someone, didn't want them tracing the sports car.

"Meanwhile," she said. "I've spoken to one of Emma's flatmates this morning. She's not home. Not that I expected her to be. And I've heard from Kay."

"Kay Holinshed?"

She nodded and filled him in. "None of us thought Kay was anything other than an honest, dedicated worker. You think you know people, Aaron, but they can always surprise you."

Maybe she was right. But Harry Oldman. Aaron closed his eyes again, trying to picture the man, trying to remember more about him than his patient walk, his slow greetings, the way he had of making you feel like you had all the time in the world...

The boss was on the phone. When had that happened? She was looking at him, mouthing something.

Post-mortem. She raised her eyebrows. A question.

He nodded.

"Thanks, Chris," she said into her phone. "DS Keyes will join you shortly."

CHAPTER THIRTY

TOM HAD FORGOTTEN about the antimacassar, but he could hardly miss it, walking to his desk with his backpack hanging from one hand and a coffee in the other. It had been a stupid bet.

But you couldn't just take the sensible ones.

"Morning, Sarge," he called as he sat down, without turning round. "All OK?"

"Yes, Tom," replied the sarge. "Why wouldn't it be?"

Someone had clearly got up on the wrong side of bed this morning.

"No reason, Sarge." He tried to think of something to add and was saved by his phone's ringtone.

"Caroline," he said. "How's things?"

"*Things* are fine. Got some results for you."

From what he'd heard, they'd been back on the site for most of yesterday afternoon, and still hadn't recovered everything they wanted.

"That's quick."

"Not really. I'm talking about Cawter Hough, not Fell Barn."

"Oh, right."

Cawter Hough was the barn fire he'd looked into a few months back. Nothing had come of it, but there hadn't been any dead bodies on the scene to make it worthwhile.

There had been traces of drugs, though, and the similarities with Fell Barn had been enough to get Caroline to retrieve the Cawter Hough material for testing.

"Anything interesting?" he asked.

"Prints and DNA. Lots of them. Ones you'll recognise, too."

"Names?"

"I've got the late Neil Colvin, to start with."

"Right." So whatever it was Neil had been doing at Fell Barn, he'd been doing it at Cawter Hough, too. Just with less lethal consequences. "Anyone else?"

"Tony Harris, Steve Walker, Eddie Driver."

Tom frowned. "Are you sure?"

"The science doesn't lie, Tom."

"I could have sworn Steve and Eddie are clean."

Caroline laughed. "Did they tell you that themselves?"

"Well." Tom paused. "As it happens, they told Nina, about a year ago. But I gather they were very convincing."

"Maybe they were telling the truth. This is just a few months ago, Tom. Maybe they went straight, and then fell back into it."

"And Topper – Tony Harris. Last I heard, he was serving a year down south. Is it possible there's been some contamination or something?"

There was a noise on the other end of the phone, a bang,

something like a grunt, which didn't sound like Caroline, and then a shout, which definitely wasn't.

"Who the fuck said that?" he heard, and then more noise, the sound of the phone being snatched from Caroline's hand.

"Hello?" he said.

"DC Willis, is it?"

Stella. Of course. His heart sank. "Yes, Stella. I was just—"

"I heard what you were *just*, Tom, and if you think I'm going to stand here and listen to you making allegations about my lab, you'd better—"

"I wasn't alleging anything, Stella. I was just—"

"*Contamination*, you said. *Contamination*. Which implies either incompetence or corruption. So which one is it you think we're guilty of here, DC Willis?"

"Anyone can make mistakes, Stella. And look, I'm sorry if I... I was only—"

"You might well make mistakes in your job, but we don't make them here. Huz did that work, and he's very thorough. If Caroline says someone was there, they were there."

"OK, OK," he said, but the line was dead already.

There was a snort from behind him. He turned to see Nina standing in the doorway.

"You hear that?" he asked.

She raised an eyebrow. "Every word." The sarge had left with DI Finch, presumably heading down to interview Theo Georgiou. "Doesn't take much to put Stella's nose out of joint, but that was a masterpiece. How to not win friends and influence people, by Tom Willis."

"But don't you think it's a bit odd?"

She shrugged. "It's been ages since we saw Eddie and

Steve. Yes, I think they were telling the truth, but anything could have happened since."

"And Topper?"

"Topper's out. Don't you remember?"

Tom shook his head.

Nina sighed. "Morris Keane told us. Right here. No? A few months ago. Said he'd been seen in the area."

"Dealing?"

"Not that Inspector Keane knew. But it's Tony Harris, Tom. What else is he gonna do?"

CHAPTER THIRTY-ONE

AARON SAW the boss raise an eyebrow as she entered Interview Room Two. "Been away?" she asked.

Stan Basham was sitting next to Theo Georgiou, looking tanned and relaxed and more like a human being than Aaron remembered him looking.

Basham nodded. "Tenerife," he said. "Which was lovely, but anywhere's lovely compared to this place. I'd rather be in fucking Wales than sitting here."

He looked pointedly around. Interview Room Two was functional. Bare walls, metal chairs, plastic table. Theo's last set of interviews had been in Room Four, the comfortable one.

"And so would my client," continued Basham, gesturing to the young man seated beside him. "So let's get on with it and we can all go home."

The boss ran through the formalities and reminded Theo that he was still under arrest, but hadn't yet been charged. Theo looked tired, but not as tired as Aaron felt. Perhaps the cells were more comfortable than the sofa.

Basham hadn't looked at Aaron once. Fine. Basham liked to play games.

This time, Aaron intended to win.

"What were you doing at Fell Barn?" he asked, to get things going.

Basham leaned over to whisper in Theo's ear.

"No comment," replied Theo.

"Can you tell us about the drugs we found there?" added the DI, looking Theo straight in the eye.

"No comment."

"We know about Emma Hudson," Aaron said.

"What do you mean?" asked Theo. It wasn't much, but it wasn't 'no comment.'

"Where is she, Theo?" asked the boss.

"I don't understand," replied Theo, turning to Aaron.

"Can you tell us where Emma is?" said the boss.

They'd decided on this before they'd come in. Alternate the questioning, get him used to a rhythm, then disrupt it. Unsettle him.

Theo seemed unsettled enough. "Isn't... Isn't she at home?"

Aaron leaned forward. "Our colleagues told you yesterday she was missing, and you didn't seem to want to help, despite the fact that one man's been murdered and Emma's clearly at risk. She's your girlfriend, isn't she?"

Theo nodded.

"For the recording, please," said the boss.

"Yes."

"But you don't seem to care what happens to her. Is that right, Theo?" she pressed.

"I don't understand. Is she... She's still not home?"

"No sign of her," Aaron said. "She didn't come home the

night of the murder. She didn't come home last night. So, to summarise, Emma Hudson's missing, Neil Colvin's dead, and the only other person who we know for sure was with them that night is you, Theo. So if you've got anything to tell us, now would be a good time."

Basham leaned towards Theo again and muttered, "Say nowt," but Theo had turned pale and Aaron could feel the vibrations of his leg shaking under the table.

It wasn't quite over, but it was nearly done.

"I just thought..."

Theo stopped, looked at Basham, then back across the table at DI Finch and Aaron. Basham was shaking his head.

"I just thought she'd turn up eventually. Yesterday, you know? Thought she was probably on a bender somewhere. But... two nights. That's not like her."

Aaron glanced at the boss. She nodded almost imperceptibly.

"Theo," Aaron said, leaning forward. "Why don't you tell us what you were doing at Fell Barn, and what happened when you got there?"

Theo nodded. "She asked me to come along," he said.

"Come along where?"

"Fell Barn. It was... Look, you know all this already, right?"

Aaron said nothing.

"Well, it's drugs, isn't it? You know that. She gets them delivered in the middle of nowhere by some bloke, calls him her 'contact,' and then she tests them, repackages them, brings them back to Preston, sells them. Neil does the same at Lancaster."

"Neil's dead," DI Finch reminded him. Theo blinked, rapidly. He looked like he was about to cry.

"What was your role in all this?" Aaron asked.

"I've never been before. Emma needed the transport. Her car broke down. I reckon she wanted the company. And maybe a bit of security, too."

"Why? Was it dangerous? Had she said anything about being scared before?"

Theo shook his head. "No. Maybe she just wanted a lift."

"And this contact of hers," said the boss. "Do you know who that is?"

"Just some bloke. She wouldn't tell me his name, never has. And when he turned up I had to stay in the car while she spoke to him. So I didn't even get to see him."

"Did you see his car?" asked Aaron.

"Not sure." Theo frowned. "Think it was small. That's all I can remember."

"Did you see who killed Neil Colvin?" said the boss.

"Sorry. There was a fire, in the barn. I didn't like it. I..." He looked down at the table.

"You don't have to say anything," said Basham.

"What happened?" said DI Finch.

"I ran. I'm not proud of it, but fire's not good. Scares the shit out of me."

"You're a chemistry student, aren't you?" asked Aaron.

Theo shot him a look. "We try to keep our fires under control in the lab. This one wasn't. So I ran. Got in the car and drove and kept thinking about turning back, but before I knew it, I was back in Preston."

"That's, what, two hours of thinking about it and not doing it, Theo?" said the boss. "Enough time for Emma to disappear and Neil to get murdered. Have you thought about what would have happened if maybe you'd been there, with your car, instead of halfway down the M6?"

Theo shook his head and blinked again.

"Let's go back a little," Aaron prompted. "After Emma's contact left, what happened then?"

"I came out and helped her and Neil."

"Helped them with what?"

"Testing. Weighing. Repackaging."

"Shut up," said Basham. Theo ignored him.

"Testing, weighing and repackaging what, precisely?" Aaron asked.

"Weed, mostly. Bit of coke."

"Where did this contact of Emma's get it from?" asked the boss.

"Don't answer that," said Basham.

"He got them from you," replied Theo.

"From us?" repeated Aaron.

Theo stared at him. "That's right. He got them from the police."

Aaron turned towards the DI, wondering if he looked as astonished as she did. Across the table, Stan Basham was leaning down, his head in his hands.

CHAPTER THIRTY-TWO

ZOE SHOULD HAVE EXPECTED something like this.

The work experience that both Neil Colvin and Emma Hudson had supposedly been engaged in was too much of a coincidence. The fact that no one seemed to know anything about it hadn't helped.

But standing in front of Nina and Tom and having to tell them that other officers might be involved still left her feeling sick.

There was a moment's silence, and then Nina asked the question they were all thinking.

"Does this mean we'll have to hand it over to PSD?"

Zoe sighed. "I'll need to discuss it with the super. As far as I'm concerned, this is a murder investigation, and since the only thing we know about Emma's so-called contact is that he left before the murder happened, we can argue that the drugs side, and therefore the bit that might concern PSD, is secondary. And we don't know the police really are involved. Anyone can claim they're working with the police, after all. We'll have to see."

Tom stood up and coughed.

"Boss, there's something else."

"You don't have to stand, Tom."

He sat back down. "More bad news, I'm afraid. The forensics came back on Cawter Hough."

"Cawter Hough?" The words were familiar.

"The other barn fire. Couple of months ago."

Zoe nodded. "Go on."

"Prints and DNA, only they're not plausible. We've got Neil Colvin on the scene, which is interesting, but we've also got Tony Harris, Steve Walker, and Eddie Driver."

Beside her, Zoe could see Aaron frowning.

"I knew Topper was out," he said, "but I didn't know he was dealing. And Steve and Eddie are selling cars now."

"Exactly," replied Tom. "I'm worried there's been a mistake. And if there has, then is it limited to Cawter Hough? Or could there be some sort of contamination at the lab that's going to affect other results, too?"

"Does this matter?" asked Zoe. She could feel the conversation getting away from her.

"Well, boss, with respect—" Tom began.

"No, Tom," she said. "I understand you're concerned, but this sounds like an unnecessary distraction to me. We've got a murder victim and a witness who isn't really even a witness and won't tell us anything useful."

Theo had dropped his bombshell about the police, and told them he didn't know who the contact was. Emma had always been fiercely protective on that front. And no, he hadn't seen the murder, hadn't seen anyone else, didn't know what had happened. Then he'd fallen silent. He wasn't even saying 'no comment' any more. They'd terminated the interview shortly after.

"But, boss—" Tom tried again.

"I'm sorry, Tom, but no. I don't know who this Topper is, I don't know who Eddie and Steve are."

She could feel Aaron's eyes burning into her. Were these the dealers he'd told her about yesterday? The ones who'd stopped because of *supply-side issues*, whatever that meant?

Perhaps the issues had resolved themselves, and they'd gone back to their old ways.

"And frankly," she continued, "I don't really care. What I care about is finding Emma Hudson, who might have seen the whole thing, and whoever drove that fucking Land Rover."

She stopped. She took a moment to breathe and figure out what had got her so worked up.

The mention of police involvement. The possibility of PSD taking the case off her hands. All that was annoying, but it was something she could live with.

But not if it meant yet another argument with Carl. The same argument, about who should be running what cases, what they should be telling each other, what they had to keep to themselves, just with a new focus.

She gritted her teeth. "I'm sorry. I shouldn't have spoken to you all like that. But the point stands. Emma and the Land Rover driver. That's the focus. If you're really worried about the accuracy of the forensics, Tom, you can go and talk to this Eddie and Steve. I'm happy for you to do that, if only to set your mind at rest. But otherwise, let's get on with the job in hand. OK?"

She looked around. No one had replied, but they were all nodding.

"Good. Now I've got to go and see the super and tell her

we haven't got any solid leads, and we might be about to get in a jurisdiction fight with PSD. Wish me luck."

CHAPTER THIRTY-THREE

FIONA'S ASSISTANT was hovering in the corridor. When he spotted Zoe, he raised his eyebrows and gave a tiny shake of his head.

Someone was in there, then. The super had a massive plant positioned outside her door, so you couldn't see whether her office was occupied or not. But Luke, her assistant, had come to Zoe's rescue like this more than once before. She turned and began to walk away, mouthing her thanks. She'd nearly reached the lift when she heard her name called.

"Zoe. DI Finch."

She turned. Alan Markin had just stepped out of the super's office.

"Everything OK, Alan?" she asked.

He nodded. She headed back towards him, trying to read his expression. He just looked ill. The same way he always looked.

Who knew what mood he'd left the super in?

"Fine," he said. "You?"

"All good." She stepped past him and knocked on the super's door.

Whatever Markin had said to her, Fiona didn't seem to have been affected by it, or if she was, she wasn't showing it. She listened as Zoe briefed her on their progress, or lack of it, and mentioned the possible police angle.

"But I'd argue that's nothing more than rumour at this stage, and anyway, it's incidental to the murder."

"I understand you don't want to hand the case over to PSD," Fiona said.

Or anyone else. Fiona had a habit of making threats when investigations stalled. Find a decent lead, or lose the case.

"I don't think that would be appropriate at this stage. Obviously, if we find anything that backs up the suggestion of police involvement—"

"Look, Zoe. I trust you enough not to pass the case on to anyone else, including PSD, so I hope you'll be honest with me. There might not be anything concrete, but in your professional opinion, is it more likely than not that there's a PSD angle lurking somewhere in this investigation?"

Zoe hesitated.

"Yes. Yes, I think so, but I also think that the police involvement isn't the main thing here. That's the murder."

"And you don't think that's directly linked?"

"I think the police connection was Emma Hudson's contact, and whoever he was, he'd gone before the fire, long before the murder."

"OK. Fine. We'll keep this between us for now. Short term. We'll have to let PSD in soon, one way or another. Just make some progress, OK? And if you need any help, ask for it."

"Thanks, Fiona."

"Is there anything else you want to talk about?"

Zoe calculated. "There's a problem with the system," she said. "Only, I don't think it's really a problem with the system."

She explained the 'glitch' that had stopped them from tracing the sports car that she was now convinced Emma Hudson's contact had driven to the barn. All Theo could remember was that it had been small.

Fiona nodded. "That doesn't sound like a glitch. It sounds like something that's been put there to stop us interfering."

Zoe smiled despite herself. "And who do you think would have the power to do something like that?"

The super shrugged. "All manner of choices. Special Branch or the Security Services could do that. But then," she continued, staring at Zoe, unblinking, "so could PSD."

Which was precisely what Zoe had feared. She stood to leave, and remembered there was one more thing she wanted to ask about.

"Supply-side issues," she said.

"I'm sorry?"

"There was a murder, a couple of months before I started here. Dealer called Noah Cane. During the course of the investigation, DS Keyes and the team found that most of the local dealers had either moved away or gone straight. One of them referred to *supply-side issues*, but I don't think we ever got to the bottom of that."

The super frowned. "That sounds familiar. I think DS Keyes mentioned it at the time."

"I was wondering about a connection between that murder and this one," Zoe said.

"I suppose that's possible," Fiona replied. "And if there

is, I hope I can count on you to find it. Now, tell me, is Alistair Freeburn still being helpful?"

"Freeburn?"

"With your financial investigation. Is he helping?"

"Oh, yes. Well, we'll have to see. I'll be getting in touch with him to ask him to cooperate with the forensic accountant. Hopefully he'll be willing."

"I'm sure he will, Zoe. And if he proves difficult, make sure you let me know."

Zoe turned to leave. *Why the sudden change of subject?*

CHAPTER THIRTY-FOUR

"PETER," announced Dr Robertson, gesturing at the man standing beside him.

"Patrick," corrected the man. He wore a surgical mask – all three of them did – but Aaron could see the exasperation in his eyes.

"Anyway, DS Keyes, lovely to see you down here and all that jazz, but shall we get on with looking into what killed our friend here?"

"Let's," replied Aaron. Neil Colvin – 'our friend here' – lay on his back, on a gurney. Under the bright striplight he looked even worse than he had in the flickering flames of Fell Barn.

"That was a joke, DS Keyes." The pathologist shook his head, solemnly. "It's fairly obvious what killed him. Let's get cracking, shall we, Peter?"

Aaron listened as Dr Robertson ran through the contents of Neil's lungs and air passages. It was obvious even to a layman that they were the wrong colour.

"Soot soiling in the nares and oropharynx," the pathologist said. "Look, here. Soot-stained mucus in the lining of the main bronchi. Not enough to kill him, but enough to make him very ill indeed."

As for what had killed Neil Colvin, Dr Robertson was right. It was obvious. The smoke might have weakened him, but the pathologist and his assistant counted forty-three separate stab wounds.

"Some of these would have been fatal on their own," the doctor pointed out. "There's damage to so many of the major organs it's difficult to work out which one's which."

It was a mess in there. Aaron had attended enough post-mortems to know that what he was looking at was unusual.

"As for the weapon, sharp and long is as good as I can get at this point. Eight inches, at a guess. When I've had more of a chance to examine the wounds, I might be able to narrow down the type of blade used." He stopped, and moved his head closer to the cavity. "Oh, hang on. They're all puncture wounds. Very little by way of tissue bridges. Not serrated, I think. A narrow blade. Thinner than a kitchen knife. That help?"

"I don't know. We don't have anything that might be a weapon yet."

"He was left to die, by the look of it. The organ damage would have killed him eventually, but the blood loss got there first. Astonishingly, no major arteries were hit, so it could have taken an hour, maybe two."

He'd still been alive when the hikers had found him. Dying, but not yet dead.

"See here?" The pathologist waved a gloved hand at some lumps of tissue that Aaron might have recognised under different circumstances.

"What am I looking at?"

"That, DS Keyes, is a kidney."

"It's very pale."

"Indeed it is. As the rest of him would be, if you could see past the soot damage. The pallor is from the blood loss."

When the pathologist had finished, Aaron walked back through the long underground corridors to the stairs and the world of living, breathing human beings, trying to work out what he felt.

After a minute or so, he realised that what he felt was nothing. He'd just attended the post-mortem of a man who'd been brutally murdered, and he'd come away cold. Not sickened, or angry, or sad. Just cold.

It was the tiredness. It had to be the tiredness.

Before he drove away from the hospital, he spent a few minutes tracking down a phone number. He was pleased to hear it answered on the second ring.

"Hello?"

Aaron was taken back two, five, ten years. The man sounded exactly as he'd sounded the whole time Aaron had known him. "Who's this, then?"

"Harry, it's Aaron Keyes. From—"

"Aaron? Little DC Keyes? From Whitehaven nick?"

"It's DS Keyes now, and we're at the new place out by Frizington, but yes, that's me."

"Bloody hell, Aaron. I'd say it's nice to hear your voice, but this isn't a social call, is it?"

"I'm afraid not, Harry. I was wondering if I might stop by and have a chat."

CHAPTER THIRTY-FIVE

OUTSIDE ZOE's office the cloud had turned into a fine mist, cutting the Hub off from the distant fells and giving her the impression that she was suspended here, three floors up, isolated from the outside world.

She picked up her phone, pondering the conversation she'd had with Fiona. The discussion about Noah Cane. *Supply-side issues.*

Fiona could be like that when she decided she had nothing left to contribute to a topic. It was one of the things Zoe liked about her boss.

But had there been more to it this time?

Alistair Freeburn answered immediately, and once again she was struck by the difference between the man she was speaking to now, and the one she'd first met less than a year earlier, when she was investigating the murder of Bernard Dearborn. Back then, he'd been as obstructive as he could be, without actually breaking the law.

Lately, he seemed to be bending over backwards to help.

"DI Finch. Pleasure to hear from you."

It sounded genuine. There had been a recent incident, with the murder in his office. He'd been helpful then, too, but Zoe and her team had played their part in making sure his life and his business weren't disrupted any more than they needed to be.

"Mr Freeburn," she replied. He preferred formality. "I'm afraid I'm calling to ask for your help again."

"Your forensic accountant?" he said. "I've just heard from Detective Superintendent Kendrick. You know, you don't need to go running to her if you want my help. I'm more than willing."

"I wasn't," she began, then smiled. "Thank you. I'll give Mr Zhang your number, then, shall I?"

"Please, go ahead. And take care."

She nodded. It felt good to make a little headway on the Carter front, but she knew she was only distracting herself from the lack of progress on Neil Colvin's murder.

She stood and walked quietly to the team room, where Tom was staring at his screen and Nina was reading something out loud from hers, her phone tucked under her chin. No sign of Aaron. He'd probably be on his way back from the post-mortem.

He'd have called her if there had been any surprises. And Nina and Tom would have come looking for her if they'd stumbled across anything interesting. They had nothing: no Emma Hudson, no Land Rover driver, and they were further than ever from finding out who'd been driving the sports car that night.

She walked back to her office and picked up her phone again.

"Zoe. Good to hear from you. What's it like up there?"

There was something about the sound of DCI Lesley

Clarke's voice that relaxed her a little, and she wondered whether this was what other people felt like when they had their first beer or glass of wine at the end of the working week. Lesley had been her boss back in Birmingham, but had moved down to Dorset after she'd been injured in an explosion.

She'd been an excellent DCI, and a friend, too. Zoe still missed her.

"Do you really want to know?" Zoe asked. "It's all a bit shit. Don't want to put you in a bad mood."

"You couldn't put me in a bad mood. Not today. I've been given permission to set up a new team."

Zoe sat up. This was new.

"Tell me more."

"Cold cases. The stuff that went on here back in the eighties, the nineties, you wouldn't believe it."

"Worse than Birmingham?"

"Who knows? There's never been a coordinated effort to look back and put all this stuff together. There were units that combed through it all in West Midlands, and if anything new came to light, they'd reopen it. But down here, it's like they gave a case a couple of months, then gave up if they hadn't solved it."

"So, what, you've got loads of old bodies and nobody knows who killed them?"

"Something like that. Anyway, I'm putting a team together, and I'm looking for someone to come in and run the day-to-day on my old team. Don't suppose you fancy relocating again?"

Zoe closed her eyes, and for a moment, she saw herself there, in Dorset, in a calmer place, a warmer place, with someone she understood.

She shook her head, smiling. "I think the last move will be enough for the next few years. But thanks. How's Dennis?"

"Officially retired, now, which was probably on the cards even before his injury. But you know what? I miss him."

"He drove you mad!" Zoe pointed out.

Back when DS Dennis Frampton had been working for Lesley, she'd complained about him constantly: his seriousness, his hesitancy, his bloody swear jar. But he'd risked his life trying to rescue Lesley's daughter. That sort of thing would improve a relationship.

"He got on my nerves, Zoe. But he was a good man. Now, what's going on?"

Zoe spent a few minutes complaining about the case, and Markin, but steered clear of talking about Carl and PSD. There were some things she wouldn't discuss over the phone.

The fact that she was in contact with David Randle was top of that list.

As she was winding up the call, feeling a little better for it, her door burst open and Nina rushed in, her eyes wide.

"Boss," she said.

Zoe raised a finger, said her goodbyes to Lesley, and put the phone down. "What is it, Nina?"

"Just had a call from the West Cumberland Hospital. They've got a patient they thought we might want to know about."

Zoe put a hand flat on the desk between them.

"It's her, boss. She's only half conscious, on a drip. Dehydrated and a bit scratched up, but otherwise fine. But it's her. It's Emma Hudson."

CHAPTER THIRTY-SIX

On a weekday afternoon, the Henry Bessemer was a different place. The crowd was thin, and the only noise was the clink of glasses and the buzz of conversation.

Aaron had half a pint of bitter in front of him. Harry Oldman had a full pint, and beside it, an empty one, but Harry Oldman was retired and lived a five-minute walk away. He could drink what he wanted.

They spent a few minutes catching up and reminiscing about old colleagues. Aaron hadn't worked alongside Oldman more than a handful of times – they'd been in different teams – but he'd always liked and respected the older man.

"So what's this all about then, Aaron?" asked Oldman.

"It's your old credentials," replied Aaron. "They've been used to access sensitive data."

Oldman took a sip from his glass, put it down, and looked Aaron directly in the eyes.

"I don't even know what that means. I know I'm an old

man, and it's possible I've drunk more than I should, but you might as well be talking Chinese there."

Oldman was only just past sixty, and Aaron had seen him sink a dozen pints and still be as sharp as ever.

"The details you used to have," Aaron said. "To log into the computers. They should have been wiped clean when you left, but they weren't. Mistakes happen. It's usually not a problem."

Oldman nodded. "But you're saying someone's been using them lately, then. Pretending to be me?"

"We know it's not you. I was just wondering if you knew who it might be."

"How would I know, Aaron? I haven't worked there in years."

"Is there anyone who might have access to your old login details?"

Oldman took a long drink; Aaron watched him closely.

"Look," he said, finally. "I didn't take all that stuff too seriously. Password security, that kind of nonsense. Maybe I was wrong. But the truth is, I never really got to grips with the old computer. I used to let the younger cops do the geek work. And maybe I gave them my details so they could do it."

"Which cops?"

Oldman took another long drink.

"Sorry," he said, putting his near-empty glass back down on the wooden table. "I don't remember."

Was he lying? No point confronting him about it. Aaron finished his own drink and offered to buy Oldman another before he left.

At the bar, he felt a tap on his shoulder, and there beside him was a familiar face. Aaron frowned, trying to place it, then smiled.

"Bobby," he said. "How are things?"

Bobby Silver had been a colleague of Victor Parlick, the man Aaron had been trying to recruit as a confidential informant before he'd died in an apparent accident, probably orchestrated by Myron Carter. Aaron had bumped into Bobby and her friends a few months after Victor's death and ended up getting drunk with them, toasting the memory of their old colleague.

"Join us," Bobby said, pointing to a table at the far end of the pub. Aaron looked around, and saw two hands raised in greeting. Miles, wasn't it? Miles and Stacey. Miles, Stacey, and Bobby, all three of them workers at the port, employees of Myron Carter, and as far as Aaron could tell, completely uninvolved in Carter's criminal enterprise.

That was the trouble with people like Carter. So much of what they did was legitimate, it was easy to miss the parts that weren't.

Aaron deposited Harry Oldman's pint with him, and said his goodbyes, then stopped briefly with Bobby and the others. He'd ordered himself a Diet Coke, and he could see Stacey frowning as he raised it to his lips.

"On the hard stuff, are you?" she asked.

"On duty," he told her, and she nodded.

"Aaron," said Bobby from beside him. "Tell me something. How come a cop like you was friends with Victor Parlick?"

Aaron opened his mouth to say something, then stopped. Was there an implication there?

Bobby didn't sound aggressive or unfriendly. Just interested. People like Victor Parlick weren't usually friends with police officers.

"Cops are people too, you know," he said. "I'm friends

with all sorts of people. They even tell me I'm quite likeable, as it happens."

The three of them laughed. They toasted Victor Parlick one more time, and as Aaron raised his glass, he found himself wondering.

He *had* been likeable, back before things had started to go wrong. Before Victor had died. Before Serge had made some minor mistakes, and he'd jumped on them like they were serious crimes.

But was he likeable any more?

CHAPTER THIRTY-SEVEN

NINA SAT DOWN OPPOSITE TOM. The break room was empty, but there would be teams coming off shift in the next few minutes, which meant the snack machine would soon be empty too. If you wanted a packet of crisps, it was now or tomorrow.

"Well, this is a proper shit show," she said.

"What do you mean?"

"I mean all of it. This case. We've got nothing."

"You've found Emma Hudson," Tom reminded her. "That's something."

Nina ripped open her crisps and crammed a handful into her mouth. "The boss'll go and talk to her, and she won't know a thing." She spoke through the crisps. "It'll be Theo Georgiou all over again. Trust me. And as for the sarge, don't get me started."

"What's up with him? I've never seen him looking so miserable."

"You asked him?"

"Come on, Nina. Sarge isn't really the type to open up.

Not to me, anyway."

Nina nodded and grabbed another handful of crisps. She could talk to most people in the station and wasn't afraid of any of them. But talking about the sarge's personal problems, whatever they were, felt a step too far.

But the sarge's bad mood wasn't the thing that had affected the atmosphere in the team room.

"You know," she said, "she might have freaked me out when she first started, but I sort of miss Kay."

"Yup. Just feels like she's the kind of person we need right now. And it doesn't help that Stella's lot have started making mistakes."

"You really think so?" Nina asked.

Tom reached out and grabbed two crisps from Nina's pack before she could stop him. After a moment, he nodded.

"I do. Topper's... I don't know about Topper. But it seems unlikely. And as for Eddie and Steve... What do you think?"

The door opened and half a dozen uniformed officers walked in. A lean woman with short, dark hair and a slender, almost elfin face approached their table. She grinned at Tom and shook her head.

"Crisps, DC Willis?" she said. "Don't you want to keep that perfect figure?"

She turned and walked away again.

"Who's that?" Nina asked. The room was filling up now, and she and Tom stood and headed out and towards the lift.

"Who's what?"

"The woman who was just talking to you. I recognise her, from the Lowther Street thing."

"Oh, yeah. That's Martinez. D shift."

"I think she likes you, Tom."

He shrugged. "You're imagining things. Trying to distract from your own love life."

Nina pulled a face. She'd been on one date in the last three months, with a man she'd met when she'd been interviewing the witnesses at the Great Borne murder. Romit Chandra. He was a runner, older than her, and probably too thin for her taste, but not bad looking. And he'd been the perfect way to put a stop to her mum's attempts to set her up with the sons, nephews and neighbours of her friends.

Nina's mum had a lot of friends. And those friends had an inexhaustible supply of sons, nephews and neighbours.

"Don't talk to me about that," she said.

"So you definitely won't be seeing him again?"

She pulled another face. They'd gone for dinner, at a cheap and cheerful grill place Romit had assured her served the perfect meat. The food had been fine, but Romit had spent the first half of their date talking about the way the meat was prepared, the different cuts, the fact that you could tell, if you really knew your stuff, and of course, Romit knew his stuff.

The second half of their date he'd spent talking about himself and his job. Nina had been so bored that when he'd finished, she still wasn't sure what he did for a living. When he suggested coming back again the following week, she'd seriously considered vegetarianism, but had instead resorted to putting him off.

She'd been putting him off for weeks now, but he still hadn't got the message.

"Definitely not," she said, as the lift arrived.

"You didn't answer my question, though," Tom pointed out as they headed up. "Eddie and Steve. You really think they've started dealing again?"

"No. It doesn't seem right to me, either. And you heard what the boss said."

"What did she say?"

"She said you could go and talk to them. Set your mind at rest."

"Do you really think she meant that?" Tom asked, as they emerged onto their floor and headed towards the team room.

"If she didn't," Nina pointed out, "then she shouldn't have said it."

CHAPTER THIRTY-EIGHT

IT WAS A NOVELTY, parking up at the West Cumberland Hospital and heading somewhere that wasn't the mortuary. Zoe had visited Roddy Chen here a few months back, and she'd had to get herself patched up after Dean Somerville had injured her, but most of her trips to the place had been to see dead people.

Of course, dead people didn't get quite the same levels of privacy and security as living ones.

"I'm sorry," said the nurse, sitting behind a narrow desk, beside the double doors that led into the third-floor ward. "You can't see her."

"Why not?"

"Visiting hours are over." The nurse pointed to a sign on the doors. But Zoe didn't really think of herself as a visitor.

"I understand that," she said. "But I've just shown you my warrant card. I'm with Cumbria CID, and we're investigating a serious crime that Emma might have witnessed. We've been looking for her for more than twenty-four hours, and it really is crucial that I speak to her as soon as possible."

Zoe smiled and waited for the man to press the little button that would allow her to push through the double doors and find Emma Hudson.

"I'm sorry," he said. "She's really not well enough to talk to anybody."

"Can you get one of her doctors here for me to speak to, please? This is a police emergency, after all. I hope you understand."

"The doctors are all busy, Sergeant," said the man, who'd spent nearly thirty seconds looking at Zoe's warrant card and knew full well she wasn't a sergeant.

"Right. Since you're convinced she's not well enough to speak to me, can you tell me precisely what's wrong with her?"

"Sorry, Sergeant. I—"

"It's Detective Inspector."

"Sorry, Detective Inspector. I can't do that. Patient confidentiality, you see."

Zoe sighed. "I'll be back shortly with a warrant." She turned and started to walk away, then stopped and looked back at the nurse. "And it'll have your name on it."

"Wait," he called. "OK. She said she didn't want to speak to anyone."

"I'm not 'anyone.' I'm the police."

"She said she didn't want to talk to the police."

Zoe walked back to the desk. She leaned forward, resting her palms on it. She looked the nurse in the eye and spoke slowly.

"A man has been murdered. Your colleagues in the mortuary have only just finished his post-mortem. The woman in there," she pointed through the doors, "was on the scene. She's the best hope we have of finding out who the murderer is and stopping him before he murders someone else. So in the circumstances, I'm sure you'll understand, I don't really care whether she wants to talk to me or not."

She stepped back again. The nurse stared at her and nodded. As Zoe walked towards the double doors, she heard the buzz of the unlocking mechanism being activated.

CHAPTER THIRTY-NINE

More than a year had passed since Nina had visited Mint Condition Motors, with the sarge accompanying her. In the intervening months, the KFC and McDonald's opposite had been joined by a Subway.

At least some industries were booming.

As they walked in, Nina spotted Steve Walker, leaning against the main reception desk, picking his fingernails and chatting to the woman sitting behind it. He wore different glasses from the last pair she'd seen him in. Smarter. And the suit— she shook her head in surprise.

Steve Walker looked good.

"Steve," she called.

He looked round fast, as if he'd been caught doing something he shouldn't have done. When he saw who had called him, his face fell.

"Hang on," he said. He strode to a glass-panelled door at the back of the showroom, tapping once and walking in.

"We'll give it thirty seconds," Nina told Tom. The woman behind the desk was staring at them, her mouth open, her face creased in confusion. "We're old friends," Nina called out to her as she approached the office door.

It opened before she got there. Steve emerged, followed by Eddie Driver.

Eddie still had the same mop of thick red-brown hair, but he walked with more confidence than before. It was as if finally, in his twenties, he'd grown into his outsized body. Nina's gaze slid over the plaque on the door Eddie had just walked out through, and stopped.

Edward Driver, Director of Sales.

The two of them had come up in the world.

"Get in here," hissed Eddie. "Fuck's sake. Thought you lot would have given up on us by now."

Nina and Tom followed Driver and Walker into the office, a small, plain room with a fake wood desk and three uncomfortable-looking chairs. Driver shut the door.

"Good to see you, Eddie, Steve," said Nina. Tom walked over to one of the chairs, pressed his hand onto it, as if to test its solidity, and grimaced.

"Yeah, yeah," said Eddie. "Oi, you. DC Willis, isn't it? Don't get comfortable. What do you want?"

Steve Walker was leaning against the wall, his eyes flicking between his friend, and Nina and Tom. Driver would be doing the talking, then. Some things hadn't changed.

"Cawter Hough," said Tom.

"What?" said Driver.

"Cawter Hough," Tom repeated.

Driver shook his head. "Speak English, will you?"

"It's a barn. North of Parton. Fire there, a few months back."

"Hope they were insured," replied Driver. "But it's nothing to do with me."

"Traces of cocaine were found. Cannabis."

Driver had been leaning back against his desk, but now he straightened up and pointed back out, through the glass panel in the door. "We sell cars, DC Willis."

Tom nodded. "The thing is, your prints were found there."

There was sharp intake of breath from Nina's right. She turned to see Steve Walker, his mouth open, his eyes wide.

"What the fuck are you playing at?" Driver stepped closer to Tom. Nina took a step towards them. Driver raised his hands and moved back.

"Your prints, Eddie," she said. "And yours, Steve. They were on the scene. Care to explain why?"

"Oh yeah," Driver said. "It's quite simple, really. One of your lot's trying to fit us up."

Nina shook her head and gave a small laugh. "Do you really think that would be worth our while, Eddie?"

"You explain it, then."

"You're dealing again. Both of you. You packaged the drugs there, there was a fire, you found somewhere else. Am I getting warm?"

Eddie Driver shook his head.

"We sell cars," said Steve, echoing Eddie's earlier comment.

Nina turned to him. "Remember when we dropped by last year, Steve?"

Walker nodded.

"We asked you why you'd stopped dealing. And you said something that's stuck in my head since then."

"What?" asked Walker.

"'Supply-side issues'. That's what you said. 'Supply-side issues.' Care to tell me anything more about that?"

Eddie Driver shook his head gently. Nina moved to stand between the two men, but it was too late. Walker had spotted the signal.

"Erm," he said, as Driver coughed. "No. No, I don't have anything to say."

"The thing is," said Tom, "there was another fire the other day. At a different barn. And this time, someone died. Driven out by the fire, then stabbed to death. That sound familiar?"

This time both of them looked surprised, two mouths hanging open, four eyes wide. Walker shut his mouth, then opened it again.

"I'm sorry someone's died," Driver said. "And we'd help you if we could. But we can't. And we don't want to lose our jobs. So if you don't mind, I'd be grateful if you'd fuck off."

On the way out, Nina pointed out the KFC. Tom shrugged, then sat and watched her while she wolfed down a Zinger Burger.

"That was a waste of time," she said between mouthfuls.

Tom looked thoughtful. "I don't think so."

"No?"

"We'll be hearing from them. One of them, anyway. Probably Steve. But possibly Eddie."

"Nah. They're too scared of losing their jobs. They don't know anything. And they don't want to be involved, either. They're clean, Tom. Someone's fucked up at the lab."

"We'll be hearing from them," he repeated.

Nina shook her head.

He grinned at her. "I think this one's worth a bet," he said.

CHAPTER FORTY

"Emma Hudson?"

What?

Emma tried to open her eyes, screwed them shut, then tried again. It was bright, and everything still hurt, but not as much as it had hurt earlier.

"Emma?"

And who the fuck was saying her name?

She blinked and tried to make out the shapes in front of her, but she couldn't lift her head properly.

"Let me help," said the same voice, closer now. There was a whirring noise, and she felt herself move, the upper half of her body lifting. Her head rose until she was looking at a tall woman with reddish hair and the face of someone who was used to asking questions.

A cop. She'd said no cops – no visitors was what she'd said, but that included cops – and one of them was already here.

"That's better," said the woman. "I'm Detective Inspector Zoe Finch, from Cumbria CID."

The woman had an accent. Not local, though. Emma could feel something tugging at her arm and moved her eyes to the right. Tubes. There were tubes and wires running into her.

She was dehydrated. That was what they'd told her. She'd not eaten, she'd hardly drunk. She was on a drip.

"I know you've had a hard couple of days, but I'm afraid I need to ask you some questions."

Emma finally remembered how to speak.

"No."

It hurt, a little, but not as much as it had hurt earlier, when she'd had to tell them who she was.

"I'm really sorry, Emma, but we really do need to talk. It's serious."

The laugh bubbled up through Emma's chest.

It's serious. She'd just spent a day hiding in a fucking shed after watching her friend get stabbed to death. Yeah. You could say it was serious.

"It's not funny, Emma. I don't know if you're aware of what happened to Neil Colvin."

Emma nodded. She was tired.

Too tired to fight it.

"Neil's dead," she said. Hoarse, but hardly painful at all.

"Did you witness the murder?" asked the woman. DI Finch.

Emma nodded.

"Do you know who it was? Do you know who killed him?"

Emma shook her head. Something occurred to her.

"What's happened to Theo?" she said.

The woman smiled. "Don't worry. Theo's safe."

Emma tightened her lips as a wave of anger surged through her. Theo was *safe*, was he?

Fucking coward.

"The person who killed Neil," said the DI.

"Man," muttered Emma. "It was a man."

The tiredness was washing through her again, filling the spaces the anger had just surged past. She blinked, and realised a moment later that her eyes were still shut. Opening them again felt like hard work.

"Emma?" said the woman. Midlands accent. What was she doing here?

What were any of them doing here?

"Emma, would you recognise the man who did it? If you saw him again?"

Emma said nothing.

"Emma? Would you recognise him?"

"Not sure," muttered Emma.

"Can you describe him, at least?"

Go away.

"Emma?"

"Maybe." It was hard work, just making her mouth move the right way. Maybe. Maybe. Maybe if she pretended to fall asleep…

"Emma? Please? Whoever he is, this man's still out there and if we don't stop him, he might kill someone else."

Someone else. Emma forced her eyes open. She was *someone else.* That was why she'd spent a night in a shed. The woman was leaning over her, frowning.

"Brown hair," Emma said. "Medium height."

"Anything else?"

Emma let her eyes fall shut. She shook her head. "There was smoke. It was dark."

"Do you know why? Did he say anything?"

Emma shook her head again, and she could have sworn she felt her brain moving about inside her skull. Everything was fuzzy. Black and fuzzy at the same time.

"What about your contact?" said the woman.

Who was this woman, again? Why was she here?

Where were they?

"Who did you get the drugs from?" said a voice. A woman. Funny voice. Funny accent. What was that?

"Emma?"

Go away.

"Who did you get the drugs from?" asked the voice again.

Maybe if she answered, they'd leave her alone.

"CSI man," she said.

"Do you know his name?" said the voice, as the darkness grew thicker and the fuzziness grew fuzzier.

Man who brought drugs. Did she know his name? She did know his name. Yes.

"Emma?" said a voice from the darkness. "His name. The man who gives you the drugs. Who is he?"

"Huz," said Emma, and succumbed to the darkness.

CHAPTER FORTY-ONE

AARON WALKED into an empty team room just as Nina texted, explaining that she and Tom were on their way back from Mint Condition Motors.

Hopefully they hadn't been wasting their time.

His phone rang. He answered without saying anything, and was surprised to hear not Nina or Tom, but the boss.

"Aaron, are you on your own?"

He looked around the room. It wasn't like there was anyone hiding there.

"Yes, boss. Just back from the PM. And I spoke to—"

"Stop talking for a moment and listen to me, and if anyone comes in, act casually, OK?"

He frowned.

"Aaron?"

"OK, boss."

"I've just spoken to Emma Hudson," she said. "She's at the hospital. She's OK, just dehydrated. She saw the murder, but she doesn't know who did it."

"Right." Aaron knew there was more. The echo of footsteps told him the DI was in one of the stairwells at the hospital.

"But she gave me a name. Her contact. The one who gets her the drugs."

Aaron felt his heart quicken. "Who?"

"It's Huz, Aaron. Huz, from the lab."

"Shit." He looked around the team room. "What are we—"

"I've had a few minutes to think about it, and I've made a decision. I want to bring him in."

"OK. Shall I speak to Inspector Keane? Get Uniform—"

"No. Just you and me."

"But boss—"

"Listen to me, Aaron. Don't say anything, just listen. OK?"

"OK." He made his way out of the team room to the stairs. Behind her voice, he could hear the wind. She was outside.

"The lab's just round the corner, but I've spoken to Stella. Huz isn't there. He's got a day off today. I've got his home address. Clitheroe Drive, in Whitehaven. You know it?"

"Yes," he told her.

"I want you to meet me there. Just you. Don't tell anyone else."

"What about Uniform? And shouldn't we tell PSD?"

"No. In normal circumstances I'd say of course, but we don't have time to get PSD involved and we don't know who we can trust at the Hub."

Aaron had been about to protest. But what the boss had said, it was true. It wasn't just Streeting. If Huz was involved in something, anyone could be. Someone at the Hub had been using Harry Oldman's login credentials to blackmail people. He could trust the DCs. The super. Morris Keane. Clive Moor in the Custody Suite. Maybe a handful of others.

But the rest?

And as for PSD, well, the DI knew the way they worked better than anyone else at the Hub did. If she said they didn't have time to get PSD involved, she was probably right.

"You understand me, Aaron?" she asked.

"I think so, boss."

"Good." She read out the address again. "This is an operational decision being taken to prevent serious prejudice to a murder investigation, Aaron. I'm comfortable it's the right decision, and I'll stand by it if I have to."

CHAPTER FORTY-TWO

CLITHEROE DRIVE WAS a tiny road off Park Drive, part of a little estate hemmed in by woods on both sides, just a couple of minutes from where Zoe lived and not much further from the hospital. There weren't many more than a dozen houses on the road – Huz's was number fourteen, right at the end – all of them smart semis with rounded, double-storey bays.

The bottom half of the road, the bit where Huz lived, was sealed off with police tape.

Zoe parked just outside the cordon, blocking someone's drive, but it was hard not to. There were only four or five places to put a car, and they were all taken up with other vehicles.

Unmarked. But police issue. After a while, you could tell.

Zoe approached the cordon. A man stood there, young, not in uniform, but he held up a hand with an air of authority and asked her to stop.

As she showed him her ID, she heard a car pull up and turned to see Aaron parking his Volvo just behind her Mini. Blocking the neighbour's drive too, now.

"I'm sorry, DI Finch, but I can't let you through," said the man.

"Who are you?" Zoe asked, fighting back anger.

"I..." He looked down, then back up at her. He turned around, to face Huz's house, and she followed his gaze.

A woman was emerging from the house, pulling off a forensic suit and mask, dragging her hand across her forehead. Zoe recognised that woman. Dark hair, sharp, almost striking features.

Aaron had reached her. "What's going on, boss?"

"PS fucking D," she told him. "That's what's going on."

Denise Gaskill was walking towards the cordon, but when she spotted Zoe and Aaron she stopped, then nodded, and carried on.

"DI Finch," she said.

"DS Gaskill," Zoe replied. "This is my colleague, DS Aaron Keyes. What's going on?"

She knew the answer, but she had to ask.

"We've taken Hussein Mahmoud into custody, DI Finch."

"Right," Zoe replied. *Of course they had.* "When precisely did this happen?"

"Earlier this morning," Denise told her.

Zoe tried to read the woman's face. DS Gaskill worked for Carl, but she'd only met her once, and briefly at that. Perhaps this was the way she always looked.

But Zoe was still struggling to control her anger.

"We need to talk to him."

"This is a PSD matter now, DI Finch."

"We're investigating a murder. He might well be able to lead us to the killer."

"Look, I'm sorry." Denise chewed one side of her lip. "I

wish I could help. But you know the rules. And really, you should have told us you were looking into him."

"Did you know?" Aaron asked from behind Zoe. He paused for a moment, and added, "Oh."

Zoe turned to him. He was pointing at the driveway in front of Huz's house, where a blue Audi TT was parked.

"I knew I recognised it, boss," he said, but Zoe was already walking back to her car, away from the house, away from Aaron and Denise Gaskill, anxious to shut herself away before she said or did something she'd regret.

Because the truth was, DS Gaskill was right. PSD were in charge now.

CHAPTER FORTY-THREE

ZOE LOOKED UP. Aaron was standing on the pavement, looking at her, a concerned expression on his face.

She started the engine and lowered the window. "Let's head back to the Hub, Aaron."

"You OK, boss?"

"I will be. I'll see you in the team room. Just... I need to think for a minute, OK?"

She started the car, drove up to the cordon. The unidentified young man took a step back in obvious alarm before she stopped and made a three-point turn.

Stupid. It wasn't his fault. It wasn't even Denise Gaskill's fault. Not really.

It was a short drive. She'd dialled Carl's number before she was off Park Drive, and when he answered, she could tell he knew.

"Zoe?" he said. "Everything OK?"

"What the fuck is going on?"

"Look, I understand you're angry, but—"

"How long?"

"How long what?"

"How long have you known we were looking into him? Did you know last night?"

"I—"

"It was your flag, wasn't it? On the TT? You were already looking at him. You didn't want anyone else involved."

"Yes, that's true."

"So you must have seen we were looking. And you didn't say anything."

"Look, Zoe. I didn't realise it was you, OK? But you know how this works."

She blinked. She was driving too fast. She was letting her emotions take control, and that wasn't like her. She had to calm down.

"You have your job to do," she said. "And even if I don't always agree with the rules, they're the rules. We can't discuss this now. Not on the phone. Not while I'm in the car."

"Agreed. And for what it's worth—"

"Don't say you're sorry, Carl. I just had that from your DS Gaskill, and believe me, it doesn't make things any better. We'll talk about all this later."

"Understood."

"In the meantime, see if you can do something more helpful than just being sorry."

"If I can, I will."

She was heading out of Whitehaven on the Moresby Road, her usual route to work. She hadn't even realised she was doing it.

"I'm working on a murder case," she said.

"I'm aware."

"And the actual murder, as far as we know, doesn't involve any police officers or civilian police workers."

"As far as you know."

"Neil Colvin was murdered. Unless you think Huz was the murderer, the murder itself doesn't actually concern you."

"That's not unreasonable."

"Thank you." She forced herself to slow down, both the car and her breathing. "But Huz was at the crime scene. Earlier. He left before it all happened. We've got CCTV."

"I know."

She took a sharp breath, prepared to shout again, and stopped herself.

"That means he might know something. Which means, I'm going to need to be involved when you question him. Surely you can see that?"

She'd almost reached Steel Brow, and she still hadn't got what she wanted.

"It does make sense," said Carl.

She breathed out, slowly.

"But it's not up to me," he continued. "DCI Branthwaite will make the final decision."

"Please, Carl."

"I'll do what I can. I can't promise anything, but I'll put in a word."

CHAPTER FORTY-FOUR

THE BOSS WAS MISSING, which wasn't unusual. Tom had got used to the way DI Finch disappeared, sometimes for a whole day, and then walked back in as if nothing had happened.

But there was no sign of the sarge, either, and no message. That was more unusual.

Annoying, too. Because even if he couldn't prove it, Tom was convinced Eddie and Steve were on the level. And when they got in touch with him and he *did* prove it, he'd be getting rid of the antimacassar currently draped over the back of his chair.

He'd just turned to Nina, to remind her of that, when the door burst open and DI Finch strode in, closely followed by the sarge.

Tom had seen the boss in a bad mood more than once. He'd been the focus of that bad mood himself. But he didn't think he'd ever seen her this angry. Her face was twisted into a scowl. And the way she was moving – he was glad he wasn't the carpet.

"Right," she said.

Tom glanced at Nina, who gave a tiny shake of her head, not that he needed it. Yes, he wanted to tell them about Mint Condition Motors. But now wasn't the time.

The boss stopped, and turned to face them, Nina and Tom, standing side by side, the sarge, who'd stopped himself, just the other side of Nina. "You need to know what's just happened."

Tom held his breath.

"We've just been to arrest Huz," she continued.

Had she really just said that? Huz?

Huz?

He had to say something.

She clenched a fist against her side. "Emma Hudson informed me this morning that he was her contact, and it turns out it was his Audi on the CCTV."

"Where is he?" asked Nina.

The boss turned to Nina. "PSD got to him before we did. That's why we couldn't trace the car. They had a flag on it. But Huz was the one who got the drugs for Neil and Emma to distribute. I've put in a request to be involved in the questioning, but we'll have to wait and see."

Silence.

Huz.

It didn't make sense. Only, it did. A lot of things that hadn't made sense suddenly did. Not just the glitch in the system that had stopped them from tracing the car.

"The evidence," Tom said.

The other three stared at him.

"I mean, the other barn. Cawter Hough. The prints and DNA that didn't make sense. Topper. Eddie Driver and

Steve Walker. It was Huz who analysed it all. If he's involved..."

The boss nodded. "If he was involved, then he'd have removed evidence of his own presence, and muddied the waters by shoving something else in."

"Christ," said Nina. "That's just one scene. They're going to have to go through everything else he's worked on. I'll call Stella."

She'd taken a single step back towards her desk when the boss shouted, "No!" and everything went still again.

"Sorry," said DI Finch. "But Stella doesn't know yet. And I don't think we can tell her. Not until we have to. In the meantime, though, I've got to brief the super."

If she'd stormed in like a woman bent on murder, the way she left the room was more like someone heading to their own execution.

CHAPTER FORTY-FIVE

ZOE TRUDGED UPSTAIRS, Nina's words – and her own – echoing through her brain.

Stella was one of the few people in Whitehaven she absolutely trusted. Zoe had confided in Stella, had told her what she'd suspected about Streeting. Stella had even helped her set the scene for the non-existent evidence that implicated Carter in the death of Victor Parlick. The non-existent evidence that had gone up in flames shortly after Streeting found out about it.

Stella was clean. Zoe had come across enough people who weren't to be sure of it.

But she couldn't tell Stella about Huz. Not yet. And she didn't feel good about that.

Upstairs, there was no sign of Luke. Zoe stood for a moment outside Fiona's door, waiting, listening.

She knocked, and heard the familiar tones. "Come in."

Fiona was alone, at least. Zoe fell into one of the empty chairs with a sigh. "I've got bad news, Fiona."

The super stared at her, her mouth set in a thin line. "What is it, Zoe?"

What's your team done now?

"We've just found out that Hussein Mahmoud's been taken in by PSD."

"Hussein Mahmoud? You mean Huz? From Stella's lab?"

Zoe nodded.

"What... Why... How did this happen? What's he done?"

"I don't know what PSD wants with him, but we were there to talk to him about drugs. Turns out he's the contact who was supplying product to Emma Hudson and Neil Colvin."

"Shit. OK. Tell me the rest."

Zoe told her the rest, then sat back and waited. She'd managed to interview people, search houses, speak to bereaved relatives in three different locations in Lancashire without anyone getting possessive or territorial. But now things were going just the way she'd feared.

"We can't do much about PSD," Fiona warned her. "Wait and see what they say. I'll see what I can do, but my authority is limited. As it should be."

Zoe nodded. No surprises there.

"Of course," Fiona continued, "now you're starting to expose more details here, another angle comes into play."

Here it comes. Zoe waited.

"Organised crime. If Huz was involved, and we've got people coming from elsewhere in the region to package and distribute the product, then—"

"They're a bunch of chemistry students, Fiona. We're not talking about the Krays here."

The super shrugged. "I hear what you're saying, but still.

There's been a murder, there are significant numbers of people involved, there's corruption, there's geographic spread, and you know as well as I do what that points to. Probably better, given your experience."

Zoe nodded again, glum. "Has Streeting been in touch already, then?"

"Yes. But not in the way you're thinking."

Fiona was smiling. Zoe leaned forward, surprised.

"What do you mean?"

"He called earlier. Said he'd heard some interesting things about your case. Did his usual waffling along until I asked him if Specialist Crime and Intel would be trying to take it over. He said no."

"He did?"

"He did. Well, not for now, at least. He's happy for this to play out, but he wants to be kept updated."

Of course he did. Intel on a case like this, with murder, corruption in the police, and a drugs operation that seemed to have been running under their noses without anyone spotting it, would be worth its weight in gold.

And whatever Zoe did find out, Ralph Streeting was the last person she planned to share it with.

CHAPTER FORTY-SIX

PSD MOVED FAST when they had to.

They'd taken Huz in before Zoe could get to him. And now, just minutes after she'd returned to her desk, her phone rang with an unfamiliar number. She answered it, and found herself talking to DCI Branthwaite.

"Zoe?" she heard. "Doug Branthwaite. PSD."

"Oh," she said. She'd been expecting to hear from PSD, but she'd assumed it would be Carl calling her. And not until later in the day, if it was going to be that day at all. "Hello, Sir."

She'd not met Douglas Branthwaite before, or even spoken to him. The way Carl talked about him, he sounded like a decent cop, and a decent boss.

"We'll have none of that 'Sir' nonsense," Branthwaite said. "Your other half, he has to call me that. But you don't work for me. Lucky you, eh?"

The accent was thick, and the voice reminded her of someone. She closed her eyes for an instant, and it came to her.

Solomon Frimpton. Him and all the others, the elderly former miners who congregated in the Anchor Vaults, and the Miner's Yard, from time to time. Proper Cumbria, as she liked to think of it.

But most of them would be in their eighties. Branthwaite was thirty years younger.

"Thanks for calling," she said.

"I gather you want to talk to one of our pulls?"

'Pulls.' She'd not heard that in a while. Branthwaite really was one of the old school.

"If I can, DCI Branthwaite. I'm working on a murder case, and—"

"No need for all that, lass. I've heard it all from Carl. And I think it's fair enough. We'll want to be in on it too, of course. In case he says anything that tickles our antennae. But I don't see why you can't be there. So how's about you and Carl question Hussein Mahmoud together?"

"Oh," she said, taken aback, not only by how easy it had been, but by the way Branthwaite had pronounced Huz's name. Not a dinosaur, after all.

"I won't lie to you, we've already tried to get him to say something. Not about your murder. More general. But he's doing an excellent impression of a mime artist right now, right down to the bit where I'd like to get hold of the little bastard and slam his face into a desk, only I can't. Bloody rules, eh?"

Was he joking? Zoe had good reason to hate corrupt cops, but this seemed a bit much.

"So, I was thinking," Branthwaite continued, "we'd let him stew overnight, and then send in the big guns in the morning."

Zoe raised an eyebrow. "That sounds excellent, Sir."

"And the big guns are you and that lad of yours, for the avoidance of doubt, Zoe. Now, I've got an urgent appointment with four pints of Cumbria's finest, so I'll be off now, but it's been a pleasure speaking to you."

"Thank you," Zoe replied, but the line was already dead.

On the stairway, between the first and second floor, she passed Tracy Giller-Jones, Alan Markin's DS, coming the other way. She stopped, said "Hello," and realised immediately that had been the wrong thing to do, because Giller-Jones stopped too, and turned.

For thirty seconds, the two women engaged in what could best be described as excruciating small talk: *How are you? Very well. Interesting weather. Have you settled in yet?*

Zoe couldn't have been more relieved when her phone rang. She lifted it apologetically to her ear, heading down the stairs and answering without checking the display.

"What's going on?" asked the voice on the other end of the line.

"Stella?"

"Zoe, I need to know what's going on. You've got your ear to the ground."

"What do you mean?"

"I mean, I've had a call from PSD. They've said they want to talk to me later. They'll be coming into the lab, too."

"Oh," said Zoe. She'd spent most of the last half hour saying *Oh* into her phone.

"And what with you being an important DI, with a partner who's also an important DI, in PSD no less, I thought you might be able to tell me what I should expect."

Stella was a friend. Friends looked out for each other.

"Stella," she said, "are you sitting down?"

CHAPTER FORTY-SEVEN

ZOE AND CARL had been tiptoeing around each other for weeks. First over the Randle messages. Then over Elena's stay at the house. Even after Elena had left, there had been tension. She'd pushed it aside and pretended it wasn't there.

But suddenly, she felt like she'd never loved him more.

Yoda wasn't for leaving the sofa, but Zoe scooted her over and sat down, and Carl fell into the spot beside her. They sat with their kebabs and drinks, and accused each other of ruining investigations, having messed-up priorities, not understanding what being a cop was really about. It was wonderful.

"So those searches," she said. "The ones Aaron was running, on the Audi. Is that why you pulled Huz in?"

She was resting her head on his chest, and felt him nod.

"We'd been looking at him, but we weren't quite ready. Then we realised someone else was interested and wouldn't let it go, so we had to bring him in."

"Someone else?"

"I promise you, I didn't realise it was you – not until this morning, and by then, the decision had been made."

Zoe turned her head upwards. He might not tell her everything, but he wouldn't lie to her.

"So, you were looking into him, were you? What for?"

"Zoe..."

"No, I think the least we can do is tell each other the full story on this. You asked me a while back what the local dealing scene was like. Which I have to say was a strange question to hear from PSD, but I didn't think anything of it at the time. Is that what you've pulled Huz in over?"

There was a long silence, and Zoe looked up again, to see Carl frowning in concentration.

"Sorry," he said. "I don't even remember what that was about. But OK. You want to spill all the secrets, I'm game. But you first."

"Fine. You know about our murder, right? Fell Barn?" She felt him nod again. "From what we've pieced together, the victim was one of a handful of students who used remote barns to take delivery of drugs from a source, then test them, repackage them, and take them back to university for distribution. We still don't know who the killer is, or the motive. But we've found the other student who was there that night. And she told us her source was Huz."

"Bloody hell." Carl had shifted, so he could look down into her face. "I knew it was something serious, but... well, I can see why you wanted him."

"You only had to ask, Carl. I could have told you this earlier."

"You didn't know it was Huz earlier, though, did you? And I didn't know it was you that was looking into the Audi. Anyway, what you've got, it's a lot more than we have."

Zoe pulled herself away from him and took a swig of Diet Coke. "Are you serious?"

Carl nodded. "He's been flashing the cash. General erratic behaviour. Coming in late and a bit the worse for wear. It wasn't a lot, but it was enough."

"That's ridiculous," Zoe said, but a memory jolted through her mind. Huz, outside Freeburn's office, wearing an Armani suit and shoes that normal people wouldn't be able to afford in a lifetime.

But it wasn't enough.

"So you haven't even got a proper investigation going?"

"Not yet, not really, but—"

"And I suppose now you're just going to use what we've got?"

She turned to stare at him.

He shrugged and swallowed the last of his kebab. "I'm sorry, Zoe. But that's how it is in PSD. Sometimes we investigate cops and they turn out to be crooks. Sometimes you investigate crooks and they turn out to be cops, and it becomes our case."

"That's not fair, Carl."

"Why not? And why does it matter? Does it really bother you that we're talking to him at the same time you are?"

"No. I'm happy to share. But I'm not happy about the secrecy and I'm not happy our murder investigation is being delayed because you've swooped in and done your thing. And frankly, I'm worried the small detail of that murder's going to be forgotten in all the excitement of pulling in a CSI."

There was a silence, broken by Yoda miaowing loudly at Carl. The cat had had her eye on the last of the kebab, and hadn't been happy to see it disappear into a human mouth.

Carl sighed.

"That's fair, Zoe. And I'm sorry. I'll do what I can to keep your case front and centre. But it's not my place to decide who gets to do what. Your super and my DCI are going to have to sort that out between themselves."

Zoe nodded. So far, Branthwaite seemed to be doing the right thing. She could only hope that would continue.

CHAPTER FORTY-EIGHT

AARON PAUSED IN THE LOBBY. There were two figures ahead of him. PSD. DI Whaley, the boss's partner, and the woman he'd seen outside Huz's house yesterday.

He took a breath. The boss had left a message; she'd heard from DI Whaley's senior officer, and she was going to be allowed to question Huz alongside him. She'd made the best of a bad situation.

He caught up with the two officers as they entered the stairwell. DI Whaley noticed him immediately. His brow furrowed briefly, then cleared.

"Aaron, isn't it?"

"Good to see you, Sir," Aaron replied, then turned to the woman. "DS Gaskill," he said, smiling.

DS Gaskill gave a small grunt of acknowledgement, and continued up the stairs.

The boss had told him PSD were to be granted full access to the team room, so when they reached the fourth floor, he moved ahead of them and beckoned them to follow.

The team room was empty. The boss would be in her office, preparing for the day. Nina and Tom weren't in yet. DI Whaley looked around the room slowly, taking in details, nodding appreciatively. DS Gaskill grunted again, then sighed.

"Something wrong, Denise?" asked DI Whaley.

Aaron took a step back. It felt like he was intruding on something here. He glanced longingly at the door, took another step towards it, then stopped.

This was his office. His team room. He ran this team, when the DI wasn't around, and for all those months when there'd been no DI at all.

He was staying.

"I just don't know why they have to be involved, boss," said DS Gaskill.

Aaron couldn't hold back a gasp.

If you've got something you want to tell me, say it to my face.

He looked at DI Whaley, wondering how he would react to his sergeant's rudeness.

"Now, now," said DI Whaley. "You're just annoyed you're not going to be running the interview. But everyone has to sit the odd one out, Denise. You know that."

"I suppose I can sit around twiddling my thumbs somewhere and hope we get something good out of the little shit."

DI Whaley frowned at her. "DS Keyes here is in the same position. Aren't you, Aaron?"

Aaron nodded. "It's really not that bad," he said. "And if it gets boring, we can be bored together."

DS Gaskill turned the full force of her gaze on him, and he resisted the urge to take yet another step backwards.

Withering. You saw her staring at you, and you withered.

He forced himself to stand up a little straighter and stare back, and tried to think of something else to say. But the words wouldn't come.

He was saved by the sound of the door opening. He turned to see the boss walking in, her head buried in her phone, looking up and seeing the three of them there, frozen in position.

"Here already? Excellent," she said. "Carl, I think they'll be ready for us soon."

DI Whaley nodded. Aaron had seen his face lighten as the boss entered the room. He'd seen that before, on Serge's face, months ago, years ago.

"Denise," said the boss. "I hope we can make you comfortable while you wait."

"I'll need somewhere to work, Ma'am," she replied. "I'm not sure it would be appropriate for me to take up space in here."

There was a sneer in that last word, that *here*.

Aaron's eyes followed DS Gaskill's and lit on the back of Tom's chair. The antimacassar. The bloody antimacassar.

Maybe DS Gaskill had a point.

"That's fine," said DI Finch, looking back down at her phone. "I'm sure we can find you a terminal and an empty office. Aaron can call Resources and see what's available, if you want?"

DS Gaskill smiled at DI Finch, then turned the same insincere smile on Aaron.

The boss hadn't even noticed it.

"That's OK, DI Finch," she said. "I know this place well enough to find my way around. I've been visiting the Hub since it was built, thank you."

She turned and walked away, and when Aaron looked

over to the boss, to see how she'd react, her face was pointing down at her phone. After a moment, she looked back up.

"OK," she said. "Huz's lawyer's here. They're ready for us, Carl."

CHAPTER FORTY-NINE

Standing outside the interview room, Zoe felt a touch on her shoulder.

"This is weird," he said. "Isn't this weird?"

She nodded. "But not in a bad way." They'd done interviews together before, in Birmingham. But not here.

Carl smiled. "OK. Let's do this thing." He pushed the door open.

They were on the sixth floor of the Hub, walking past corridors lined with solid, unmarked doors. Zoe hadn't been this high up, hadn't known what was here, and for the most part, she still didn't.

Except for three things.

The first was that there was a Custody Suite up here. A separate Custody Suite from the one downstairs, a brand new facility that only opened when it was needed, so the people being pulled in didn't have to be seen by others who might recognise them.

The last of the corridors they'd marched down opened up into a wide reception area, behind which stood a man in plain clothes and a serious-looking set of muscles. He'd checked their ID and ushered them through, but he'd spent more time checking hers than Carl's, and Zoe knew immediately that Carl had been here before, had questioned people here before.

Had he questioned Kay here?

The second thing was that there was a separate lift, which, Carl informed her, ran straight from the back of the delivery entrance and meant people like Huz could come all the way up without anyone spotting them.

And the third, as she realised when she walked in, was that the interview rooms up here were somehow much more intimidating than the ones downstairs.

There was a table in the middle of the room, two chairs on either side. Huz blinked at her. Beside him was a woman Zoe didn't recognise. The table was made of wood, or a decent veneer, and the chairs were upholstered. There was a carpet, too, and the walls were painted a shade of pale blue that in another place might have been described as 'calming.' The contents of the room were fine.

It was just so clean. So professional-looking. Glancing around, she had the sense that when they finished in here, it could all be packed away and used to host a seminar on Equality and Diversity or a surprise birthday party.

That was it. A feeling that everything in here could be forgotten about. Wiped away. Erased from history.

Including the person being questioned.

From the look on his face, the same thought had occurred to Huz. Were those tear stains on his cheeks?

She looked at Carl, who'd raised an eyebrow. They hadn't planned this, not any of it. They hadn't even decided which of them would kick things off. Was that a mistake?

Zoe read out the formalities. Huz had been arrested on suspicion of Misconduct in Public Office, which would be wide enough to catch anything he had done, assuming he'd done anything. Zoe had questioned plenty of suspects over the years, clever ones, stupid ones, brave ones, and cowards. The innocent and the guilty.

Huz's expression screamed *guilty*.

He confirmed his name, and his role, then turned to his lawyer, who'd introduced herself as Paula Vernon and seemed to know Carl already. They whispered to one another for a moment.

"Can you explain what you were doing at Fell Barn three nights ago, Mr Mahmoud?" Zoe asked.

"No comment." His eyes had widened when she'd referred to him as 'Mr Mahmoud.'

"We have evidence you were there," Carl added. Huz's gaze darted over to Carl. His lower lip was trembling slightly.

"No comment."

"That's fine, Mr Mahmoud," Zoe said. "My colleague here has a number of questions relating to your recent behaviour, and your lifestyle. We'll come to those shortly. In the meantime, I'd like to ask you about your relationship with Emma Hudson."

"No comment."

"What about the late Neil Colvin?"

"No comment." But this time, had there been a trace of a wince?

Carl leaned across the table, fixed Huz with a probing stare, and said, "What about Theo Georgiou?"

"Never heard of him. No comment."

Zoe waited while Carl asked questions about Huz's bank account, his car, his clothes. Every now and then she'd ask something of her own, just to vary things a little. She remembered the Armani suit he'd been wearing in the summer. She asked where he got the drugs from. She asked if he knew who'd been driving the Land Rover that had been behind him as he'd driven up to Fell Barn.

"No comment," to everything, although there was a flicker of something like fear when she mentioned the Land Rover. Did he know who it was? Or had he not realised anyone was behind him at all?

"Do you know who killed Neil Colvin?" she asked.

"No comment."

"Did you kill Neil Colvin?" added Carl casually.

"No." Not even the customary, 'No comment.'

They hadn't learned anything. But as an exercise, it had gone well. They'd worked well as a team, her and Carl. They'd seemed to know instinctively when to say something, when to remain silent, what direction the other wanted to go in. As they stood to leave, she caught Carl grinning at her, and she couldn't help returning it.

It had gone well, regardless of the results. And the fact that Carl clearly felt the same made it even better.

CHAPTER FIFTY

Nina had nodded when the boss suggested she speak to Emma Hudson. But now, sitting in a plastic chair beside the woman's hospital bed, she wasn't so sure.

Emma lay there, pale, frowning and stifling her yawns with the back of her hand. She clearly wasn't pleased to see Nina.

"I need to sleep," she said as soon as Nina introduced herself. "The doctors say I need rest."

"I appreciate that," Nina replied. "I wouldn't be here if I didn't have to be. But if we're going to find whoever killed your friend—"

"He wasn't my friend."

"He wasn't?"

A shrug, followed by a wince. "Well, I suppose we got on well enough. But it wasn't like we hung out together. I'd see him in a barn every now and then, we'd sort out... Well, you know what we did. And then we'd go our separate ways. I'm sorry he's dead, but..."

Emma paled and shook her head.

"I'm sorry. It was so horrible." She fell silent, her eyes closed.

"We've arrested Huz," Nina said.

Emma looked up and then away. Was that guilt? "Is he OK?"

"He's in custody. He's being questioned by Professional Standards. Do you know who they are?"

Emma shook her head.

"They're the cops who investigate the cops. You get pulled in by them, you know you're in trouble."

"Shit." Emma was still looking away. "I didn't mean for that—"

"They were looking at him already," Nina told her.

"Why?"

"Because the idiot was driving a new TT and wandering about in Armani suits. Like a bank robber buying a fur coat."

Emma looked back at Nina. She gave a nervous laugh. Nina smiled at her. Emma smiled back.

"I know you don't want to get in any more trouble," Nina said. "But there's a murderer out there, Emma. If there's anything you can tell us that might help us catch him, you should probably do that."

Emma nodded. "It was such a blur, though."

"I know. Just start at the beginning, from when you arrived at the barn. Take me through it, bit by bit. Maybe something'll jump out."

It wasn't a long story, in the end. A drive, an annoying boyfriend who kept fidgeting and scowled when he was told he had to wait in the car, Huz arriving, Huz leaving. Neil, Theo, and Emma in the barn.

"Then the fire started. Just a funny smell, at first," Emma said. "I think it was Neil who saw the smoke, and Theo shouted something, I don't remember what, and the next I knew, he was gone, and we could hear the motor as he drove away."

She shook her head.

"I remember looking at Neil and laughing, and he laughed too. It was so ridiculous. But the smoke was still coming and then there were the flames."

"Where?"

"Everywhere. Well, both ends, and the other walls, too. It was so sudden. A bit of smoke, a bit more smoke, and then there's flames on all sides, not big, but enough. We had a couple of towels, just cloths, really. A couple of bottles of water. I watched Neil, he poured some water onto a cloth and then tried to put the flames out in one corner, and it worked, so I did the same thing."

She stopped, and looked away again, then closed her eyes.

"But there weren't enough cloths. Or water. Neil pulled off his jumper, and I used my coat, but there was too much. Then we gave up. I was at the far end of the barn where there was a little door with a metal latch, and I turned to Neil and he was looking at me and shaking his head." She opened her eyes. "I shouted, 'It's not working' or something like that, and he shouted, 'Get out.' Luckily the latch wasn't hot yet, and I got the door open. Neil was running out the main double doors, he just pushed them, and I thought it would all be OK. I'd got out. He'd got out. I coughed a bit and walked around the side of the barn. It was difficult to see what was going on."

"Try, Emma. Try to remember."

"I could see Neil. There was so much fire, so much smoke, and it was pitch black. I remember feeling for my torch, but then suddenly there was someone else."

She shook her head.

"He was on top of Neil, and I could see him bringing his hands down. I could even see the knife."

She stopped, closing her eyes. "I ran. If I'd stayed, maybe..."

Nina looked at her. "If you'd stayed, you'd be dead too. Neil's wounds— you couldn't have done anything to save him, Emma. Believe me."

Emma nodded, tears in her eyes.

"You told my colleague the man had brown hair and was of medium height. Do you think you can describe him for me in any more detail?"

She screwed her eyes shut. A moment later, she was shaking – not just her head, but her whole body, in tiny spasms, her limbs so clearly out of control that Nina reached forward and held her shoulders until the shaking had subsided and Emma had opened her eyes again.

"I'm sorry," Emma said. "I can't do it. I can't see it in any more detail."

"What about the knife? Anything distinctive? Size? Shape?" Nina hated herself, but it had to be done.

"It was pointy. Sharp. I don't know." She shook her head.

Nina smiled at her. Maybe things would improve later. Maybe tomorrow.

"But I'd know him if I saw him," Emma said.

Nina's smile broadened.

"In that case," she said, "do you mind if I send a colleague over later? Someone who can use the digital composite software, make up a face from even the vaguest descriptions, and then they show you alternative versions and keep going until it gets closer to the real thing?"

Emma nodded. "That's fine." She closed her eyes.

It was time to go.

CHAPTER FIFTY-ONE

ZOE LOOKED AT HER TEAM, feeling optimistic at last. The interview with Carl had gone well, and Nina had returned from the hospital and filled them in on Emma Hudson.

"Good work. Sadly, we got nothing out of Huz, but we'll keep pushing. In the meantime, I..."

She stopped. Nina was staring at her phone.

"Anything interesting, Nina?"

"Sorry, boss. I think this might be—"

"Take it."

The three of them waited while Nina answered her phone, walked to the end of the team room, and spoke quietly to whoever had interrupted one of the most pointless briefings Zoe had ever run. The three of them watched as Nina walked back to her own desk and sat down, pen in hand, her phone wedged between shoulder and ear, jotting down notes.

There was an animation in her movements that lifted Zoe's spirits. Nina thanked the caller and said goodbye.

"That was Steve Walker, boss."

"Which means," Tom said, "that you lose the bet."

Nina nodded.

"The dealer whose prints turned up at the other barn?" Zoe asked, realising where she'd heard that name before.

"That's right. We went to see them yesterday, they said it couldn't be them, wouldn't really say any more, but... well, it looks like Steve's changed his mind."

Tom lifted the antimacassar from the back of his chair, and draped it, with a flourish, over Nina's.

Nina was grinning. "He gave me a name, boss."

"What do you mean?" Zoe said.

"The *supply-side issues* thing. He said they kept getting busted, losing their product. Every time they took a delivery, they lost it again within a couple of days. They tried shifting things around, changing their delivery dates, but it kept happening. Like clockwork. Take a delivery, lose it, slap on the wrist. They weren't getting arrested, let alone charged, and they couldn't figure out what was going on."

"Who was it?" Zoe asked. In the space of a minute, she'd moved from resigned to excited.

"Same cop every time. Carrie Wright."

The name meant nothing to Zoe.

"You know her?" she asked.

Tom and Nina shook their heads. Aaron nodded. "Sergeant. Based here, these days. Always thought she seemed OK. Walker might be winding us up, boss."

Zoe turned to Nina.

"I don't think so, boss. He seemed scared, if anything. And what would be the point?"

"OK," said Zoe. "We've got a name. It's another copper. Another link in the chain. We'll have to move slowly. And we'll have to keep PSD involved."

CHAPTER FIFTY-TWO

IF INTERVIEWING alongside Carl had seemed natural, working with Denise Gaskill was something else entirely.

Zoe was her senior, with more experience, investigating a different, more serious offence. And DS Gaskill was sitting next to her, on the same side of the table.

But every time Denise asked a question, every time she left a pause, for Zoe to ask one of her own, Zoe couldn't help feeling like she was the one being interviewed.

It was probably just a PSD thing. She'd felt much the same with DS Layla Kaur, back in Birmingham. They had a way of putting you on the defensive, making you second guess yourself, overanalyse everything to the extent that you were practically paralysed. It was unsettling and unpleasant, and probably deliberate. And Denise Gaskill was a master at it.

Zoe glanced over at Huz. If she was feeling uncomfortable, he'd be in his own personal hell.

They'd opened with the same questions as last time, and received the same answers, with no variation on the standard "no comment." Paula Vernon sat silently beside her client, nodding every time he refused to tell them anything.

What was the point of her, exactly?

"Carrie Wright," said DS Gaskill, suddenly. She'd just been asking Huz about his car, producing receipts and bank statements, and it had seemed as if the conversation was going nowhere.

Huz made a noise somewhere between a cough and a gasp.

"She's the one who gets you the drugs, right?"

Huz stared at her, then turned to Zoe, who hadn't spoken.

"PS Carrie Wright," Zoe said. "Can you confirm that she's your supply?"

"I... I don't..." said Huz. Paula Vernon leaned towards him and whispered urgently in his ear, but he didn't tear his eyes away from Zoe's. Not for a second.

Was that fear?

"It's just that we're planning to have a little chat with Carrie shortly," Denise said. "And if she's got any sense, she'll be a lot more forthcoming than you've been."

More whispering from Paula Vernon. Huz nodded, shook his head, nodded again. Denise had gone in hard, but not so hard anyone would be able to complain about it afterwards, because the threat she wasn't really allowed to make had been implied rather than spoken.

If you don't tell us, she will. If you don't land her in it, she'll land you in it.

"Yes," said Huz.

Zoe resisted the urge to punch the air. "Yes, what?" she asked.

"Yes. Carrie Wright is my supply."

Once that had come out, the rest followed as easily as if Huz were confessing to a minor driving offence. He'd recruited the students through their universities – there were dozens who claimed to be interested in working with the police when they'd finished their degrees, and of those dozens, there were a handful who wanted to make a bit of money in the meantime, too.

"Where does Carrie get the drugs?" Zoe asked.

"I don't know," Huz said, "but I'm not an idiot."

"What does that mean?" asked Denise.

"I know she's a copper. So I assume it's from her busts."

"Right," said Denise. She sat back and nodded, then picked up a sheet of paper. Carrie Wright's information summary. They'd been through it together, not that there was much to go through. Carrie Wright's career had been as close to uneventful as you could hope for.

"You've explained how you brought these students into your little operation, and I can see how that worked," Denise continued. "It's actually quite clever of you."

Huz opened his mouth to say something, then stopped as Denise went on.

"But how exactly did you recruit a serving police officer with an unblemished record?"

"I didn't," Huz said. "And it's not my operation. She recruited me."

Zoe sat forward. So did Denise.

"Please explain," Zoe said.

"I was doing a little dealing on the side. Just weed. Nothing big. Not even using the evidence. Just people I knew. She was the one who busted me. She knew who I was, said I could lose my job, or I could help her out."

"And you decided to help her out?"

Huz nodded. Zoe thought of something else.

"You've been covering things up, haven't you?"

Huz frowned. "What do you mean?"

"DNA, prints. Cawter Hough, for example."

Denise Gaskill turned to stare at her. Zoe hadn't told anyone about Cawter Hough. Hadn't thought it was important. But Steve Walker had been telling the truth about Carrie Wright, which meant he'd probably been telling the truth about not being at the other burnt-out barn.

Which meant the evidence had been tampered with.

Huz said nothing, so Zoe went on.

"There was another barn fire, a few months back. No one died that time, but there were drugs present. You were there, weren't you?"

After a long silence, Huz nodded.

"For the recording, please," Denise said.

"Yes."

"And when you were tasked with examining the physical evidence you had to make sure your own prints and DNA weren't found, didn't you?" Zoe continued.

A nod. "I was the one doing the analysis, so it was easy. Just removed the records that matched with me. Replaced them with others. People who wouldn't have been a surprise."

Zoe could have told him that he'd made a stupid mistake, setting up two lads who'd stopped dealing a year ago and another who'd only just been released from prison in another county.

But there was no point. They had what they needed.

CHAPTER FIFTY-THREE

AARON SAT in a tiny room beside the interview room, in front of a screen that took up a whole wall. Beside him was DI Whaley. He'd met DI Whaley before, a handful of times, but he still wasn't sure how to behave with the man.

It wasn't that he was the boss's partner, although that didn't help. It was that he was PSD.

He'd found himself fidgeting, talking too much, talking too little, and realised suddenly that this was what ordinary members of the public felt like when they were talking to him.

On the screen, they could see the boss and DS Gaskill, and Huz and his lawyer. And they could hear every word.

Aaron sat forward, frowning.

"What?" DI Whaley said.

"The blackmail," Aaron replied. Huz had just revealed that he'd been blackmailed into the operation. "I want to know more. I think someone should push on that."

"Why?"

It was a good question. It had rung some bells, that was

all. Margaret Hooper. The images that had been captured and stored at the Bassenthwaite Manor Hotel. Nothing concrete. Just vague connections.

DI Whaley was sympathetic, at least. "I'll call DCI Branthwaite," he said, standing and heading out of the room when the interview had finished. "I'll tell him you want to question Huz a little more on the blackmail angle."

He returned just two minutes later, shaking his head. "I'm sorry, Aaron. The DCI's being territorial."

"He's refused?"

"If it's not directly related to our investigation or your murder, it'll have to wait. I'm sure it'll be looked into, eventually, but it's not a priority."

Aaron frowned. "But it must be related," he said. "You've just heard Huz tell us he was blackmailed."

DI Whaley shook his head. "That's a side angle, Aaron. Yes, it's interesting. But for the moment, we don't care about *why* Huz is crooked, and we don't care about other people who aren't cops who've been caught in similar stings."

How could they not care? It was all linked. Surely that was obvious?

Aaron sighed. DCI Branthwaite had made his decision.

"I really am sorry." DI Whaley clapped an arm on his back, and he winced. It ached. Too many nights on the sofa. "We're here to find out about cops dealing. You're allowed to be involved because you're investigating a murder that might be related. And that's all we're going to be asking about until we've got to the bottom of it."

CHAPTER FIFTY-FOUR

ZOE HAD WALKED out of that interview with a spring in her step. Even Denise Gaskill had been smiling. The two of them had congratulated each other and disappeared in opposite directions, and a minute later Aaron was in her office, sitting opposite her, and shaking his head.

"They're pulling Carrie in now," Zoe told him. "PSD will question her alone, and then they'll make a decision on whether we'll get to speak to her."

"They're gonna say no, boss," Aaron said. He still looked rough. He'd fallen into the chair on the other side of her desk like a man who'd just run a marathon rather than someone who'd walked down a few flights of stairs.

"Why d'you say that?"

"I asked if we could push Huz on the blackmail angle," he explained. He'd been looking into that a few months back. Nothing had come of it, but it was still there. "DI Whaley asked DCI Branthwaite, DCI Branthwaite said no. Apparently, if it's not directly related to the PSD investigation or the murder, it'll have to wait."

"He's right. If it turns out the blackmail's a key part of this whole thing, I'm sure we'll revisit it sooner rather than later. If it doesn't, you'll get your chance. Just not yet."

"I don't know, boss." Aaron was shaking his head again. "I'm worried they're going to take the whole case off us now."

"What, the murder?"

Aaron nodded.

"They won't." She smiled at him, hoping for a reassuring look. "Neither Carrie nor Huz seem to have been targeted, so the obvious conclusion is that the murder is about the drugs, not the fact they work for the police. Huz and Carrie might have information that helps the investigation, but it's a different investigation from PSD's case."

"Does DCI Branthwaite agree with that assessment, boss?"

"I don't know," Zoe admitted. "But Carl does, and he's got Branthwaite's ear. Is there anything else, Aaron?"

There was, apparently. He'd been to visit the retired DS Oldman the previous day. Oldman hadn't said much, but he had told Aaron that he hadn't taken security very seriously. His login details could have been used by a number of other officers.

And he didn't have any names.

Zoe shook her head. The mood in the room had shifted. Her phone rang.

Unknown number. Aaron stood up, but she waved him back down again.

If it was Randle, she could ask Aaron to leave, and take the call. If it was anyone else, it wouldn't hurt for Aaron to hear it.

It wasn't Randle.

"Hello, DI Finch."

She put the phone down on her desk and turned on the speakers.

"Hello, Olivia," she replied. Aaron's eyes widened. "I'm here with DS Keyes. You remember him?"

"I do. I was calling to ask if you'd come up with anything."

Zoe thought back to her last conversation with Randle. *Sometimes it's about finding clues. Getting information to steer an investigation.*

"The photographs," she said. "Send them. If you send them to me, they won't have any reason to go after you."

Zoe swallowed. She could hear her heartbeat.

If Olivia Bagsby sent her the photos, they might have something to work with. Somewhere to start.

"No," said Olivia. "Those photos are my only leverage. If I release them, they won't leave me alone. They'll just hunt me down to make a point."

Zoe wanted to argue. She could see Aaron looking at her, pleading with her to argue.

But Aaron didn't know about Ahmed Iqbal.

Ahmed hadn't been much of a threat. He'd been in witness protection. And he hadn't just been killed. His eyes had been removed from their sockets while he was still alive.

Hunted down to make a point.

"I hope you change your mind," Zoe said. But she didn't add anything that might change it.

CHAPTER FIFTY-FIVE

AARON SAT BACK in his chair and closed his eyes. He tried to empty his mind of everything that was distracting him, to make a space he could fill with something useful.

When he opened his eyes again, he was in darkness. At this time of day, the lights shut down when there was no movement for five minutes, or ten.

He must have fallen asleep. He should go home. Have a coffee first, then go home.

Talk to his husband. Watch his daughter as she slept. Take things back to the way they'd been a year ago. To the way they'd been before Victor Parlick had died and he'd decided to blame himself, and allowed that blame to spread over every aspect of his life.

But how?

He still hadn't moved. Everyone else had left hours ago, either to go home, or to follow up on things that couldn't be done at the Hub. He waved an arm and the lights flickered on.

The case. He had to find something, before PSD came in and he lost that too, along with his daughter and husband.

Twenty minutes later, a steaming cup of instant coffee on his desk, he was watching the same footage he'd already seen half a dozen times. The Audi TT, driven, he now knew, by Huz. Behind it, the Land Rover.

There was more footage now. Back when they'd first spotted the cars, he'd requested everything available. He hadn't noticed it slipping into the team inbox earlier that day. Probably while he'd been watching Huz's interview.

CCTV from further back. Captures of Huz in the TT. It had been blocked, when PSD didn't want them looking into it. Now they were all on the same team, for the time being, at least, and the floodgates had opened.

Here it was, heading south alongside Mosser Beck. And the Land Rover, just behind it.

Here again, cutting east through Pardshaw. The Audi TT, and close on its tail, the Land Rover.

Close, but not so close you'd notice it. Not unless you were looking for it.

There was nothing after that – or before that, as it would have been in real time – until Dean. Both vehicles. The same in Winscales. Then on the main road, heading north through Distington. The Land Rover hung back a little further here. It could afford to. All the way to Parton, the two vehicles were together, and after that – before that – there was nothing.

But Aaron had seen what he'd needed to see. The Land Rover driver had been following Huz all the way from Whitehaven to Fell Barn. And the way he'd fallen back on the main road, the way he seemed to keep a distance whenever the road was straight enough to allow him to, without losing sight of his quarry, Aaron didn't think Huz knew a thing about it.

Aaron shut his eyes again and ran through everything he'd seen.

He thought he knew what had happened.

The Land Rover driver had followed Huz to find out where he was going. When he'd got there, he'd waited. And when he was ready, he'd set fire to Fell Barn, waited for Neil Colvin to come out, and stabbed the poor lad to death.

CHAPTER FIFTY-SIX

"Back, are you?" Emma said. She was looking at Nina, but was that the hint of a smile on her face? Then she glanced at Zoe, and the smile fell away.

But it didn't matter which cop she was willing to talk to, as long as she was willing to talk to one of them.

The nurse had let them in without an argument, although he hadn't looked happy about it. Zoe could see why when they reached the bed.

Emma was leaning forward, peering through half-closed eyes at a screen. Bai Lanfen, the digital sketch artist, was pointing and shaking her head.

Emma looked exhausted. And if Bai's expression was anything to go on, the whole exercise had been a waste of time.

"What have you got?" Zoe asked. Bai turned the screen towards her, and Zoe's heart sank.

"I'm sorry," Emma said. "I just can't do it. Not with words, and I'm not criticising Bai, I just don't think I can do it unless I actually see him."

The image on a screen was of a man. Somewhere between twenty and fifty, by the look of it – the features were smooth, but not because the man himself had smooth features.

The features were smooth because the whole thing was a cross between a cartoon and a blur.

Brown hair, quite short. "She told me she could see the ears," Bai explained. There was a hint of a beard. "And the facial hair. Also short, we think. Maybe he'd just not shaved for a couple of days."

Bai was trying to sound upbeat. But Emma Hudson wasn't stupid. That face – it could be a million people.

"I'm sorry," Emma said. "I wish I could do better. I kept thinking I'd seen the right one, but then the next one looked like the right one, too. It was just too dark. The smoke. And the fire. And..."

Zoe watched her closely. Eyes closed again. Her body tensing, shaking briefly, then relaxing. Eyes open. A wan, apologetic smile.

Nina was staring at the screen, frowning. "You know, boss, there is something familiar about that face."

Of course there was. There must have been fifty thousand men in Cumbria who looked like that.

Zoe had seen Bai Lanfen in action before, watched her coax a perfect image out of someone who'd started off saying they weren't sure if it was a man or a woman who'd stabbed them. The problem wasn't the expert, or the software.

The problem was Emma Hudson's memory. And there was no reason to believe that was going to improve any time soon.

CHAPTER FIFTY-SEVEN

It had been weeks now, months even, and Nina was starting to feel that she was never going to get anywhere.

Elena Marin came from the town of Bârlad, in Romania. She'd been staying with Nina in the little spare room usually reserved for Tom after a big night out. She'd been there since she'd left the boss's house. They'd thought maybe Elena would open up to her in a way she hadn't opened up to DI Finch and DI Whaley.

But in all that time, Elena had hardly said a word, and it wasn't because of the language barrier.

It was clear the woman was suffering. Maybe PTSD, maybe something else. Nina wasn't an expert. But Elena had been trafficked to the UK with the promise of a decent job, and then she'd become someone's property. She hadn't told anyone what had happened to her, but it wasn't going to be anything good. Her friend, Daria, had been murdered. Elena might have survived, but that didn't mean things were easy.

Nina had come home straight from the hospital. On the way out, she'd suggested the boss come too. Maybe between the two of them they'd have more chance of getting Elena to talk. So now they were in the kitchen, which was neater and cleaner than it had been in all the time since Nina had moved in.

Elena wouldn't stop tidying things away. Nina had laughed at first, told her to relax, she didn't need to do it, she didn't need to earn her keep.

But it was compulsive. So Nina let her tidy up. It was nice, living in a place where you actually knew where things were.

"Cheers," she said, and lifted the beer to her lips. The boss was drinking water. Elena was having red wine.

"So, Elena," said the boss, "how are things?"

"It's nice here. Thank you very much," Elena added, turning to Nina.

Nina smiled, and cursed inwardly. Months. And they still hadn't got beyond *Thank you very much*.

"It's lovely having you here," she replied.

There was a silence.

"So, Elena," said the boss again, "is there anything you've remembered? Anything you think you could tell us about – well, about all of it?"

They'd been trying the subtle approach for too long, and it hadn't worked.

"No," said Elena. She was tall, had been blonde, when the dye had been there, but she'd chosen not to replace it as it grew out. Even though Nina had offered to buy whatever products she wanted. Nina had, at least, been allowed to cut it. Three times, now, with barely a word spoken between them, but still, it was as close as she'd managed to get to Elena.

"OK," said the boss. Nina tried not to meet her eye.

They had to give Elena time. With time, she'd speak.

But Carter, Streeting, the people who would come after Elena because they feared she might talk, they thought she'd headed down to Liverpool. Nina wasn't just putting Elena up in the hope that they'd learn something from her. She was putting Elena up to keep her safe.

"Only," said Elena, "I remember a big building."

"Yes?" said DI Finch.

"Building where things are kept. Herehouse?"

"Warehouse," suggested Nina.

Elena turned to her and nodded. "Yes. Warehouse."

Nina's phone rang. Romit Chandra. She let it ring out, but whatever moment they'd reached, it had ended. Elena fell silent again. Ten minutes later, the boss got up to leave.

As DI Finch opened the door, a woman was standing outside, her hand poised to knock.

"Mum," said Nina. Her mother didn't usually turn up without warning. She'd call, and Nina would arrange for Elena to tuck herself away upstairs.

"Oh," said Nina's mum. "It's DI Finch, isn't it?"

The boss nodded, turned back to Nina, and mouthed something Nina didn't quite get. Nina swallowed.

"Mum, you've met DI Finch. She was just leaving. Why don't you come in and meet Elena? Boss, I'll see you tomorrow."

The boss mouthed something else. *Are you sure?* Was that it? Nina nodded.

"See you tomorrow, Nina."

In the kitchen, Mrs Kapoor was introducing herself to Elena, who stood awkwardly, held out a hand, and said, "I am Elena."

"Where do you live, Elena?" asked Mrs Kapoor.

Elena turned to Nina, her eyes wide.

"Elena's staying here," said Nina, moving to stand beside the Romanian woman. "She's been here for weeks, Mum."

Her mum's face moved between confusion, surprise, and embarrassment, before she nodded.

"That's lovely," she said. "Well, why didn't you say, Nina? I'll tell you what," she went on, turning, stepping back into the hall, her hand now on the handle to the front door. "Why don't I leave you to it, eh?"

"No, Mum—"

"I'll get out of your way," said Mrs Kapoor, "and we can have a nice catch-up when we've all got more time."

She opened the front door, stepped outside, and pushed it shut again before Nina could even say goodbye.

When Nina turned around, Elena was standing in the hallway, her mouth open.

"I am sorry," said Elena.

"It's not your fault. And anyway. It's quite funny, really."

"Yes," said Elena. A smile spread across her face. "Yes, I think actually, it is."

CHAPTER FIFTY-EIGHT

ZOE WASN'T SURPRISED to see Carl's Skoda in the car park when she pulled into the Hub next morning. He'd been asleep on the sofa, occupying Yoda's favourite spot, when she'd got back from Nina's. Not like him, but he'd been up all hours lately, driving between Carlisle and Whitehaven four times a day or even more.

She'd woken him gently, and they'd chatted for a couple of minutes, Yoda watching on with narrowed eyes, and then he'd gone up to bed. When she'd joined him there an hour later, he was dead to the world. This morning he'd woken her with a coffee, told her he'd see her at the Hub, and been gone before she'd taken her first sip.

She'd barely made it to her desk when Fiona called. She trudged upstairs to sit opposite the super. Fiona would want to know how things were going with PSD, would tell her to tread carefully, would make all the right noises and probably ask about Alistair Freeburn again.

"I'm sorry," said Fiona, as Zoe took her seat. There was a

coffee waiting for her, which she was pleased to see, because the super always insisted on good coffee.

But the super's opening words were enough to tell her this wasn't going to be a happy meeting.

"It's DCI Branthwaite. He's being difficult."

Zoe's heart sank. She waited for Fiona to elaborate.

"He's been through the transcripts of the interview with Hussein Mahmoud," Fiona continued. "He agrees that the murder itself is your case."

When Aaron had expressed his fear that PSD were about to take the murder away from them, she'd thought he was overreacting. PSD didn't investigate murders. They didn't have the expertise.

But now, Zoe was worried.

"But on the basis of Huz's interview," the super continued, "he doesn't see that Carrie Wright is directly connected to the murder. So he's told me that PSD will be interviewing Carrie alone. You can have her afterwards, but only after they're finished with her."

Zoe stared at the super, waiting. There had to be something else. Something that would make this make sense.

Fiona stared back at her.

"I'm sorry, Zoe," she said. "Branthwaite believes you're on a fishing expedition. He doesn't think there's anything there for you. There's nothing I can do."

"But this is absurd," Zoe said. "There's a murderer out there. And yes, it might be unrelated to the PSD investigation, but Carrie Wright could well have information that would lead us to him."

Fiona said nothing.

"You outrank DCI Branthwaite," Zoe pointed out.

"You know it doesn't work like that, Zoe. I can't pull rank

on PSD. Although…" A thoughtful expression played across her face. "I could always talk to Little Joe."

'Little Joe' was Assistant Chief Constable Joseph Carghillie. Bald, broad, and six foot six, he'd earned the nickname to distinguish him from Joanne Ainsworth, the Chief Constable. Zoe didn't know what the relationship was between the super and the ACC, but she'd seen them talking. They seemed friendly.

And if Fiona couldn't pull rank, Little Joe could.

"That would help, Fiona. I'd be so grate—"

"Spare me the pleading, Zoe." Fiona waved a hand. "I can't promise anything. But I'll see what I can do."

CHAPTER FIFTY-NINE

THE SARGE HADN'T LOOKED up when Tom had entered the team room. He'd waved a hand in Tom's direction, but he hadn't taken his eyes off his screen, even when Tom called out, "Morning, Sarge."

Nina walked in fifteen minutes later, which was a relief, because Tom couldn't hold it back much longer.

"You were right," he said.

"Morning, Tom," she replied. "I usually am. What was it this time?"

"Martinez. You said she liked me. I took a chance and asked her out for a drink last night after work."

Nina raised an eyebrow. "And?"

"And it turns out she's a vodka-and-coke girl with a liking for doner kebabs when the clock's struck midnight. Good laugh. Very friendly. You'd like her."

Nina nodded slowly. "But do *you* like her, Tom? That's the important thing."

He shrugged. "Not sure. I think she's fun, but..."

The words dried in his mouth as he saw Nina's lip curl

into a familiar expression, and he readied himself for the onslaught. What had he done now?

"Fuck's sake, Tom. Don't mess the woman around."

"I'm not—"

"If you're not interested, don't waste her time."

"That's not fair. I didn't say I wasn't interested." He turned towards the sarge, hoping for some support, but DS Keyes was still staring at his screen.

He turned back to Nina. "You told me I was an idiot for not calling Sue Bracewell. You've been on at me for months to get out there. Now I finally have done, and you're having a go at me?"

He had been an idiot for not calling Sue Bracewell after the Lowther Street murder, Nina had been right about that, but he hadn't been ready at the time. Now, finally, he was ready, and Nina was wrong. Just because he hadn't fallen head over heels after one night out didn't mean he was wasting his time. Or Martinez's, for that matter.

"Look at this," said the sarge, and Tom turned towards him, grateful for something to break the moment. The same relief was on Nina's face. "It's the Land Rover."

"The one that we spotted behind Huz?" asked Tom.

"The one I spotted behind Huz," corrected the sarge. "As I recall, you two missed it. Anyway, take a look."

The sarge stepped away from his desk, and Nina and Tom approached and leaned in. Tom glanced over at Nina, who gave him a brief but unmistakable roll of her eyes.

"This is the approach to the barn," the sarge said.

Tom watched Huz's car move in and then out of view, followed a moment later by the Land Rover. "We've seen this."

"Yes. Keep watching."

The same thing was repeated a moment later, on a different road.

"Where's this?" Nina asked.

"The road by Mosser Beck. It's a few minutes earlier. And this one's Pardshaw, heading east."

All three sets of footage showed the same thing. The Audi, then the Land Rover.

"So you've got footage of the whole journey?" Nina asked.

"Not the whole journey, no. Look. Here they are in Dean. And a bit further back in Winscales."

The same thing, again and again. Audi. Land Rover. Why were they watching this? Tom glanced over at Nina, expecting to see the same confusion he was feeling, but she was nodding thoughtfully.

"How far back?" she asked.

"Nearly there. Same thing. Distington, on the main road. And here, back as far as Parton. Then we lose them."

"Close," said Nina. "But not too close."

Ah. *Of course.*

"You think the Land Rover was following him?" asked Tom.

"We always thought the Land Rover was following him," the sarge pointed out. "Now I think the Land Rover was following him without him knowing about it. Which implies..."

He turned around. The sarge was looking at him, at Nina, monitoring their expressions.

Tom nodded, wondering why the sarge hadn't said it. "We still haven't found the driver, so yes. Odds are, he's our killer."

CHAPTER SIXTY

ZOE LEFT the super's office, trying to look on the bright side. It was hard. They might not have lost the case, but there was no guarantee they were going to keep it. And if they couldn't interview Carrie Wright, that might be a whole promising angle of investigation shut down before it had even begun.

Before she'd reached the lift, she walked past Denise Gaskill, who smirked at her as if she knew precisely what Zoe had just learned.

Zoe fought back her irritation and smiled broadly at the woman.

"Carl here?" she asked.

Denise nodded. "Upstairs. In the reception area."

"Thanks." She'd go and find Carl once she'd had a chance to calm down. She'd brief the team first. Find out if there was any news.

She made it to the team room without further interruption, to find Nina and Tom standing behind Aaron's desk, peering over the DS's head at his screen.

"Hope you're not watching anything inappropriate," Zoe said.

Nina gave a low chuckle. Tom stepped back, like he'd been caught watching something inappropriate.

Aaron didn't react, but went on staring at his screen as if she hadn't even spoken.

"Look at this, boss," he said. The DCs moved out of her way, and she stood behind Aaron and watched as he pulled up footage of Huz's Audi TT, and behind it the mystery Land Rover.

Three different locations. Five. Seven. Aaron turned to look up at her, his eyes wide.

"So Huz was being followed," she said.

He nodded. "It's got to be him, hasn't it?"

She realised she was chewing her lower lip, stopped and nodded.

"Good odds, I'd say."

When she told the three of them about Fiona's news, the reactions were exactly as she'd have predicted. Nina was angry. Tom was quietly frustrated. And Aaron was simply resigned.

She pointed at Aaron's screen. "This was good work. I'm going to talk to DI Whaley. I'll tell him what you've found here. Maybe it'll make a difference."

It wouldn't make a difference. But Little Joe might.

It was just three floors up to where she hoped to find Carl, but there was a nasty surprise on the way.

Two men heading down the stairs, one of them Ralph Streeting.

"Zoe," he said, his smile wide. "What a pleasant surprise!"

Zoe forced on a smile. "Hello, Ralph."

Streeting gestured at the man beside him. "This is young Mulligan. My DS. Say hello to DI Finch, Mulligan."

"Hello," said Mulligan. He had the same dark hair as Streeting, the same stature. They'd make an intimidating pair, if you were the sort to be intimidated. Mulligan extended a hand and Zoe took it without thinking. "Pleasure to meet you," he added.

Zoe nodded, then looked Mulligan in the eye, because that was what you did with people like him. She'd been expecting the same cold steel she'd always seen in Streeting, but there was a warmth. Almost friendliness.

But what could you tell from a person's eyes?

"I hear you've run into some problems with our friends from PSD," said Streeting.

Zoe felt herself tense. "Yes. You know how it can be."

Mulligan gave a quiet cough and a not-so-subtle tap on his watch.

"I'm afraid we have to leave you," Streeting said, and continued his downward journey, Mulligan behind him. Just before the turn in the stairs, Streeting turned to face Zoe.

"Good luck, DI Finch," he said.

"Thank you."

"And don't forget to keep me in the loop," he added, then turned and disappeared.

CHAPTER SIXTY-ONE

BEING in bed was all very well, but the bastards wouldn't bloody leave Emma alone long enough to sleep.

She opened one eye as a bed trundled by with a shrivelled-looking woman on it. How old was she? A hundred? No idea what was wrong with her. At that age, it was all just falling apart, wasn't it?

She glanced down at the shape of her own body under the sheets, and smiled to herself. She was recovering well. Feeling fine. She'd got up and walked to the door and back earlier, dragging that trolley with the tube sticking into her arm from it. But that was coming out this afternoon, the nurse had said. She'd be up and out of here in no time.

If they let her.

Would the police come back for her? She'd been as helpful as she could, but there was no getting around the problem. She'd been dealing. They'd been to her room, seen her stuff. That tall woman. The Detective Inspector. She hadn't liked Emma very much. The younger one with the weird quiff hairdo seemed friendlier, but still. They were cops.

How much trouble was she in?

And there was a man out there who'd butchered Neil Colvin while she stood there and watched. She still didn't know if he'd seen her. Was he coming for her too?

She had to get out. She leaned over to the little table by her bed and picked up her phone. Fully charged. She dialled Theo's number.

Answer the fucking phone, you coward.

Voicemail. Little shit.

When she looked up, the nurse was standing in front of her. The young one. She smiled at him, and he smiled back.

He was an ugly bastard, greasy black hair and spots on his face that should have disappeared a decade ago, but at least he was friendly.

"Good morning, Ash," she said.

"Morning, Emma. How are you feeling?"

She leaned her head to one side and blinked slowly at him. "I'm bored. When do you think I'll be able to go home?"

"I can find out for you," he said, and turned to walk away.

"Wait," she said. "I've... Well, it's a little embarrassing, but I was wondering if you could help me."

She tilted her head and tried to look sad. Men liked that.

"What is it?" he asked, leaning over her.

"I want to go, of course I do, but my clothes are all ruined. I'd ask my boyfriend to bring something for me, but he won't answer the phone. I don't think," she said, looking down, as if embarrassed, "he wants anything to do with me now."

Ash shook his head. Emma opened her eyes as wide as she could and launched into the big plea.

"Do you think you might be able to pop out and buy me something to wear?" she asked. "I've got some cash somewhere here."

She waited. It took a moment, but it when it came, it was just what she expected.

"Oh no," he said. "It'll be my pleasure."

She smiled at him.

"As long as you promise to give me your number before you leave," he added.

Idiot.

"Play your cards right, and I will," she told him, and he blushed again.

Christ. It was like a dog with a treat.

CHAPTER SIXTY-TWO

Zoe found Carl at a small round table in the reception area by the sixth-floor Custody Suite. She was still shaking the image of Ralph Streeting's smile out of her head, and rounding the corner to find Carl deep in conversation with Denise Gaskill didn't help.

She walked towards them, then felt a hand on her arm.

"Sorry, Ma'am, I'll need—"

It wasn't the same man as yesterday, but he was just as burly. Zoe held out her ID, and the man looked briefly at it before releasing her arm.

"I am sorry—"

"It's fine," she told him. "I shouldn't have just walked past."

Carl and Denise were looking up now, waiting for her. As she approached, Carl took a step back and raised his hands.

"Look," he said. "I know what you—"

She shook her head. "Don't worry about it."

Carl frowned. Denise was still sitting, examining her fingernails as if they held the secrets Huz wasn't spilling.

"But I'm sorry, Zoe. I know you wanted to question her. I wish I could do something."

She shook her head again, this time in exasperation. It was irritating, this apologising. It was Carl's team that had got in the way, that had slowed down her investigation, that was now reaching into her car, grabbing the keys, and chucking them in the gutter.

Figuratively speaking, of course. Although, when it came to Denise Gaskill...

"It's not that," she said. "We need to talk to Huz again."

"Why? What's happened?" Carl asked. Denise angled her head in Zoe's direction.

"He was followed. To the barn. We think the man who followed him is the killer. I want to know if he's aware of this."

Carl nodded. He turned to Denise, hesitated, then turned back to Zoe.

"Do you need to clear this with DCI Branthwaite?" she asked. She hadn't meant to lace the question with anything poisonous, but she could hear it in her voice, and couldn't help noticing Carl wince as he heard it too.

"No," he said. "Come on. We'll go and talk to him now."

Zoe shook her head. "Not me," she said. "I'll get Aaron up."

She'd go back downstairs and try to regain her composure. Because if she was put in a room with Carl, or Denise Gaskill, she wasn't sure she'd be able to keep from losing her temper.

And they were supposed to be on the same side, after all.

CHAPTER SIXTY-THREE

AARON HAD LOST count of the number of suspects he'd questioned over the years. Gangsters, groomers, murderers: he'd been through the lot.

So why was he feeling so nervous now? Was it the prospect of interviewing Huz, someone he knew, someone he'd worked with before?

No. Aaron entered the reception area and showed the giant there his ID. Sitting at a small round table, waiting for him, was the reason he was nervous.

DS Denise Gaskill.

She stood, walked over to him, and smiled.

"DS Keyes," she said. "Good to see you."

He searched her face for a sign of sarcasm. But there was nothing.

"DS Gaskill," he said.

"Why not Denise, when it's just the two of us? We're working together, after all."

He smiled.

"Why not? Aaron, then."

"Good. Let's see if we can get Mr Mahmoud to open up a little then, shall we? I'm happy to take a back seat on this one."

"You are?"

"Well, the whole point of this interview is to find the murderer. So yes. I'll back you up. We haven't got anything out of Carrie Wright yet. She seems to think it's all a game. Maybe we'll have more luck with the CSI."

Aaron followed her into the interview room. He'd already seen it on-screen, and the lawyer, Paula Vernon. Huz was waiting beside her, looking tired and scared.

He'd had two nights here. Fiona had authorised the first extension of his custody; apparently a magistrate had agreed to a further extension. Huz knew he wasn't getting out without a charge. But PSD were taking their time.

Denise ran through the formalities and asked a handful of questions that had already been asked, just to get things warmed up.

All Huz said was, "No comment." The talkative phase of the previous day was looking like a one-off.

"Mr Mahmoud," said Aaron. Huz turned towards him. Was that a smile?

If he thought Aaron being here meant things were about to get easier, he was in for a shock.

"I'd like to show you some footage," Aaron said. He'd brought a laptop up with him, and now he laid it flat and explained what they were about to see.

"Is that your car?" he asked, freezing the video and pointing at the Audi.

"No comment," said Huz.

Aaron sighed and restarted the video. The Land Rover came into view. He paused it again.

"Do you recognise this vehicle?"

"No comment," again.

Aaron continued with the footage. He paused between each location, explained where the footage was from, and when, then pressed play. He didn't ask any more questions, but he watched Huz's expression as the video progressed.

He looked resigned at first. Uninterested. Then he sat forward and frowned. By the time they'd reached the end, he was staring at the screen.

"Do you understand what you've just seen, Mr Mahmoud?" Aaron asked.

Huz remained silent.

"OK. Well, as you know, Neil Colvin was murdered at Fell Barn. We believe the murderer drove to the location in the stolen Land Rover I've just shown you, and we believe the murderer found the location by following you there from Whitehaven. Do you have anything to say about that?"

Paula Vernon finally remembered she had a tongue. "That's a rather broad question, DS Keyes," she said.

He ignored her.

"Mr Mahmoud," he repeated.

"No," said Huz. "Does that mean..."

Denise leaned forward. "Does that mean what?"

"Does that mean they know who I am?"

Aaron turned to Denise, who shrugged.

"We can't be sure," he said. "But it's likely. The way we see it, there are two possibilities. The first is that the killer's known about your involvement all along, and if that's the case, we'll need to look into all your recent movements. The other possibility is that the killer knew about Carrie Wright, and followed the drugs from her, which is how they found you."

Huz was nodding.

"Have you seen this Land Rover before?" Aaron asked.

"No," Huz replied. "I don't know." He looked around the room, as if someone else might suddenly appear, someone with the answers.

"As we've explained, it's likely the killer knows who you are. So it's in your interest to help us find them. So let me ask again. Have you seen this Land Rover before?"

"I really don't know." Huz looked like he was about to cry.

"Fine. Then we need to see if you were traced through Carrie. Where did you get your most recent supply of drugs?"

"No," said Paula Vernon, leaning forward. "I don't think my client needs to answer—"

"Your client seems to understand that there's more at stake here than one drugs delivery," Denise Gaskill said, her tone so eminently reasonable that Aaron found himself nodding along as she spoke. Paula Vernon sat back again.

"It was... hang on."

Huz frowned. Aaron waited.

"Yes. Six nights ago. Around... around ten."

"In the evening?" asked Denise.

"Yes."

"And the location?" Aaron prompted.

Huz nodded. "Parton Beach Car Park. By the station."

"Thank you."

"We kept out of sight, though," Huz added. "I mean, I know there's cameras, but I don't know if you'll see us. But I'm not lying. Seriously."

"We'll see," said Aaron. It didn't really matter whether Huz and his supplier knew about the cameras. It didn't matter if they showed up on film at all.

All that mattered was whether the Land Rover driver did.

CHAPTER SIXTY-FOUR

ZOE HAD JUST PUT down the phone on another unsuccessful attempt to get hold of Ryan Tobin, the man who'd once worked for Myron Carter and had lived to tell the tale.

Ryan Tobin hadn't just worked for Myron Carter. He'd worked for Jenson & Marley Offshore Services, one of the companies Zhang Chen was looking into on Zoe's behalf. The fact that he'd caused damage to his workplace before leaving, and Carter hadn't pressed charges or had him killed, was something Zoe had spent a lot of time thinking about.

Ryan had something on Myron Carter. He'd as good as admitted it, when he'd been arrested in connection with a murder he hadn't committed. But he wouldn't tell Zoe what. And now, he wouldn't answer his phone.

So Aaron coming downstairs to tell her Huz had named a location was a welcome treat. And while Aaron was sitting there, talking about how Denise Gaskill had been very helpful, Fiona called.

Aaron stood to leave; Zoe waved him back down and answered with the speaker on.

"Detective Superintendent," she said. "I've got DS Keyes here with me."

"That's fine. I just wanted to let you know. I've had a word with Little Joe, and he's brokered a compromise."

Zoe smiled as she watched Aaron's eyes widen. Senior police politics was still alien to him.

"Thank you," she said, and waited.

"They're still doing the interview. PSD. Not you. But you and DS Keyes will be allowed to watch it live. And between sessions, you can have input into the line of questioning. PSD won't have to follow your suggestions, but they will have to consider them and account for their decisions."

Zoe nodded. It wasn't great, but it would do. And those last few words made all the difference. Because if PSD had to account for their decisions, they'd have to weigh things carefully. If they chose not to follow a line of questioning Zoe had suggested, and there was any delay in apprehending the killer, they'd have to explain why, and hope they didn't get the blame.

It wasn't a bad result at all.

"Thanks," she said again. "We'll get started right away."

Two minutes later she was in the reception area upstairs again, at the round table, all four of them sitting there now, her and Aaron and Carl and Denise Gaskill. For a few minutes, she could almost convince herself they were a team.

"You need to ask her about the blackmail angle," she said.

"DCI Branthwaite's already said he doesn't want to pursue that," Carl replied.

"That was before Little Joe got involved," Zoe shot back. Carl sat back and nodded. "Look," she said, "I can't be sure that's connected to the murder. But none of us can be sure it isn't, either. Someone followed Huz to the barn and then killed Neil Colvin, which means there's probably a connection between this network Carrie Wright's involved in, and the murder. Right?"

"Right," said Denise Gaskill, with a little too much eagerness. If the connection was too obvious, too direct, then the whole case would end up with PSD.

"So the more we know about the network, the better our chances are of finding out something about the killer," Zoe finished.

"OK," Carl said. "We'll see what we can find out. What are you looking for, precisely?"

She told him what they knew. Someone had accessed confidential information through the login credentials of a retired DS, and used that information to blackmail members of the public. Margaret Hooper, the teacher who'd been a target, a few months ago. And along the way, Kay Holinshed had somehow found herself in the firing line.

"That's a live investigation," Denise said. "I'm not sure we—"

"If it's a live investigation, then you'll be killing two birds with one stone, won't you?" Zoe said.

Denise shut up.

Once Carl had agreed to all that, getting him to ask Carrie if she'd noticed a Land Rover Defender following her about was the easiest thing she'd done all day.

Now she just had to hope Carrie Wright was willing to talk.

CHAPTER SIXTY-FIVE

BEING BACK in the side room didn't feel quite so bad when Aaron was there with the boss.

And it felt like they'd had a few wins, too. The footage of the Land Rover. The interview with Huz. The compromise. There were difficulties in the way this case was working, sure. But when weren't there?

Aaron watched as Carrie Wright was brought in. She had a lawyer with her, a tired-looking grey-haired man Aaron didn't recognise. But he was focused on Carrie Wright. And glancing to his left, he could see the boss was, too.

"She looks relaxed enough," he said. It wasn't that she was smiling, or betraying any significant emotion at all. She just looked bored.

As if being arrested at your own police station was the sort of thing that happened every day.

"She won't be," replied DI Finch, as DI Whaley and DS Gaskill entered the room.

They listened as DI Whaley went through the formalities. What had Denise Gaskill said?

She seems to think it's all a game.

She was about his age, Aaron thought. Medium height, blonde hair, a nose and eyes that seemed slightly too small for her face, if you had to find something to say about her. Unremarkable. Something that might have been a sneer played across her lips as Denise explained that her name had been mentioned by more than one source in connection with the distribution of drugs.

"Look," said the DI. She was pointing at the bottom of the screen. The table obscured the legs of the two people furthest from the camera, Denise and the lawyer. But you could see Carl's legs, and Carrie Wright's.

Carrie's left leg was shaking.

It was the barest tremor. You wouldn't have noticed it unless you were looking right at it. The table wasn't moving, the chair wasn't moving. There was no sound.

But Carrie Wright's left leg was shaking.

"Not as tough as she makes out," Aaron observed.

"No one's tough when they're face to face with PSD," Zoe replied, and Aaron nodded. He stopped and looked at her.

How would she know?

He returned his attention to the screen, where Carrie Wright was continuing to give the impression that she didn't really care what was going on, only now he'd seen the leg, there were other signs, too.

The smile. She'd thrown it on after the first couple of questions, all of which she was refusing to answer. But there was a fixed quality to it, a sense that if she let it go, something else would burst out from underneath, and she wouldn't be able to stop herself from crying or shouting or saying whatever it was she was so desperate not to say now.

And her right fist was clenched. Hard. Aaron hadn't had a chance to observe her nails, but whatever condition they were in, he could bet there would be deep marks in Carrie Wright's palm by the time this was over.

The boss's phone lit up on the tiny table in front of them, and Aaron couldn't help glancing down and seeing the name on the display. Nina. The boss shook her head and ignored it. A moment later, Aaron's phone vibrated gently.

They could wait. At the moment, his attention was all on Carrie Wright.

She was the worst kind of person, he reminded himself. A cop who'd sold out. It was people like her who ruined everything, who gave the rest a bad name. People like her who made it so the public didn't trust the police any more. People like her who made PSD necessary.

But despite all that, a part of him couldn't help feeling a little sorry for Carrie Wright.

From the sound of it, she'd thought it would all disappear when she'd been pulled in. Thought it would come to nothing. She'd explain it away as a mistake, a bit of confusion, no harm done.

She'd been clutching at straws. She'd been face-to-face with PSD and not known what she was dealing with.

After a night in custody, she still wasn't saying anything. But at least she had a better idea what sort of trouble she was in.

And it wasn't going away any time soon.

CHAPTER SIXTY-SIX

"WHAT TIME DID HE SAY?" Nina asked, staring at her screen.

"Ten," Tom replied. "I've got one set here. Just by the track. You keep looking."

This was Tom's kind of thing more than it was hers, but now they had a lead, Nina wasn't about to let him steal all the glory.

"Got another one," he added. "South end of the car park."

While the boss and the sarge were busy watching Carrie Wright's interview, Nina and Tom had decided to track down whatever footage they could get of the last drugs handover, the one Huz had mentioned in his interview.

Six nights ago, around ten. Parton Beach Car Park.

It had been Nina's idea, but Tom had grabbed it and run. So far, he'd found two cameras which would have been operating at the time and would hopefully still have footage available.

"It's quiet at that end," Tom said. "He didn't say which bit of the car park, did he?"

Nina shook her head and stared at her screen. She was scanning a local CCTV database, but somehow Tom just had a feel for this. Could spot the right location in a sea of wrong ones.

"Got one," she said, and sat back, grinning. She looked closer and sighed.

It was the same one Tom had just found. She leaned forward again, but the strain was starting to make her eyes hurt.

Her phone rang, and she snatched it up in relief. It was Clive Moor, the Custody Sergeant.

"All OK down there, Sarge?" she asked.

"I've just heard something I thought you might want to know."

He was speaking quietly. Barely audible, in fact, but Clive 'Ilkley' Moor was a useful source of information.

"What is it?"

"Upstairs," he said. "The other suite. One of the guests is checking out."

Nina frowned. "You're going to have to be less cryptic."

There was a moment's silence, then the sound of footsteps.

"Right," Ilkley said. "Now I'm by myself. Look, I'm not supposed to know this."

"Know what?"

"The other custody suite. Sixth floor. I'm not even supposed to know it exists."

"We didn't know about it till the other day, Clive. I wonder what else they've got in here. Think there's a swimming pool on seven?"

Clive didn't laugh. "The word is, Hussein Mahmoud is being released on bail. It's being dealt with by PSD. I don't think your DI knows anything about it. So I thought I'd better let you know."

Nina felt her face freeze. "Thanks, Sarge."

She ended the call and turned to Tom.

"Shit," he said, when she'd explained it. "That doesn't seem wise to me."

"Maybe they've got a plan. Hang on."

She tried the boss. No answer. Same thing with the sarge.

"I'm going to call DCI Branthwaite."

Tom looked like she'd just told him she was going to punch the super.

"Are you sure?"

She wasn't sure at all. But the longer she thought about it, the less likely she'd be to do it. She opened the directory, found the number, and dialled before she could talk herself out of it.

"Branthwaite," said a voice she hadn't heard before. Strong accent. Pure Cumbria.

"DCI Branthwaite, this is DC Kapoor, from Cumbria CID."

"Do I know you, DC Kapoor?" He sounded friendly enough.

"No. But I'm in DI Finch's team."

"Ah. Well, DC Kapoor from Cumbria CID, what can I do for you?"

"I understand Hussein Mahmoud's being released," she said. There was a pause. "I just wanted to check this is..."

She stopped, looked around. Tom pulled a face and shrugged.

"... all OK," she finished, for lack of anything better.

"You wanted to check it's all OK that Hussein Mahmoud is released," repeated DCI Branthwaite. Was there the faintest edge to his voice, beneath the accent?

"Yes, Sir."

"Well, DC Kapoor, it is OK, because I've approved it. Is there something about this suspect you're aware of but haven't told anyone about?"

"No, Sir," she said. "But—"

"In that case, please don't waste my time. Mr Mahmoud is neither a flight risk nor a danger to society."

There was a brief pause, and Nina felt she had to fill it.

"I—"

"I didn't ask for your opinion, DC Kapoor," added DCI Branthwaite. "Mahmoud is a techie. He's small game, and we've already got something bigger in custody. Now, off you go, and do your job. And DC Kapoor?"

"Yes, Sir?"

"Don't second guess me again, or you'll find I'm not quite so polite."

The line went dead.

CHAPTER SIXTY-SEVEN

CARRIE WRIGHT WASN'T SAYING a word.

When suspects spoke, even if what they said was nothing more than "No comment," Zoe could hear something in it, or at least imagine something in it.

But silence left nothing to play with except body language, and Carrie Wright had calmed down. The smile was gone, the shaking had stopped, the fist wasn't clenched.

Because once Carrie Wright had figured out she was in serious trouble, she'd also figured out that saying something might not make that trouble any better, and saying nothing wouldn't make it worse.

The lawyer, who Zoe hadn't seen before, didn't even need to be there.

"Where did you get the drugs, Carrie?" asked DS Gaskill.

Nothing.

"How did you persuade Hussein Mahmoud to help you distribute them?" asked Carl.

Nothing.

This had been going on for ten minutes.

"You know the drugs aren't the important thing here, don't you?" said DS Gaskill. Beside Zoe, Aaron stopped fidgeting. On the screen, Carl turned to his colleague and frowned.

Carrie Wright said nothing.

"It's about the murder of Neil Colvin," DS Gaskill said. "The man who was stabbed to death while testing and repackaging the drugs you supplied him with. Aren't you interested in finding out how and why that happened?"

Nothing.

"Do you think you might bear a little responsibility for Neil's death, Carrie?" asked Denise, her tone conversational.

Nothing.

"I don't know if you've seen the photos of his body," Denise went on, "but it wasn't a pretty sight. Forty-three separate stab wounds. I have images, if you'd like to see them."

Was that a slight movement in her upper body? Towards Carl? Away from Denise?

Beside Zoe, Aaron was sitting up straight, staring at the screen, no longer bored.

"Branthwaite won't be happy if she caves in on the murder and doesn't say anything about the drugs," he observed.

"But we will," Zoe replied.

Carl had clearly noticed the same body movement they had, and decided to join in the attack.

"The thing is, Carrie, even if you don't think it was your fault, you've got to be worried you might be a target."

Nothing, now. No movement.

"Unless you know who the killer was, of course."

Still nothing.

"Have you noticed anyone following you lately, Carrie? I'm talking specifically about a black Land Rover Defender. But anything else out of the ordinary?"

Zoe watched closely, stared into Carrie Wright's face like she might find the answer there to life itself.

Nothing.

Carl turned and faced Zoe and Aaron. Faced the camera. He raised his eyebrows, as if to say, 'We're getting nowhere here.'

When he turned back to Carrie Wright, it was with a very different set of questions.

"Tell me, Carrie, are you familiar with DS Oldman? Harry Oldman? He used to work here, I understand."

Carrie Wright blinked. It seemed more deliberate than the usual unconscious movement.

"Kay Holinshed," added Carl. "Do you know Kay?"

Was that the faintest tremor in her lip?

Surely Zoe was imagining it. Beside her, Aaron was leaning forward so far he wasn't even sitting in his chair any more. Staring at the same thing Zoe was. Carrie Wright's face.

"What can you tell me about blackmail, PS Wright?" asked Carl, and something passed across that face, a flicker of fear, or of knowledge.

But she'd seen it.

CHAPTER SIXTY-EIGHT

"Got it," said Tom.

He wasn't sure what it was he'd got. But it was something. And it was better than listening to Nina as she slammed her fingers onto her keyboard and muttered about bloody Branthwaite.

She shouldn't have called him. Hadn't he told her that?

You didn't second guess a DCI. And you certainly didn't second guess a DCI in the Professional Standards Division.

He watched his screen, and smiled. Now he could see figures. People.

And not just any people.

"Come and look," he said. The sound of Nina harming the hardware ended, and he sensed her moving behind him. "That's Huz, isn't it?"

"Yes," she whispered.

Huz was on foot. Walking through the southern tip of the car park, right to the very edge, which wasn't captured by the camera. But he was in view for twenty seconds or more, and the ambient light captured his face clearly enough to be confident it was him.

There was nothing for a couple of minutes. Then another figure, also on foot. Tom turned and grinned at Nina. She grinned back.

If he'd been chewed out by Branthwaite the way she had, it would have taken more than a small victory on the CCTV front to put a smile on his face.

But both of them had spent enough time on Carrie Wright's police file in the last day to know the person they were looking at, approaching the point at which Huz had disappeared from the screen, was Carrie Wright.

"OK," said Tom. "Now we keep looking."

"What for? You're not going to see a Land Rover there. You'd struggle to park a bike."

The open ground was narrow. If there had been sound, they'd have been able to hear the pounding of the waves against the rocks, just a few metres away. If Carrie Wright had been followed to this meeting...

"Fuck," said Nina.

Tom held his breath.

There was another figure.

He – if it was a *he* – was walking the same route Huz had taken, and Carrie, a few minutes later. Moving slowly. Looking around, but keeping low. *He*, Tom thought, because Emma Hudson had said the murderer was a man, and Tom was convinced, absolutely, that the person he was watching was the murderer.

He was staying away from what little light there was, which meant his face was all but invisible. He seemed to have an instinct for the shadows. There was nothing obvious, no hair colour, or hair at all, no shape to the face, nothing.

He stopped halfway along the screen. Turned. Walked back the way he'd come.

Thirty seconds later, Carrie Wright appeared. She walked across the screen and disappeared again. A minute after that, Huz did the same. He was holding a bag. He hadn't been holding a bag before. Had Carrie?

"Play it all again," said Nina.

Tom rewound the footage and played it again. There was Huz. There was Carrie, and yes, she was holding a bag.

There was the other man. Tom watched him walk halfway across and back again. He frowned at the screen, reached forward, rewound it, played those last thirty seconds again.

"There's something familiar," he said. He turned to Nina. She was nodding.

"I know what you mean. The way he walks. It's like..."

"It's the way he rolls his shoulders," Tom said. Other people often walked like that. It expressed a sort of physical confidence he knew he lacked, and when he tried to do it himself, he stopped, quickly, conscious that on him, it would look wrong.

But this man – even though he was moving slowly, carefully, keeping to the shadows, clearly aware there were cameras about – despite all that, he walked with the gait of someone strolling casually down the street, high-fiving his friends as he went.

"I know that walk," Tom said.

Nina nodded. "I can't put my finger on it."

They stared at each other.

Who was it?

CHAPTER SIXTY-NINE

"WE'VE GOT her making the drop," Zoe said.

Carl's expression, which had been thoughtful, opened up into a grin. "Good. Can you—"

"Already sent it. Tom and Nina found it while you were talking to her. They've gone through four sets of cameras. Two of them show Carrie and Huz clearly. You can't see the actual handover, but you can see him carrying her bag back."

"That's brilliant."

They were sitting in the reception area. Zoe had been through the material sent over by Nina and Tom, and discussed it with Aaron, then sent him back down to the team room. Denise Gaskill had walked past a few minutes ago and greeted her with a nod. Carl was only just out. He'd been briefing DCI Branthwaite on the Carrie Wright interview.

"There's more," she said. "You can see the Land Rover in the car park. It drives in not far behind Carrie and parks at the opposite end. Then we've got a man on foot, watching her. Then she leaves. Then Huz leaves. Then the Land Rover leaves."

"Do you know who it is?"

"Nina and Tom think there's something familiar about him, but I don't know how they can get that from what I've seen. This guy knows what he's doing, Carl. Sticks to the shadows."

Concern flashed across his face. "Police?"

"Maybe. Or just an experienced criminal. They probably know more about cameras than we do. Listen, thanks for asking about Kay. And Oldman."

"No problem," he said, turning to look away from her.

"Carl?" she said, and he turned back. "Look, someone's set up Kay Holinshed, and they've been using DS Oldman's credentials to do it. They've accessed sensitive information, and they've used it for blackmail. You saw how Carrie reacted to the word blackmail: she's the obvious candidate. You need to push her on this again, Carl."

Carl shook his head. "That's not what we're here for."

"Listen to me, Carl. Someone's done this. You need to find out if it was Carrie Wright. Because if it wasn't, then we need to look elsewhere in the Hub."

"No. We have to be clear about our roles here, Zoe."

"What d'you mean?"

"I mean, you've got a murder to look into, and I'm happy to ask Carrie questions that might help you with that. I'm happy to do whatever it takes to find your Land Rover driver."

"Good."

"And I know you feel something personal about Kay."

"I know her, Carl. She's not perfect. But she wouldn't—"

Carl was shaking his head again.

"You can never be sure. And this, with Kay, with DS Oldman, it's not your remit. Corrupt cops is our business, not yours."

"She worked for me, Carl."

"Which is exactly why you need to step back and let other people follow it up. All this stuff you're suddenly interested in, Zoe, we've had people looking at it for a long time."

"How long?"

Carl shrugged. "Before you even got here. Weeks before. Months, in fact."

"Who?"

Carl shook his head, clearly frustrated. "She's—"

"DI Whaley."

The two of them looked up to see Denise Gaskill standing there, waiting.

"DCI Branthwaite wants a word."

Carl stood up and walked away.

"We'll take this up later," Zoe called after him. He disappeared around the corner without acknowledging her.

She'd wanted to say something about Huz being released. It didn't feel right. But there had been other priorities, and she hadn't got far with them, either.

Why was he being so obstructive?

CHAPTER SEVENTY

EMMA HELD her breath as she heard the phone ring. Finally, after all this time.

"Theo," she said, as soon as she heard his voice. "You bastard."

"Hi, Emma."

That was it? He'd abandoned her in the middle of nowhere, Neil was dead, and it was *Hi, Emma?*

"Theo," she said, coolly. "I think—"

"No, Emma. Let me say something."

She waited. This wasn't what she'd expected.

"I don't want you to contact me again."

"What the hell?"

Silence. She could hear him breathing, but that was it. Not even background noise.

"Is this why you haven't been answering my calls?" she asked.

"You know you've ruined my life, don't you?"

She shook her head. He couldn't see her, but surely he understood how ridiculous this was. *His* life?

Neil Colvin was dead.

Fuck Theo's life.

"I've been charged with drugs offences," he continued. "I'm about to be kicked out of university."

Well, boo hoo.

"So frankly, Emma, I don't want anything to do with you."

"Listen," she said, but the line was dead. She held the phone in her hand, thought for a moment about throwing it across the ward, then stopped.

She'd need that phone. Instead of throwing it, she just scowled at it, and she was still scowling at it five minutes later when the nurse approached, carrying a bag.

What was his name again?

"Hi," she said, forcing a smile.

"It's Ash," he reminded her. "I've got your clothes. The ones you wanted."

Cheap jeans, a cheap top, a cheap jacket. Plus underwear. She'd taken a perverse pleasure in describing the underwear she wanted. If he'd gone any redder, someone would have called the fire brigade.

"And you were asking when you can leave?" he said.

"I was."

"Whenever you want, apparently. They're preparing your discharge right now."

"Thank you so much, Ash," she said. "You're a real lifesaver."

He took a step closer to her, then another, and bent down.

What would she do if he tried to kiss her? He was repulsive, but she might still need his help.

Instead, he dropped the bag of clothes onto the chair beside her bed and stepped back.

She took a deep breath. "Listen, Ash," she said, "I need your help."

He nodded.

"My boyfriend's abandoned me."

Should she cry? No. She sniffed instead and looked back up at him.

"Well, he's an idiot," said Ash. It was all so predictable.

"He's not coming to pick me up, Ash. I don't suppose you have a car?"

He nodded, and mentioned a make, a model, and a bunch of letters that meant nothing to her. "Done it up myself," he added.

"Could you give me a lift to the station?"

She waited.

A different look came over his face. One she hadn't seen before. If he'd been intelligent enough to hide it, she'd have called it crafty.

"If you come out for a drink with me first," he said. "My mates would love to meet you."

Was that it? Let him show off the new bird, job done. And if she wanted to, she could lose him easily enough.

"Yeah, OK." She smiled. "That would be nice."

"Great." Poor lad. He looked like he'd just won the lottery. "I'll see you downstairs in an hour then, will I?"

"You certainly will," she told him, and watched as he walked away.

Fuck this place. Fuck all of it.

The police didn't care, now she'd given them her best shot at a description. She wasn't going to be welcome back at university. And as for Theo...

She'd be getting herself on a train out of this dump, and she'd never come north again.

CHAPTER SEVENTY-ONE

As she turned into Holly Bank, Zoe glanced at her phone, almost expecting it to ring.

She'd just tried Ryan Tobin again, with no luck. Now, when she was thirty seconds from home, it would be just about typical for David Randle to call. But there was only silence as she pulled into the drive.

Carl's car was already there.

It was so quiet here. She'd liked that, at first, but as the months went by, she missed the buzz of living in the heart of a big city.

Whitehaven would never be a big city. But she was warming to the place. Maybe living closer to its centre would be the answer.

"I'm back," she called.

"In here," Carl replied. She could smell something. A kebab?

A curry. She could feel her mouth watering as she dropped her bag in the hall and walked through to where Carl was unpacking the foil containers.

"I stopped by Akash on the way back," he said.

She shook her head and grinned. Akash wasn't on the way back. It was ten minutes the wrong way, and he'd have had to order and wait.

But their usual delivery driver was on holiday and the replacement was sick. Zoe had resigned herself to no curry at all this week. If this was some sort of peace offering, it was a good one.

But not good enough for her to forget what they'd discussed earlier. And where that conversation had ended. She poured the drinks and plated the naan as he dealt with her jalfrezi, his madras, the shared saag aloo. He turned to walk into the living room, and she shook her head and pointed to the kitchen table.

It was too easy to relax in the living room. Too easy to forget there was anything wrong.

He shrugged and sat down. They ate in silence for a minute.

"What did you mean," she said finally, "when you said you've had people looking at this for months before I got here?"

She waited as he chewed slowly.

"Nothing much," he said.

"Nothing much?"

He grinned.

"That's not really good enough, Carl," she said.

"It'll have to be," he replied, and took another mouthful of lamb madras.

This wasn't like him. He'd never been rude about it before. Never so... unpleasant. She'd just opened her mouth to object when her phone rang.

"Nicholas," she said. A video call. She forced herself to smile as his face appeared.

"Mum! How are you?"

She glanced up at Carl. He was ignoring her. Chewing slowly through his meal.

"All the better for seeing you," she told him. She peered closer at the screen.

Were those dark rings around his eyes?

"How about you?" she said. "Are you OK?"

"Fine." Nick shrugged. "Just, you know, getting on with things."

Zoe glanced up again. Somehow, despite the pace of his chewing, Carl had finished his curry already and was standing up.

She couldn't let him get away. Not like that.

"I'm sorry, Nick. Something's come up. Can I call you back in a few minutes?"

He smiled at her. Those *were* circles under his eyes. But he was a student. He'd probably just had a few late nights with friends.

"Carl," she said. He was halfway to the door. He turned and looked at her.

"Don't, Zoe," he replied.

She stared at him. There was a wounded look to him.

Had she been pushing things too far? Was this why he'd snapped? She thought back to what he said. Someone had been looking into things. Into 'all this stuff,' as he'd put it. Someone he'd started to refer to as 'she,' before he'd stopped.

What stuff, though?

And was she right to want to know who?

"No," she said. "I understand."

She wasn't going to get the truth out of him. She hadn't asked about Huz's release, either.

But now wasn't the time.

Carl headed into the living room, and Zoe sat in silence in the kitchen for a few minutes, before clearing up and going to join him.

They watched the news. Then they went to bed and read.

She didn't mention the case. She could think of little else, but she didn't mention it, and by the time he reached up and switched off his light, she thought he might, perhaps, have relaxed a little.

It wasn't until she was drifting off to sleep that she realised she'd forgotten to call Nicholas back.

CHAPTER SEVENTY-TWO

Zoe slept badly, and when she woke, Carl was gone.

She found him an hour later, in the reception area on the sixth floor. The way things had gone between them the previous evening, she half expected the security guard to stop her, but he looked at her ID and waved her through.

Carl was sitting at the round table with DS Gaskill, who offered her the familiar smirk.

She'd found herself warming to Denise Gaskill. But that smirk put her right back where she'd been before. Carl turned to see what the DS was looking at, and Zoe looked for some sign in his expression.

Nothing. It was like questioning Carrie Wright, only without the body language.

"DI Finch," he said. "We've just spoken to Carrie Wright again."

Zoe sat down. "Did she say anything?"

Carl shook his head. "Much the same. I'm not sure if she's protecting herself, or someone else."

Zoe looked into his eyes. But he just stared back, unblinking.

"Can we have a word in private, please?" she said.

Carl sniffed. "I'm not sure that would be appropriate."

"We live together, Carl. We can talk in private as much as we like at home. It's—"

"OK." Denise Gaskill stood and walked away without a word.

Zoe waited until she was out of earshot before she spoke. When she did, everything she'd thought she was going to say disappeared. All of it. Carrie Wright. Huz being released. The blackmail, the murder, the investigations that had been going on since before she'd even started in Cumbria. Instead, she said two simple, easy words.

"I'm sorry."

Carl had been sitting back, preparing to take whatever it was she was going to throw at him. He closed his eyes, and Zoe could see a faint tremor in his lip, just like the one she'd seen in Carrie Wright's.

"What for?" he asked, after a few seconds' silence.

"I'm sorry I pushed you. I should have known you can't do any more than you already have."

He nodded. She hadn't expected the conversation to turn in this direction, but she meant every word.

He seemed to be taking all this very coolly. But she'd seen that tremor. He wasn't cool at all.

"I mean it," she added.

"I know." He sighed, and reached out and put his hand over hers.

They stayed like that for nearly five minutes, in silence. She looked up every now and then, at his face, and was relieved to see him looking back at her, half a smile on his face.

After the silence, she spoke.

"Look, I know this isn't ideal," she said.

"You're telling me." He was more like his old self. More open. More immediate.

"I knew we'd be coming up against each other like this a little. I just wasn't ready for it."

"It's not just you," he told her. "I'm not exactly brilliant at finding the right boundaries myself."

Zoe smiled.

He was right. There were boundaries between them at work, and there was nothing, absolutely nothing, they could do about that. If she put pressure on him to break those boundaries, what sort of person did that make her? What sort of police officer? And what sort of partner?

"No," she said. "You've... Well, I'm not going to say you've done nothing wrong. I don't want you to get big-headed, or anything. But I think you're right. And I think you're right about the boundaries. And next time I push too hard to try to get past them, just remind me. Say 'boundaries.'"

"And you'll understand?"

"I'll probably still argue with you. But I'll regret it later."

He laughed.

Zoe smiled at him and stood up. As she walked away, she tried to silence the little voice in her head, reminding her that she'd been talking to David Randle and not told Carl about it.

CHAPTER SEVENTY-THREE

BACK AT HER DESK, Zoe spotted an email from Zhang Chen.

Might you be available for a video call, at your convenience?

She replied, one word, *Now*, and five minutes later his face was filling her screen again.

He'd had a haircut, but he was still sitting too close to the camera, still wearing the same glasses, still unable to keep that infectious smile off his face.

"DI Finch. A pleasure to see you again," he began.

That accent. It brought everything back. Her childhood. Her father. Her mother. Force CID.

"You too. How are you getting on?"

He nodded. "I've been talking to your friend Alistair Freeburn."

"I hope he's been helpful."

"He's an interesting person." Zhang pursed his lips and narrowed his eyes.

She laughed. "I'm sorry. He is a little strange," she admitted.

"He certainly thinks a lot of himself," Zhang said. "Very hung up on honour and tradition and... he reminded me of some of my more traditional elderly relatives."

She smiled.

"I've been exposed to far too many relatives who harp on about honour and tradition when, for me, honour is beating Aston Villa and tradition is getting a decent Balti afterwards."

Now her laughter was genuine. Zhang Chen might have been two hundred miles away, but he was a breath of fresh air.

"The important thing is that Mr Freeburn has done what he said he would. He's provided me with everything I've asked for."

Once again, Zoe marvelled at the transformation in the man. When she'd first met Alistair Freeburn, he'd refused to hand over the will of a murder victim without a warrant. Now he was throwing confidential financial statements about like confetti.

"And is any of it useful?"

Zhang nodded, suddenly serious.

"Very much so," he said. "It's still early in my analysis, but I think it's likely that when I've finished, you'll have enough evidence to link the payments."

She blinked. "All of them?"

He nodded again. "All of them. From Hair by Dee, through Mills Allen Begbie Alliance, through Dagon, River, Samuels, to Jenson & Marley Offshore Services."

Zoe sat back. She'd thought...

It had been a long shot, all this. She'd hoped she'd get something, perhaps a little leverage, but she hadn't really expected Zhang to make a connection so quickly or so clearly. She'd assumed she was going to need help from other quarters. Which was why she'd been trying to get hold of Ryan Tobin.

"Do you think the connection's clear enough for court?"

"I'm not there yet. But it's likely. If you can get some other form of corroboration, so much the better. But there is something else."

"There is?"

"Once the payments reach Jenson & Marley, they stay there. The company is full of cash, Zoe. It seems your Mr Carter is just leaving it there. It's like a piggy bank."

"And? It's still his company. If we can prove—"

"I think we can prove that the money in it came from Dean Somerville's brothels. But unless you have a way of proving Mr Carter knows all about this money and its provenance, you may be stuck there. I'd imagine the National Crime Agency will be able to confiscate it, and you can make Mr Carter's life difficult, but that's as far as it will go."

Zoe nodded. That was fair enough. She thanked Zhang and ended the call.

It looked like she was going to have to get hold of Ryan Tobin after all.

CHAPTER SEVENTY-FOUR

AARON HAD HOPED THAT SOMEHOW, overnight, the mysterious figure in the car park would emerge from the shadows.

Not literally, of course. But both Nina and Tom had said there was something familiar about him. About the way he walked.

"Like someone who's used to walking," Nina had said, and Aaron agreed. Perhaps that familiarity would grow more solid with the benefit of time.

But now the three of them were sitting in the team room, and Aaron was at a loss. They'd found Emma. They had Huz, or they'd had him and let him go. PSD had Carrie Wright. They'd traced the Land Rover and found its driver, and now...

Now what?

He scanned through the team inbox, looking for something he hadn't already read.

Cawter Hough. The results of the analysis Huz had

supposedly carried out on the barn fire a few months back. The results he'd rigged.

It was worth a look, at least. Aaron scanned through the description of the damage, the description of where prints and DNA had been found, levels of degradation, probability of accuracy. Steve Walker. Eddie Driver. Tony Harris.

But Huz had admitted to tampering with this. What use was it? He shook his head and read the names aloud.

"Steve Walker. Eddie Driver. Tony Harris."

"Stop," said Nina.

Aaron looked up at her, frowning.

"Say that again," she added.

"Steve Walker. Eddie Driver. Tony Harris."

"Tony Harris." She was out of her seat now, and so was Tom, both of them wide-eyed with... was that excitement?

"Topper," said Tom. "Yes."

"Will one of you please explain what you're talking about?" Aaron asked.

"That's him." Tom was tapping on his keyboard, then pointing at his screen, where the footage of the car park handover was running.

"Hang on," said Nina. She was on her own keyboard, working more slowly, but a moment later she turned and pointed to the big screen that dominated one wall of the team room.

A vertical line split the screen into two. On the left, the Photofit that had been created on the basis of Emma Hudson's description. It was vague, a poor representation of a human being, but it had some features, at least.

On the right, the most recent mugshot they had of Tony Harris.

"That could be him, couldn't it?" said Nina.

Tom looked from the big screen back to his own, where a figure walked carefully but confidently across the car park.

"Yes," he agreed. "It's him. It's Topper."

"You're sure?" asked Aaron, and both DCs nodded. He picked up his phone to call the boss.

No answer. *Fuck.*

When he put his phone back down again, Nina was already out of the door.

"Where are you going?" he called out.

"Hospital," she shouted. And then she was gone.

CHAPTER SEVENTY-FIVE

WHAT DID the super want now?

Zoe had been summoned, again. Another debrief. But then, Fiona was a hands-on sort of boss. Always wanted to know the details, and more of them than Zoe was used to sharing.

No sign of Luke outside, but Fiona was alone, standing with her back to the door, gazing out of the window.

Fiona turned to look at her. "Zoe. Take a seat."

Zoe sat. "Everything OK?" In her jacket pocket, her phone buzzed. She ignored it.

"I hope so," replied the super. "I'm just conscious that this investigation is spilling out a little. I wanted to make sure you were still on top of things. Still focusing on the right areas."

Spilling out a little? Focusing on the right areas?

"Is this about PSD?" Zoe asked. She'd been worried, briefly, that it was about Streeting.

"In part, yes. But even if they weren't involved, I'm aware that we've now got a drugs network, police corruption, talk of blackmail. I know – and don't ask me *how* I know – that Kay Holinshed's name has been mentioned, too."

The super stared at her meaningfully. Zoe looked back as casually as she could.

Was that what this was, then? Had she been summoned to the super's office to be told off?

"Fiona—" she began, but the super raised a hand.

"Don't get me wrong, Zoe. I'm on your side."

Zoe raised an eyebrow. Fiona had said this to her before. It had taken a while for Zoe to believe her.

"And these are all absolutely legitimate areas to follow up on. But I'm concerned that they're dragging you further away from the principal objective. Which, in case you've forgotten, is finding out who murdered Neil Colvin."

"I'm aware of that." Zoe kept her gaze steady. "And I can assure you that the full focus of our team is on finding the killer. My team has just managed to get some footage of the man himself, in fact. It's not clean enough to make an ID, but it's a start."

Fiona nodded, pleased. So she hadn't known this. Zoe pressed on.

"But do you know how we found that footage, Fiona?"

"No. Do I want to?"

"We found it by following leads we'd got through Huz Mahmoud and Carrie Wright. The interviews PSD didn't want us to be involved in. Whatever this network is, it's clear the murderer was interested in it. And that's the only reason *I'm* interested in it. So no, Ma'am. I haven't forgotten what our principal objective is. I'd just be grateful if other people would stop getting in the way of us reaching it."

Fiona didn't like being called *ma'am* any more than Zoe did. But that had stung, that *in case you've forgotten*.

"Fair." Fiona smiled.

All the anger that had been building up inside Zoe evaporated. There was little point staying angry with the super. She was on Zoe's side. Unlike, for instance...

"I saw Ralph Streeting here yesterday," she said. "Has he been calling you?"

"Yes," replied Fiona. Zoe sat up. "But only to remind me to remind you to keep him in the loop."

Zoe nodded. Keeping Ralph Streeting in the loop was the last thing she'd be doing. And from the way Fiona was smiling, the super knew it.

The conversation had started on difficult ground, but Zoe had steered it towards firmer territory. If she was going to ask, now was probably the time.

"PSD," she said. "Here. What's your thinking on that?"

"Well, they're here with my agreement. That was the deal when we came to the Hub. They'd have access to the sixth-floor custody suite, plus any other available areas. You can't argue with them, Zoe. If they want something, they usually get it."

"That's not what I meant." Zoe stopped. What she was about to say, she wasn't even sure of herself. "Not that," she continued. "I meant undercover."

Fiona gazed straight at Zoe. "Are you saying there's a PSD officer undercover in one of my teams?" she asked.

Was she?

"Not necessarily. I'm just wondering what you'd make of that. Would you countenance that happening here?"

Fiona shrugged. "I wouldn't have a lot of choice, would I?"

Zoe shook her head, and the super went on.

"I know it's hard, Zoe, but they have a job to do, and we

have to let them get on with it. Because if we didn't, things would be a lot worse."

Fiona was right. Without PSD, people like Randle would get away with it. The police would be no better than the criminals they were supposed to be going after. Probably worse.

But it was somehow unsatisfactory. The sort of thing she'd heard from Carl, and others, over too many years.

Was there a PSD officer embedded at the Hub? A lot of things had been said over recent months, things she'd thought nothing of. But now she was piecing them together.

And if there was a PSD officer here, she was starting to have an idea who that might be.

CHAPTER SEVENTY-SIX

NINA HAD RUN from the car park, into the building, and up the stairs, and the words came out in a rush. She didn't have time for this. They were trying to catch a killer.

"She's gone," the nurse said. "She's not here any more."

Nina examined the man's face.

Emma might not have been much use when it came to describing the man she'd seen kill Neil Colvin, but she'd been confident that she'd recognise him if she saw him. And Nina had plenty of photos of Topper to show her.

"How's that possible?"

"She discharged herself, didn't she?"

"But wasn't there a police presence, or someone else to stop this happening?"

A shrug. The idea hadn't even crossed anyone's mind. Emma had disappeared, and hidden, but when she'd turned up again, she hadn't given the impression of someone about to run. They hadn't arrested her, much less charged her. And the police didn't have that many spare people hanging around to do the job.

"Do you know where she went?" she asked.

He shook his head and shrugged. Nina eyed him. This was the man who'd been obstructive when the boss had first shown up. People like that wanted to look good, to demonstrate their power.

"If you know anything at all, Ash, you'd be doing us a huge favour."

"Not sure I'm that into doing people favours. Not after what she did."

"She?"

"Emma Hudson."

Nina nodded.

"She didn't even give me her real number," the nurse continued. And now the expression was clear.

He was embarrassed. And there was only one way to deal with that.

Nina reached out and touched his arm. "We've all been there, mate," she said. She blinked, and saw the little shit who'd snogged her in a bar on her eighteenth birthday, then given her the number of a local taxi firm. She wouldn't forget him in a hurry. "Why don't you come and have a coffee, and tell me what happened?"

He looked around, suddenly furtive. "I'm on duty."

Nina smiled. "Come on," she said, steering him onto the corridor and towards the canteen before he could raise an objection.

The whole story came out over tea and toast smeared with marmalade, which stuck to the man's face as he ate and gave him the appearance more of an escaped patient than of a member of staff.

"Took her to the pub, I did. She said she wanted a lift to the station. I thought maybe a drink first. I thought..."

He chewed for a minute before completing the sentence.

"I thought she liked me. So anyway, I introduced her to a couple of mates, bought her a drink, we even had a table. Then I went for a piss. When I came back, she was gone. Took all the cash in my wallet, too."

"Which pub?" Nina asked.

"The Vagabond."

She'd be able to get CCTV, for what it was worth, but picking out one face in the crowd wouldn't be easy.

"Did she tell you where she was going?"

He shook his head. "Just that she wanted a lift to the station."

Which could mean anything. University. Home in Reading. Or somewhere else entirely, if she was smart.

Which, it seemed, she was.

"Can you describe what she was wearing?" Nina asked.

She expected another shake of the head. So she was surprised when he listed not just the style, but the brand, size, and colour of each item of clothing. Black jeans, a navy top, black fake leather jacket with gold zips.

"I bought them for her," he explained ruefully. "She had this line about some boyfriend who didn't want anything to do with her. Can't believe I fell for it."

"If it's any consolation, that bit's true."

He frowned.

"Can you tell me what you talked about during the evening?" she asked.

Another frown.

"Did she tell you anything about herself, Ash?"

"I told her about my car. How I'd done it up. And the flat. And the lads trip to Dublin last year. Made her laugh with that one, I think."

Nina could see where this was going.

"But she didn't really talk about herself," the man continued.

Another Romit Chandra. The town was full of them.

"Thanks for your help," she said.

She tried Emma's mobile as she walked back to her car, but there was no answer.

Emma Hudson was gone.

CHAPTER SEVENTY-SEVEN

Zoe was walking towards her office when her phone rang. She glanced at the display and smiled.

"Mo!" she said, answering. "How are you?"

"Not bad. Hasn't rained here for nearly a day, Zo. I think it might be a record."

Mo didn't really care about the weather, not like she did. But it was one of those easy things they could talk about, like Carl, and Catriona and the girls, and not like David Randle, who she'd mentioned in another conversation, a while back. Mo hadn't reacted well. They spent a couple of minutes idly chatting before Mo's voice turned serious.

"Zo," he said. She felt her stomach dip. "Have you spoken to Nicholas lately?"

"Yes." She nodded. "Last night. I..."

Shit. She hadn't called him back.

"Why? What's wrong?" she asked.

"I'm just a little concerned about him," Mo told her.

She leaned against the wall of the corridor, tried to

conjure the image of her son on the phone the previous evening.

He'd looked rough, hadn't he? Even in the middle of everything else, she'd noticed that.

"Why?" she said.

"He came over at the weekend, but he wasn't himself, Zo. Quieter than usual."

"That happens to teenage boys."

"He's not a teenager any more, is he? He's been through all that. And I've not seen him like this before. He didn't really engage with the girls, didn't eat, it was like he wasn't there at all."

Zoe fell silent. How had she missed this?

"If I had to put a name to it," Mo said, "I'd say he was depressed."

"Or maybe just down?"

"Maybe, yes. I don't know. Catriona's sure it's nothing, but it's been a little while now since I saw the boy enjoying himself."

"What about his partner? Fox?" Those two had been so wrapped up in each other. Surely that would help.

"They broke up. Didn't he tell you?"

Shit. "No," she said. "Why didn't he tell me?"

But she knew. She knew why she hadn't realised there was a problem, why he hadn't told her about Fox, why Mo was more in touch with what was happening with her son than she was.

She hadn't spoken to him properly for ages. Not since he'd been down to visit. And even then, it had just been brief moments in the gaps between all the time he and Fox spent in the sanctuary of his room.

Since then, just snatched moments.

"Thanks, Mo," she said. She pushed herself away from the wall and walked to her office. "I need to speak to him, don't I?"

"Yeah."

But when she tried Nicholas a minute later, there was no answer. She'd just finished leaving a message when the door burst open and Aaron stood there, his face flushed with excitement.

"What's up?" she asked.

"We've got a name, boss," he said. "I think we know who the killer is."

CHAPTER SEVENTY-EIGHT

AARON LOOKED AT THE BOSS.

There was something wrong. There was a look on her face that shouldn't have been there. Not now, not when the excitement in the room was finally growing after so much frustration.

She'd followed him back to the team room. Tom was running through what they knew about Tony Harris. Topper. The man they'd been looking for. He was highlighting images on the big screen, giving a brief personal history alongside the slightly longer criminal history.

But the boss looked like she was thinking about something else.

Aaron tapped her on the shoulder, and she turned to him, an expression of surprise flickering briefly across her face.

"You OK?" he asked.

She closed her eyes, and nodded, then shook her head.

"I will be, Aaron. Sorry. I need to focus." She looked up at the screen, where Tony Harris was gazing blankly at them in his most recent mugshot. "Say that last thing again, Tom. About the release date."

So she hadn't been completely absent. *Good.*

"Sure, boss. Yes. I've got a release date here. Topper got a year, in Bure."

"Where's Bure?" she asked.

"Norfolk, boss," Tom replied. "Thing is, he got out early. They don't have any more room down there than we do up here. And his release date, it's just a week before the fire at Cawter Hough."

"The other barn?" Aaron asked.

"Yes. So even if Huz planted the evidence from Steve and Eddie, Topper might actually have been there."

There was a brief silence, broken by the sound of Tom's phone. He looked down and picked it up.

"Caroline," he said. "I'll put you on speaker. I've got DS Keyes and DI Finch with me."

"Oh," came a voice. Caroline sounded different. "Well, DC Willis, I'm calling with the preliminary results of the analysis at Fell Barn."

"Right." Tom was frowning. He'd noticed it too. The crack in her voice, and a formality in her words, something none of them were used to. 'DC Willis,' she'd called him.

"We have prints for the following individuals." There was a pause before she went on. "Neil Colvin. Tony Harris."

Aaron looked at the boss, who returned his gaze and nodded.

Caroline cleared her throat.

"And Hussein Mahmoud," she said.

Ah. Aaron exchanged glances with the boss.

"Thanks," Tom told her.

"You're welcome," she replied, and the line went dead.

How would she be feeling? She'd worked alongside Huz every day. Aaron had been shocked, all of them had. For Caroline, the betrayal would be so much deeper.

"Topper was there, then," Tom said. "I think we can assume he's involved, at least."

"Yes." Something else had occurred to Aaron. "And there was another thing. Back when he was operating here, we struggled to get much on him. He always managed to ditch his supply when he was about to get searched."

Tom was nodding. "Usually, you'd find evidence all over the car, but Topper didn't have a car. He used to walk everywhere. Kept everything in his pockets. Easier to dump."

"Exactly. Walking. That was his thing. Someone like Topper, walking back from the barn, after he'd killed Neil Colvin and burnt out the Land Rover and his victim's car, it wouldn't have been a big deal. He's used to walking long distances."

He turned to the boss. She was nodding, but not looking at him, or at Tom. Had he lost her again? Her phone rang.

"Nina," she said. "Anything at the hospital?"

Aaron exchanged glances with Tom while the boss listened to Nina, then turned to them.

"Nina's heading back. Emma Hudson's disappeared."

CHAPTER SEVENTY-NINE

"HELLO, DEAR," said the woman sitting beside her, and Emma shuddered.

She'd done little but shudder over the last twelve hours. She'd shuddered at the clothes Ash had bought her, shuddered as she put them on, knowing he'd touched them.

Then she'd shuddered in his car, suddenly conscious that no one knew where she was, or who she was with. He'd said he was taking her to the pub, but was that true? Or was he taking her out into those same godforsaken hills she'd hidden in for what felt like a lifetime, to kill her or worse?

He hadn't killed her, although it had felt nearly as bad, making conversation with his friends until they buggered off and she had the chance to do the same. But by then, she'd missed the last train to Carlisle, which meant she was stuck in Whitehaven for the night.

Where even was Whitehaven? Before a few days ago, she'd never heard of the place. Now it was miles away, and she hoped to God she'd never hear of it again.

"Hello," she replied. The woman had white hair and was

neatly dressed in a cardigan and skirt, the very model of the kindly grandmother.

"Where are you heading then, dear?"

"Oh, just London."

Which was true, in that London was where the train was heading.

"Oh, that's nice. We'll be together all the way there, in that case."

"Yes." Emma nodded, and smiled her most insincere smile at the woman. "Won't that be lovely?"

She'd assumed the train would be nearly deserted, mid-afternoon on a weekday, but no, the previous train had been cancelled, and the one before that, so now every seat was taken. And hers was next to the very model of the kindly grandmother.

"Are you visiting friends in London, dear? Or family, perhaps?"

Christ. Not just the very model of the kindly grandmother, but the very model of the kindly grandmother who wouldn't shut the fuck up.

After the pub, and the disappointment of missing the last train out of town, she'd had to come to terms with staying in Whitehaven for the night. She'd toyed, briefly, with the idea of returning to the pub, finding Ash, taking advantage of whatever hospitality might be on offer there.

She'd dismissed that soon enough. The price would be too high. She'd considered heading back to the hospital. She could feign an injury, perhaps?

But they'd be looking out for her there. She still had her debit card, but she knew enough about the police to be wary of using that. Which meant cash, which Ash had provided in a decent quantity. A hundred and ten quid in his wallet. Not a fortune, but enough to get her away.

The old woman was looking at her quizzically, and she realised she hadn't answered her question.

"Friends," she said. Hopefully, the old dear would get the message.

It was a hostel, in the end. And the thought of that place was enough to make her shudder again.

"Are you alright, dear?" said the woman.

"Fine," she replied. She'd have to shudder more subtly in future.

"Would you like a sweet?"

Now the woman was holding out a bag of something. Little sweets, individually wrapped. If she said yes, she'd probably be making polite conversation for the rest of the journey.

But she was hungry.

"Thanks," she said.

"I like your jacket," said the woman. "Very modern."

Emma hated the jacket. It felt plasticky and cheap, probably because it was plasticky and cheap. She wanted her red cardigan back, the cardigan which had saved her life, because if she hadn't been wearing it, no one would have spotted her, and she'd have died out there in the hills, unconscious and alone. She wanted it all back, the car that didn't work, the little room in the shitty house in Preston, nights in with Meredith and Aliyah, nights out with the rest of the gang, even lectures. Even bloody Theo.

But it was gone, and all she had was this old woman and these crap clothes and her phone, which was filled with messages from that cop, Nina, asking her where she was and pleading with her to come back.

Not likely.

She didn't even have headphones. Even the old woman would have got the message if she'd shoved a pair in and started listening to something.

Instead, she leaned back, closed her eyes, and pretended to sleep.

CHAPTER EIGHTY

Focus.

Zoe stared at the face on the screen, trying to read it. She'd not seen the man before. He'd already been serving his sentence when she arrived in Whitehaven. It was a face. It meant nothing to her.

But it was the face of the man who'd killed Neil Colvin, and that should mean something. She'd seen Neil's body. Seen what Tony Harris had done to him.

She had to focus. Had to stop thinking about Nicholas and turn her attention back to the case.

"So if we're confident it's him," she said, trying to sound coherent, "what's the thinking on motive?"

Tom exchanged glances with Aaron. Had she missed something?

"Well, boss," Aaron said, "I guess Topper's been targeting the operation that took his drugs after Carrie Wright busted him."

Oh. Of course.

Get in the game.

Tom took over. "We can assume he's figured out the pattern. Carrie Wright probably kept busting him the same way she kept busting Steve and Eddie. Kept letting him off, so he could pick up another delivery, so she could get that off him too. Steve and Eddie went straight. Topper just moved to East Anglia and kept doing the only thing he knew how to do, only he got caught."

Zoe nodded. This was one of those exercises she loved. Passing ideas back and forth. Criticising. Solidifying.

"And then he had time to stew and realise what was going on," she said.

"Or some of it, at least," added Aaron. "So when he's out, instead of sticking to his new territory, he makes his way quietly back here."

"Keeps himself out of trouble," said Tom. "Under the radar. He was noticed, sure, but it wasn't like he was doing anything."

"Except he was," Zoe pointed out. "He was watching Carrie Wright. Finding out who else was involved. PSD have Carrie in custody, but she's not saying a thing. Your Tony Harris probably has a better idea of how this operation works than the police do."

Good. They were getting there. All they had to do was find out where Tony Harris was.

Assuming they were right. Assuming it *was* Tony Harris. If it wasn't him, they could waste hours, even days, looking for the wrong man, and the right man, or woman, might get away. Or even kill again.

The evidence was pointing at Topper, but there were gaps. Gaps like an actual witness.

"OK," she said. "I want confirmation that the man we're looking for is Tony Harris, and the only person who can give us that is Emma Hudson. Tom, call Emma's flatmates. Try her family in Reading. Aaron, you've already circulated her description once. Time to do it again."

"And I can tell you what she was wearing," said a voice from the door. All three of them turned to see Nina walking in. "Black jeans, a navy top, black fake leather jacket with gold zips. The nurse... Well, it's a long story. But that's what she was wearing last night, and odds are she's wearing it all again today. I've tried calling her, boss. She's not answering her phone."

She wouldn't be, not if she wanted to get away from all of it. In the meantime, there was another problem that had been nagging at Zoe.

A war.

Topper was the priority, of course. He'd already killed. But what he'd exposed had the potential to be even more violent than what he'd done himself. Carrie Wright might have been stealing from the small-scale dealers, the little guys, but if she'd been onto them whenever they got a delivery, she was stealing from someone else's customers. Someone higher up the chain.

And that meant a drugs war. Two different gangs, fighting over the same product, the same territory. And police involved, on one side, or both.

"OK," she said. "You lot, keep going. I'm off to tell PSD what we've found, and then I'm going home. Contact me if there are any developments."

CHAPTER EIGHTY-ONE

"You sound young," said Meredith Bawcombe.

"What?" replied Tom.

"For a copper. You sound young. You sure you're not just pretending?"

He could hear laughter in the background, and the sound of liquid tumbling into a glass.

"No. I'm... look. This is DC Willis. From Cumbria CID."

"You're not the one I spoke to the other day." There was a pause, then the sound of the phone being moved around. "Ali," she said, "it's a different one. Younger. Might be fit." Meredith's voice was muffled; no doubt she had her hand over the phone. Not very effective, that, but she probably didn't care. "Shall we get him over here?"

More laughter.

"What can I do for you?" said Meredith.

"Have you seen Emma?" Tom asked. "Since she went missing?"

There was a sigh, and more movement, and then another voice.

"Honestly, it's Emma this, Emma that, you'd think we had nothing better to do than tell the police we don't know where Emma is. And we don't. So unless you're getting over here and having a drink, that'll be the last we want to hear from you."

Did they not care at all about their flatmate?

At least her parents cared when he called them a few minutes later. Cared enough to panic that having been found, she'd disappeared again.

"After your colleagues told us she'd turned up, we thought that was an end to it," said Mrs Hudson. "How can this have happened?"

"I'm sure she's fine," Tom told them, trying to sound confident.

"I should bloody hope so," Mr Hudson replied. "Losing our daughter once might have been misfortune. Losing her twice sounds like carelessness."

"It's not funny, James!" shouted Mrs Hudson.

"I'm sorry, dear."

Having failed with Emma Hudson, Tom turned his attention to Tony Harris.

His first port of call was the arrest sheet for Topper's most recent offence. He'd been picked up on the street, spotted dropping a bag of cannabis, then fled before he could be arrested. But he'd been living in Norfolk long enough for the local police to know where he lived, and they'd made it into his flat before he could dispose of the significantly larger quantities of cannabis he had there.

"What's in it for us?" asked Sergeant Bryant, who'd been the arresting officer.

"I'm sorry?"

"I mean, why should we help you?"

Tom frowned. "Because we think he's killed someone, Sergeant Bryant. We'd quite like to get hold of him before he does it again."

"Fine," said the man, after a pause. "What do you want, exactly?"

"Thanks. It's possible he's left our area, which means he might be back in yours. So if you could keep a look out for him, that would be great."

"Yup."

Bryant sounded bored. Maybe violent murders were ten-a-penny down there.

"And if you know any of his friends—"

"Little toerag didn't really have any friends."

"Maybe his contacts, then?" suggested Tom. "Other dealers. Or his cellmates? See what any of them have to say about him. Any information at all—"

"Yeah, yeah. I get it. I'll have a word with the cellmates. Most of them are probably out by now, lucky little fuckers."

"Thank you," said Tom, and gave the man his contact details. Between Emma Hudson's flatmates and the Norfolk police, he wasn't sure who cared less.

CHAPTER EIGHTY-TWO

ZOE CLOSED the office door behind her. It would be just like Aaron to burst in with another bit of news. And she didn't want anyone to hear while she made the call.

Because it wasn't PSD she was calling.

"Zoe. How lovely to hear from you."

That voice. Even now, it could make her skin crawl.

"Hello, David. I wanted to talk some things through with you."

"Always happy to help." As long as he was helping himself at the same time, at least.

"We're in the middle of a murder investigation, but on the edge of it there's a copper who seems to have set up her own operation with confiscated drugs."

"Sounds like something for PSD."

"They're dealing with it. But I think it's going to get bigger than that. She's been ripping off the small fry, but they're being fed by someone bigger, and whoever that is, they're not going to be happy, are they?"

"Tell me everything."

Randle remained silent while she outlined what they'd found.

"So what do you think?" she said, finally.

"If someone's been ripping off local dealers, that probably means inside information. Which means they're connected at the source."

She knew where this was heading, just hadn't wanted to admit it to herself.

"And given where you are, that almost certainly means Myron Carter."

"Why?"

"No one else brings in drugs at a big enough scale to make finding out where they're going and stealing them worthwhile. And if they're Carter's drugs, then what you're looking at here is either Carter robbing his own middlemen, which sounds cheap and pointless for someone like him, or, more likely, someone else ripping off Myron Carter's middlemen."

Zoe sighed. She'd been thinking the same thing. "Agreed. And what happens next?"

"If Carter finds whoever it is, he'll kill them. He'll need them dead to stop them talking to police about his operation, but he'll want them dead to send the right message to anyone who might have the same idea. So you need to look out for a war, Zoe. Be ready."

She ended the call, and spent a minute staring out the window in silence.

How did you prepare for a war?

She'd said she was going to call PSD. And she needed to hear Carl's voice.

But Carl didn't answer the phone. Instead, Denise Gaskill did.

"Oh, DI Finch. Good. The boss has left his phone here. Are you still in the Hub? You can bring it home with you."

"He's left his phone?"

That wasn't like Carl.

"He was in a hurry, jumped up and said he had to leave. I'm still on the sixth floor. Do you mind coming up here to get it?"

"Thank you, Denise. I will. And while I've got you, I should let you know what we've found out."

Zoe outlined their theory about Tony Harris. Denise Gaskill was silent when she'd finished.

"The thing is," Zoe said, "this might be a way in for you. If Carrie Wright knows Neil was killed as revenge for her and her gang stealing Topper's drugs, then she might think she's a target, too."

"Yes," said Denise, slowly. "Yes, of course. And if she does, she might be more willing to talk to us."

Zoe smiled as she ended the call, then glanced at the clock on her wall and stood up, the smile falling from her face.

There were layers of guilt. There was talking to David Randle and lying to her team about who she was talking to. There was talking to David Randle and not telling Carl about it.

And there was the fact that she was running late for the same thing Carl had rushed out of the building for.

They had an appointment. A viewing. The house with the hot tub. Carl had arranged it what felt like weeks ago, before everything had blown up: Huz, Carrie Wright, their arguments, the reconciliation that morning.

Zoe had actually been looking forward to it.

And she'd forgotten all about it.

CHAPTER EIGHTY-THREE

Nina was so surprised to see the number that was calling her, she almost forgot to answer the phone. But she managed it, after half a dozen rings, to be greeted by "What do you want?"

"I just want to make sure you're OK, Emma."

As lies went, it was a plausible one. She'd built up Emma's trust, she hoped.

"Sure." Emma snorted. There was a rushing noise in the background, the murmur of voices. She was in a public place, then.

And she hadn't bought the lie.

"OK. I'll be honest with you—"

"That would make a change," Emma said.

It must have been exhausting, being her friend. Being her boyfriend. Theo had been an arse, no question, but he'd been blessed with an unusual level of tolerance to put up with this as long as he had.

There was a different noise in the background now. A high-pitched tone, followed by two more, then a voice.

"Look, why don't you just leave me alone?" Emma asked.

"We will. I will. I just need you to—"

"You won't find me. You don't know where I am, and you don't know where I'm going."

Nina resisted the urge to laugh. The voice in the background had just said, quite distinctly, that the train Emma was on would shortly be arriving at Wigan North Western, following which it would be stopping at Warrington Bank Quay before continuing directly to London Euston.

Emma Hudson was many things, but a criminal mastermind wasn't one of them.

"Please," she said, "just help us."

"Why?"

"Why not?" Nina said.

Suddenly, she'd had enough. They'd done all they could to find Emma Hudson, to protect her, and it wasn't like the woman was stupid. She had to understand.

"It's hard work, this," she added.

"What is?"

"You. Talking to you. Dealing with you. Look, can you just do something that helps someone else, for once?"

There was silence, except for the rushing noise and all those other voices. Nina tried to picture Emma on the train, heading south. Wearing the clothes Ash Emerson had bought for her, sitting there, scowling as she listened.

"We think we know who the murderer is, Emma. The man who killed Neil Colvin."

Emma said nothing.

"Your friend. Neil was your friend, wasn't he?"

Another pause, and then a small voice.

"I suppose so. Sort of."

"Well, we think we know who killed him. But we can't

be sure, and we don't want to waste time hunting the wrong person while the real killer's getting away."

Silence, again.

"Emma, are you still there?" Nina asked.

"Yeah."

"You said you'd know the killer, if you saw them again. Yes?"

"Maybe."

"I'd like to send you a photo, and then you can confirm if the person in that photo is the person you saw stabbing Neil."

"I'm not standing up in court or anything like that. I'm not doing a line-up."

This was painful. Every tiny step was like running a marathon.

"You wouldn't have to. This is in complete confidence. It's not a formal identification. I just need—"

"No," said Emma. "Leave me alone. I don't want to hear from you again."

The line went dead.

Nina called back immediately. Engaged tone. She tried again, and it went straight to voicemail.

She'd been blocked. Emma Hudson had fucking blocked her.

CHAPTER EIGHTY-FOUR

THE HOUSE on Scotch Street was empty. No furniture, nothing. The people who'd lived there had taken everything except the hot tub and the bathroom fittings, and Zoe had seen the hot tub and that remarkable bathroom in the photos. When Carl opened the door, she could almost smell the emptiness of the place.

She tried to ignore it, apologising over and over for being late, and producing his phone like some kind of peace offering.

She didn't need the peace offering. She'd missed appointments before, and so had Carl. And she didn't need to ignore the emptiness, either.

Because this empty house wasn't like an empty house at all. For all that there was nothing inside it, it was somehow full.

Was it the shape of the kitchen? The colours of the paint on the walls, vibrant reds in one room, pale blues in the next? The carpet on the stairs, a faded maroon that she knew she'd swear to get rid of the moment she moved in, if she moved in, and knew at the same time she'd be walking over for years, because it felt like...

It felt like home.

The realisation hit her like a punch in the guts.

"Are you OK?" Carl asked.

"Yes." She smiled. "Better than OK, actually."

She could hear the sound of laughter as a group walked past on the street. There was a chip shop a few doors away and a pub on the corner. As she'd driven up, there had been young people everywhere she looked.

The location. It wasn't Birmingham; it was a hundredth the size and more than two hundred miles away. But back there, she'd lived on a street full of young people. And she missed it.

"I really like this place," Carl said. "I know I should wait for you to say something. You might hate it for all I know. But there's something about it. It reminds me..."

"What?"

"It reminds me of you." He shrugged.

She took three steps towards him and kissed him full on the lips.

She grunted at the sound of her phone. Nicholas, of course. She couldn't put him off, not after Mo's call and all the worrying she'd been doing.

"Where are you?" he asked.

"Looking at a house."

"Hang on." His face disappeared from the screen briefly. "Scotch Street. Wait... Oh. Hot tub, eh?"

"How did you—"

"I can track you on the family app, Mum. Throw that together with Rightmove and it's easy."

"If you ever want a job in the police, Nicholas... No. Don't answer that. How are you, though?"

"Fine." His face was back on the screen, his eyes sliding away.

He was hiding something, then. Maybe he could join the police, but he'd be a terrible criminal.

"Really? Only I spoke to Mo earlier, and he said you and Fox weren't together any more."

"Yeah. It's not ideal. But it happens. And it wasn't the greatest love affair of all time. Plenty more fish, eh?"

His laugh was so brittle she could have smashed it to pieces.

"Seriously, Nicholas, are you OK? Why don't you come down and stay here for a bit?"

Zoe glanced up. Carl was standing in the doorway, nodding. It wasn't like she had to run it past him every time she wanted her son to stay, but it was nice to know he agreed.

"No, really, Mum. It's fine. I'm fine. I've... Listen, I've got to go. Speak soon."

She was looking at a blank screen. And Nicholas definitely wasn't fine.

Back home, they spent half an hour talking about Nicholas and what was wrong with him, and got no closer to an answer. Every now and then, Carl would smile, and eventually, she asked him why. There was nothing funny about any of it.

"Sorry," he said. "Just thinking about that house."

"Oh." She didn't say anything more about it, but for the rest of the evening, from time to time, she caught herself smiling, too.

Work had to intrude at some point, and Carl listened as she told him what she'd already told Denise Gaskill: Carrie

Wright might be more inclined to talk if she feared she was a target.

Carl nodded. "She knows she's safe in custody. Maybe if we threaten to release her..."

Zoe frowned, then examined his face. The smile, again.

Fine. He was joking.

Her phone rang before they could discuss it any further.

"Zoe, this is Zhang Chen. I'm sorry to disturb you so late."

It was half past eight.

"That's fine, Zhang. Is everything OK?"

"Ye-es, I suppose so," he said. "I just wanted to let you know that I'm almost done, and we are where we feared we'd be."

"Which is?"

"I believe I can link the payments to a decent evidential standard. But even if I can, what's to stop your Mr Carter from simply pointing out that he doesn't know what's going on in all his individual businesses? This man, if he's the sort of person I think he is, won't struggle to get someone else to take the fall."

Zoe thanked him, and ended the call as politely as she could. She needed someone who knew what had really been happening in Carter's businesses, at Jenson & Marley in particular.

She tried Ryan Tobin again. Again, no answer.

CHAPTER EIGHTY-FIVE

EMMA LAY ACROSS TWO SEATS, the old woman leaning over her with anxious eyes.

There had been a delay. They'd been stuck in the Midlands, not moving, for an hour.

They were moving now.

But she was lying down, across two seats, which was strange enough, because last thing she remembered, the train had been full.

Why was she lying down? And who were these other people? A man and a woman were talking quietly to her, asking her if she needed help, telling her to try to sit up, leaning forward alongside old woman and taking her arm and gently pulling her upright.

"Would you like some water?" asked the man.

Emma nodded. Her throat felt like shit. Felt like it had felt in that shed, in the hills, after she'd vomited and had nothing to drink.

She hadn't vomited again, had she? She scanned her

body, the seat, the floor in front. She couldn't see anything. Couldn't smell anything, either.

The old woman was leaning over her again.

"What happened?" Emma asked. The words sounded strange, like someone else's voice.

"Well, dear, I don't really know. You were looking at your phone, and then, well, you just gasped and fainted, dear."

Looking at your phone.

She remembered, now. What she'd seen. The man in the photo.

Why had that copper sent that photo? Why had she opened the image? Why had she looked, and seen what she'd seen, and then seen it all again, the fire, and Neil, and the man, and the—

"Deep breaths," said the other woman, the one she hadn't met before. "Calm. That's right. In for four, out for six. Can you do that?"

Emma nodded. Someone pressed a bottle of water into her hand. She focused on breathing until she knew she wasn't going to be sick or pass out again, then lifted the bottle to her lips and drank greedily.

"Easy, now," said the man. "You don't want to make yourself sick."

She laughed like a madwoman. No idea why, but suddenly laughter hit her. So hard it hurt. So hard she spat water all over the people in front of her.

And then it was over. All of it. Everything. The laughter. The sickness.

"I'm so sorry," she said, finally.

"It's fine," replied the man, wiping the water from his glasses. He sat down opposite her, staring at her in bewilderment.

Emma turned to the old lady beside her. "Do you know where my phone is?" she asked.

"Oh. I think you might have dropped it when you fainted, dear."

She could do this. She bent down and examined the floor. Nothing in front of her. But under the seat—

"Is this it?"

A hand appeared from above. Someone in the seat behind her. She reached up and took the phone and thanked the person, and then she turned to the old lady and swallowed.

"Will you do me a favour?" she said.

"Of course, dear." The old lady smiled at her, and suddenly she loved this woman, whose conversation she'd been so desperate to avoid that she'd pretended to sleep.

"Will you sit with me and watch me while I look at that message again?"

"Oh." The woman's smile turned into a frown of concern. "Are you sure? Because whatever it was, it didn't seem to do you much good."

Emma laughed, a sharp, bitter little laugh.

"I think we're past worrying about what's going to do me any good. Please, will you stay with me?"

The woman looked up and down the train, and nodded.

It was time. Emma looked down at the phone.

There was the message.

She tapped on it.

CHAPTER EIGHTY-SIX

"I HOPE SHE'S NOT A VEGETARIAN," said Nina's mum.

"What?"

"Your – your friend. Elena, isn't it? Where is she?"

"She's upstairs, Mum. What's with the—"

"Shhh. Stop fussing. Now, go and get Elena and leave me to sort this out."

No one ordered Nina Kapoor around in her own kitchen. No one except her mum. Nina found herself climbing the stairs, muttering to herself.

Mum had shown up at the door, unannounced, five minutes earlier, with a big bunch of flowers in her hands and a casserole dish on the ground by her feet.

"My special spiced lamb," she'd said. And then, a minute later, when Nina had carried the dish into the kitchen, she'd turned to her daughter.

"I'm not angry, you know."

"Not angry?"

"About your – your relationship. It's your life. If it makes you happy and it doesn't hurt anyone else, then it makes me happy too. But I am angry that you didn't tell me."

And now Nina was climbing the stairs and wondering whether she should just go back to the kitchen and explain to her mum that she'd got it all wrong, or whether...

There were advantages. Not just the flowers, and the home cooked food – her mum's spiced lamb really was delicious.

Now she'd stop trying to set Nina up with every young man she came across. Half the older ones, too.

But what would Elena think?

Elena, it turned out, thought it was fine.

"If you want to do this, yes, I can do this. I can pretend."

They entered the kitchen together. Nina wasn't sure what to do, but either Elena had done this before, or she was a natural actor.

She greeted Nina's mum with a broad smile and kissed her on both cheeks. She praised the flowers, smelled them, said they were divine. She sniffed appreciatively at the air, followed the scent to the casserole dish on the kitchen counter, lifted the lid, and exclaimed, "Lamb is my very favourite!"

Nina's mum loved her. It was an act, all of it, but Elena was playing the part of the daughter's partner to perfection.

Her mum stayed for a cup of tea, which became two. Nina and Elena watched her leave, waving from the window, and it wasn't until they saw the lights from her car disappearing around a corner that the two of them collapsed onto the sofa, overcome with laughter.

After the laughter, the tea was put away, and the wine came out. It was halfway through the first glass that Nina's phone rang. She looked at it and shook her head.

"Who is it?" asked Elena.

"Romit."

"The man who has been calling you and will not stop?"

Nina nodded. Before she could react, Elena had reached out, taken the phone, and answered it.

"She isn't interested in you," she said, before Romit had the chance to speak. "In fact, you have turned her off men completely. Do not call again."

She ended the call and passed the phone back to Nina. Her solemn expression lasted all of five seconds before dissolving, once more, into laughter.

By the time they were on their second glasses of wine, Elena was telling Nina stories of her childhood in Bârlad. By the time they moved onto a third, they were exchanging tales of their tearaway teenage years. Bârlad sounded a lot more exciting than Whitehaven, but Elena still seemed to be impressed by some of Nina's exploits.

And Elena was talking about herself. Even halfway drunk, Nina could recognise that for what it was.

A breakthrough.

It was near the end of that third glass of wine that Elena said something that made Nina laugh so hard she spilled her wine.

Red wine. White carpet.

"It's OK," Nina said, as Elena looked on in horror. She stumbled into the kitchen, rummaged around, returned a minute later with the cleaning solution she had for just this problem.

"See?" she said. The stain was already fading. It would be gone by morning, and if it wasn't, another treatment would finish the job.

Elena was staring at the carpet. Her mouth was hanging

open, her eyes wide. It was an impressive product, sure, but it wasn't *that* impressive.

"The smell," Elena said.

"Yeah, it's quite strong, isn't it?" Nina replied. "Ammonia."

"That was the smell."

"What smell?"

"In the... warehouse, yes?"

Nina nodded, almost afraid to move.

"That was it," Elena said. "When we were there, in the building, that was the smell. It was horrible."

She nodded, as if confirming it to herself. Nina took a breath, and at that moment her phone buzzed.

It can wait.

But it was Emma Hudson.

Yes, it said. *That's him. That's the man who killed Neil.*

CHAPTER EIGHTY-SEVEN

AARON WOKE TO A FAMILIAR SMELL. Something good that he couldn't quite place.

He was lying on the sofa, his eyes still closed, trying to figure out what it was, when he heard footsteps. He opened his eyes to see Serge standing over him, his eyes filled with worry, a plate of bacon and eggs in one hand and a cup of tea in the other.

What brought this on?

"Aaron," said Serge. "Oh good. You're awake."

Aaron twisted his mouth into what he hoped was a smile. Serge's frown deepened. It had been so long since Aaron had smiled naturally. What sort of expression was he wearing?

"Morning." He should ask why Serge had done this for him. But if he did, maybe it wouldn't have happened. Maybe he'd wake up. Maybe he wouldn't, and it would be something bad.

"Are you OK, Aaron?"

Without thinking, Aaron stretched and reached to rub

his back, and realised how that might look. Like he was complaining about the sofa.

"Yeah," he said. "Fine."

"Good." Serge was still frowning. "I'm... I don't know. I thought maybe you'd like some breakfast. I've got to head out to meet a client, and I'll drop Annabel at nursery. You sure you're OK?"

Aaron nodded. Serge deposited the bacon and eggs, turned, and walked away.

No lingering kiss. No touch of fingertip on skin. Not even a look.

But Serge was worrying about him. Did that mean there was something to worry about?

An hour later, in the team room, he was directing Nina and Tom in the hunt for Tony Harris.

"Who've we seen?"

Tom had spent part of the previous evening with Uniform, knocking on doors. He reeled off a list of names. Eight of them. Dealers, former dealers, the sort of people Topper had interacted with when he'd been local.

"Nothing, Sarge. None of them even knew he was back."

"You believe them?"

"They sounded plausible. Topper's been keeping a low profile. If he's been doing what we think he's been doing, he'll have steered clear of his former associates."

And Topper *had* been doing what they thought he'd been doing. Emma Hudson had texted Nina and confirmed it.

If he was still in the area, they had to find him before he disappeared again. Aaron was conscious of the boss watching over his shoulder as he directed Nina and Tom. She seemed to be leaving the nuts and bolts of the hunt to him, which made sense. He was the DS. He still knew the area and the people better than she did.

Aaron had to do this. Had to find the man. Because even if he was a shit dad and a shit husband, at least he was a decent police officer.

Don't think like that.

There was a whole page of names on the big screen. Tom had already been to see the obvious ones. But there were plenty more to go round.

And if they didn't find Topper there?

He'd cross that bridge when he came to it.

CHAPTER EIGHTY-EIGHT

"Well, well, look who it is."

Nina stood on the pavement and allowed herself to be subjected to the woman's examination. It was slow and uncomfortable, but she'd come here to ask for a favour. Alison Peters would be perfectly entitled to tell her to bugger off, and there wasn't a thing she could do about it.

"Come on, then. Don't just stand there like an idiot." Alison turned and walked away.

Nina followed her inside.

The former drug-dealer lived in a semi-detached house in a smart area to the south of Whitehaven. Nina hadn't visited her home before – she wasn't sure any of her colleagues had, other than the sarge. And as far as she knew, no one from the Hub had so much as spoken to Alison Peters in more than a year.

"Sit down, then." They were in a mid-sized kitchen. Everything looked clean and comparatively new. "Coffee?"

Nina hesitated.

"If it helps, I grind my own beans. Got to repurpose some of the old equipment, eh?"

Nina rose from her chair. "Hang on," she said, and then she realised Alison was laughing.

"It's a joke, DC Kapoor. Look. Proper grinder and espresso machine." She gestured to the countertop, where a lump of black and chrome squatted like a robot. "Stuff I used for the drugs, you lot got all that. Well, the bits I hadn't sold."

She threw Nina a wink.

Nina smiled. "Yes, then. To the coffee."

Alison Peters had been dealing in Whitehaven since long before Nina had even contemplated joining the police force. She'd been something of a legend: a former user who'd got clean and smartened up her act. The woman bustling around the kitchen could have been any successful professional in her early fifties. Either retired, or coming to the end of a lucrative career.

Alison Peters was a business adviser these days. She hadn't been a dealer in a long time, and when she had dealt, she'd been sensible. No one ever overdosed on Alison's products. She didn't fight over territory, or start price wars, or get kids hooked. She was clever, too clever to get anything more than a suspended sentence nearly twenty years earlier.

But her career in drugs had overlapped with Topper's. And Topper might have turned into a psychopathic killer, but back then, he'd been one of the smart ones, too. He and Alison had worked neighbouring areas, and they'd divided their territory by agreement rather than violence. By the standards of rival drug dealers, they'd almost been friends.

"Not in touch with him, no," Alison said. The two of them were sitting in metal chairs at a square kitchen table made of glass. Nina had been careful to set her coffee down on a coaster. It was clear Alison was proud of her home. "Not since I stopped dealing."

"Oh."

Nina had wasted her time, then. It was a decent coffee, but it hadn't been worth coming all the way to Sandwith. She began to rise from her chair.

"But I have seen him, though."

Nina sat back down. "Recently?"

Alison took another sip from her coffee and nodded.

"Last week, maybe? Or the week before. Probably three or four times over the last couple of months."

"What did he say? How did he seem?"

"He didn't say anything. When I've seen him, I've been in the car and he's been strolling along. In town, once or twice, but also up on the fells."

"On the fells?"

"Ennerdale way. Or Loweswater. I forget which. He's there with his little rucksack on his back, just walking and walking."

"Do you know why?"

Alison shrugged. "The word is, while he was inside, he got obsessed with open spaces. But I don't think anyone's actually asked him. It's just gossip, really."

"And you haven't been able to speak to him?"

"Oh, I stopped the car. More than once. Pulled over – only when it was safe, Officer, I assure you – and asked him how he was. Ignored me, the little bugger. Even when I shouted his name. Like he was deaf, or something. Or like I wasn't there."

Nina nodded, thanked the woman, and stood to leave.

"So you think Topper's involved with this poor lad who got stabbed outside the barn the other day, then?"

Nina turned. She hadn't mentioned the case at all. Just said they were looking for Topper, in connection with a serious matter. How did Alison know?

Alison Peters grinned at her.

"Well, you lot, you don't do the little things, do you? You do the murders. And apart from that one, there hasn't been a murder here for weeks."

CHAPTER EIGHTY-NINE

ZOE WATCHED as Aaron instructed the DCs. She was looking out for errors in judgement, him forgetting something critical, overlooking something important.

But he'd done everything right. He still looked like shit, but whatever was wrong with him, it wasn't keeping him from doing his job.

She was hitting roadblock after roadblock. She'd tried Ryan Tobin as soon as she'd woken up, again on the drive in, a third time before the morning briefing.

No answer, no answer, no answer. Which was reassuring, in its own way.

He hadn't blocked her, at least.

Now they were out, Aaron, Nina, and Tom. She'd told PSD everything she knew about Carrie and Huz. Emma Hudson was gone, but unless they found Tony Harris and brought him to court, Emma wouldn't be needed again, and that wouldn't be for a while. Plenty of time to find Emma and lose her all over again a dozen times over.

She'd done all she could. So she tried Ryan Tobin again, and after a few seconds the ringtone was replaced by a voice.

"Will you not get the message, DI Finch?" said Tobin.

Zoe was so surprised she'd have fallen over if she hadn't been sitting down already. "Ryan?"

"Seriously, you've tried to get hold of me so many times I've got the phone company checking up on me, making sure you're not some weird stalker or something."

"Really?"

A laugh. "Like the phone company would give that much of a fuck about their customers."

"Ryan, I need your help."

"Is this about Carter?"

"Yes. I need to talk to you about Jenson & Marley. What you found there. Whatever it was that meant you could damage a Myron Carter business and walk away with all your limbs intact."

There was a snort. "You know why I've got all my limbs intact, DI Finch?"

"No. That's what I need to—"

"I've got all my limbs intact because I don't speak to the police any more than I have to, that's why. So you'll forgive me if I say fuck off, and don't call again."

The line went dead. Perhaps it would have been better if he'd blocked her after all.

She stood and stared out of the window. Sun, cloud, sun, cloud. *Proper English Weather.* The same as the weather everywhere else, just more of it.

She should probably check the team inbox, make sure nothing important had come out of the morning's conversations with Topper's associates. But if it had, they'd have called her.

She should brief Fiona on the hunt, check in with Carl, find out if Carrie Wright had said anything. A whole list of things she should do, people she should speak to, and the one person she was itching to speak to was the one person she despised.

But she had the measure of the man. She could get what she could from him, gather information, probe his thoughts, do all that without being sucked into whatever schemes he was plotting. Yes, she'd spoken to him just the day before, but it wouldn't hurt to speak to him again.

She picked up her phone and stared at it.

Didn't all addicts think like that?

She shook her head. Before she could put her phone down, it rang. Not Randle.

Was that relief she felt? Or disappointment?

"Stella," she said.

"Zoe. Mind telling me what's going on?"

"What do you mean?"

"Huz. He's just turned up here." Stella sounded even more pissed off than usual.

"There? The lab?"

"Yes, Zoe. The lab. Why did no one tell me he'd been released?"

Shit. It was bad enough Huz had been let out. Even worse that none of them had thought to inform his colleagues.

"I'm so sorry, Stella. What happened?"

"He just showed up like it was a normal day, like he still works here."

"What did you do?"

"What did I do? I told him to fuck off, is what I did."

"And he left?"

"Eventually. He begged me to let him in. Said he'd do whatever anyone wanted, or wouldn't touch anything. Said he just wanted another chance."

"But you—"

"No second chances. If he turns up here again, Zoe, I won't be responsible for my actions."

CHAPTER NINETY

Baz Ingerson was a long shot, but at least he was in. Back last year, when Noah Cane had been murdered, they'd wasted too long trying to reach Baz while he was still finishing his three month sentence in HMP Moorland in South Yorkshire.

"Oh, for fuck's sake," said Baz, his Glaswegian accent somehow making him seem larger than he really was.

"Aren't you going to invite me in, Baz?" Tom asked, then pushed his way past the man before he had the chance to reply.

"You can't just barge your way in here, man. It's not like you're gonna find anything."

Baz was a whinger. All the dealers in the area were bad news, but some of them were easier to deal with than others. Some of them didn't complain every time you so much as looked at them.

Tom found himself in a narrow hallway, more of a corridor, with three closed doors off it. He pushed open the one at the far end to reveal a kitchen,

"Bloody hell, Baz. You want to get yourself some cleaning products."

Even Nina would have been horrified, and that was saying something.

"So?" Baz had followed him into the room. "Not a crime, is it?"

Tom shook his head. "Look, don't worry. I'm not here to give you any grief."

"Well in that case, why don't you sit down and have a wee dram?"

The invitation was laced with sarcasm, which was fine. Tom wouldn't have wanted to drink from any of the glasses in this kitchen anyway. Or, in fact, to sit down.

"Just tell me everything you know about Tony Harris."

"Topper?" Baz sounded surprised.

"That's the one."

"There's a name I haven't heard in a while. Last I knew, he'd fucked off down south somewhere. Went off the rails after some copper beat the shit out of him and stole his drugs."

Tom frowned. The stealing made sense. But Carrie Wright didn't seem the type to beat the shit out of anyone.

"And since then?"

"How the fuck should I know? Like I said, he lost it, went down south. End of. Now, with the greatest respect, get the fuck out of my house."

Tom was happy to comply. His phone rang before he reached his car.

"DC Willis, it's Rick Bryant. We spoke yesterday. About Tony Harris."

Tom wasn't likely to forget Sergeant Bryant. "Yes, have you found anything out?"

"I have, as it happens. And listen, I probably didn't give the right impression yesterday. Always happy to help fellow officers and all that. OK?"

"OK," Tom replied. No doubt he'd been overheard by his inspector or grassed up by a disgruntled PC. Bryant didn't sound genuine, but Tom didn't really care about the man's personal views. Just his information.

"So," Bryant continued, "me and some of the team have managed to have a chat with a couple of the people Harris was inside with. They paint an interesting picture."

"Go on," Tom said.

"Word is, your man Harris completely lost it inside. Came in angry, got even angrier during his stay."

"That's not unusual," Tom replied. But it did chime with what he'd just heard from Baz Ingerson.

"That's not the best of it, though. That was his thing about space."

"Space?"

"Yeah. The man sounds... Well, it's interesting."

"How?"

"Sounds like he was desperate for open air and big spaces in the daytime. And you get that. But at night he changed. It was the opposite. He needed tiny enclosed spaces to sleep in. One of the lads said he turned his bunk into a sort of fort."

"A fort?"

"Like kids do. With cushions. He piled stuff up."

"So, what, he was claustrophobic in the day and agoraphobic at night?"

"If you say so."

"OK. Thanks."

Tom wasn't sure if what he'd just heard might be useful.

He tapped the details into the team inbox anyway, and made one more call.

They had enough on Topper to be confident it was him. But you had to cover all the bases. And if Huz had planted Steve and Eddie's prints and DNA at the scenes, it was still possible he'd done the same for Topper, and they were chasing the wrong man.

Unlikely. But not impossible.

Huz's police-issued phone had been confiscated, but there was a home number on the system. Tom rang it.

No answer. The poor bastard probably didn't want to talk to anyone.

CHAPTER NINETY-ONE

AARON SAT in his car at the end of Westmorland Road and flicked through the team inbox.

Nothing from the boss. Nina had been to see Alison Peters, who'd actually spotted Topper, since his return. So Topper was walking the streets, the hills, wherever he wanted to go. Wouldn't respond when people called his name. Aaron was struggling himself, but he had a way to go before he reached that stage.

Tom's report explained why. Something about being beaten up by police, which wasn't particularly convincing, but it was rare that anything coming from Baz Ingerson made sense.

The arresting officer had some background that shed a little light on Topper's strange behaviour, but what use was that when it didn't tell anyone where he was now?

Where he was now was unlikely to be Westmorland Road, but it was as good a place to start as any. Aaron climbed out of the car, approached the semi-detached house, and knocked on the door.

When it opened a moment later, he found himself looking straight at nothing, and then down at the top of a bald head.

"Mr Adebola Taiwo?" he asked.

The man looked up at him and shook his head.

"Almost," he said. "It's Dr Adebola Taiwo. But I usually allow people one mistake before I get upset about it."

Adebola Taiwo was tiny. Aaron couldn't help taking a step back to look at the man properly. Less than five feet, certainly. Closer to four.

"Four foot six," said Dr Taiwo.

"I beg your pardon?"

"You were wondering how tall I am. I'm four foot six. Now, what can I do for you?"

Aaron blinked at the man, until he remembered why he was there, which prompted a polite invitation to come in.

He stumbled past a pair of boots by the front door, then followed Dr Taiwo through a short hallway to the kitchen. He stood briefly at the threshold of the room, looking around.

"Everything here is normal, DS Keyes. I am not a dwarf, I don't live in the forest, I don't have a house full of special gadgets. I'm just a specialist in acute care at the West Cumberland Hospital who happens to be unusually short."

"I'm sorry," said Aaron, taking a seat at the table and looking around the room. It was all normal, just as the doctor had said. A kettle. A toaster. A mug by the sink. An electrical cable ran through an open window, through a narrow back garden, to a tiny shed.

"Have you seen Tony Harris lately?"

Dr Taiwo shook his head. "Not for months." He frowned. "Possibly more than a year, in fact. Before he went to... Suffolk, was it?"

"Norfolk," Aaron replied. Dr Taiwo hadn't offered him any coffee, which was fine, but he could have done with one. He was exhausted. He closed his eyes, briefly, saw an image of Victor Parlick smiling at him, and opened them again.

"Norfolk, then," said Dr Taiwo. "I understand he got into some trouble there. I had assumed he was still in prison."

Aaron blinked and forced himself to focus. "You and Topper are friends, aren't you?"

"Topper?"

It was Topper's customers that had given him the nickname. No reason for the doctor to know it.

"Sorry. Tony."

"*Were* friends, DS Keyes. We were at school together. But people lose touch. I haven't seen him, not for a long time, or even heard from him. That makes it difficult to think of a person as a friend, doesn't it?"

Dr Taiwo had been picked up a few years back. A small quantity of cannabis. Personal use only. No doubt that was what was going on in the shed. Aaron didn't need to look at it.

The man was a doctor. He was doing something useful with his life. Aaron wasn't going to waste any more of his time.

CHAPTER NINETY-TWO

AARON, Nina, and Tom were assembled in the team room, looking glum, when Zoe walked in.

"What's wrong?"

"We've got nothing, boss." Nina raised her hands. "Been through every name on the list, and no one's got anything useful to tell us."

That wasn't strictly true. No one knew where Tony Harris was, but there were things people had said that might help narrow it down.

"Come on," Zoe said. "Let's go through what we've got, see if there's anything we've missed that jumps out when we're all looking at it together."

She smiled, trying to project a confidence she didn't feel. There was no reason to believe the killer was in the area at all, not now. Maybe he'd done what he'd come for and disappeared again.

But Tom and Nina were watching her eagerly. They thought this might work. And maybe it would. They'd got to the bottom of Topper's motive by throwing ideas back and forth the night before. Maybe the same thing would work now.

She glanced at Aaron, hoping to see the same interest on his face, but he just looked defeated.

Deal with Aaron later.

"So what have we got?"

Nina went first. "Alison Peters. She'd seen Topper, round and about. Called his name. He didn't respond. Walked everywhere."

"Good," said Zoe. "Doesn't tell us where he is, but explains how he got away from the barn after he'd got rid of the Land Rover. And tells us we're dealing with someone potentially unstable."

She pictured Neil Colvin's body. *Potentially unstable.* That was one way of putting it.

"Baz Ingerson thinks he lost it after he was beaten up by Carrie," said Tom. Nina snorted.

"What is it?" Zoe asked.

"Sorry, boss. It's just... I know we're talking about drug dealers, and none of them are exactly trustworthy, but Baz Ingerson's a snake. Wouldn't know the truth if it hit him in the face."

Zoe nodded. *Fine.* Carrie Wright might have taken Topper's drugs, but beaten him up? Unlikely.

"But Sergeant Bryant," Tom said, "the one who arrested him in Norfolk, he managed to speak to some of the men Topper was inside with. And they... well, I don't trust Baz any more than you do, but he used the same words. *Lost it.* Maybe Carrie didn't beat him up, but Topper wasn't balanced when he went in, and while he was inside, things got worse."

Zoe had read all this in the team inbox. But hearing it

first hand, or in this case, third hand, was always better. "Go on," she prompted.

"It was all about space. Needed lots of it in the daytime. The opposite at night, wanted to be enclosed. Wrapped up, tight. Tried to turn his bunk into a fort."

"Sounds like he was veering between claustrophobia and agoraphobia," Nina pointed out.

Tom nodded. "That's what I said to Bryant. Not sure he knew what the words meant."

"But does any of that get us any closer to figuring out where he is now?" asked Aaron.

It wasn't promising.

"Did you get anything useful from the old schoolfriend?" Zoe asked. Aaron hadn't got round to updating the file.

He shook his head. "It's a—"

Tom's phone rang. He flashed an apologetic look, then answered, and listened for a moment.

The colour drained from his face.

"What is it?" asked Zoe. It wasn't like they were getting anywhere. But being interrupted rarely helped.

"It's Huz, boss," Tom said. He stopped, shaking his head.

"What about him?"

"It's Huz," Tom repeated. "He's... He's been killed."

CHAPTER NINETY-THREE

For a few seconds, all four of them stared, in shock, three faces turned to Tom, Tom focusing on Zoe.

Huz had been murdered.

"Right," she said. "We've been working on the assumption that Topper was still in the area. Now we can be pretty much sure of it."

Her team stared back at her.

They'd be thinking about Huz. About the man they knew. She had to get them to refocus. To think about the man who'd killed him.

"Tom, where did it happen?"

"Huz's house," he said. His voice was flat. "Whitehaven. Clitheroe Drive."

"What else do we know?"

Tom moved, turning back to his screen, pulling up the call notes, then turning to the big screen on the wall.

A photo of Huz. Serious expression, but the ghost of a grin hidden underneath, waiting to come out. A couple of years younger than the Huz she knew.

This was his work ID.

A map of the location. She'd been there once already. It was easy enough to get to.

To the side, there was text. One uniformed officer on scene. One body in the house. Positive identification.

Zoe turned to Tom, to ask what she'd missed, then stopped.

Whoever it was who'd gone to the house, they probably knew Huz.

She scanned the rest of the call notes. The woman next door, and her teenage son, had heard screaming. They thought it sounded serious. She'd got on the phone to the police just as the son opened the front door to see a man emerge from Huz's house. Just walking away, down the street. He'd turned left at the top and disappeared.

Blood all over him, the boy claimed.

Medium height, brown hair, short beard. It could be almost anyone.

It was Tony Harris. They all knew it was Tony Harris.

Zoe scanned the room.

Tom was still in shock. Aaron was... Aaron was still whatever he'd been earlier.

Tony Harris was in Whitehaven. They had to find him before he got out.

Zoe turned to Nina. "Nina. Can you go?"

Nina nodded, already half out of her chair.

"Call as soon as you have anything. Everyone, stay in touch. I need to..."

Zoe felt her legs give way and slumped into the spare chair. Kay's chair.

She'd been joking. They'd all been joking. Zoe, Carl, Denise Gaskill.

Carrie Wright might be more inclined to talk if she feared she was a target.

She probably had been a target. Probably still was. They hadn't meant it. Not seriously. If they had done, they wouldn't have forgotten about Huz.

She picked up her phone and dialled Carl.

She knows she's safe in custody. Maybe if we threaten to release her...

He'd only been joking, too. But Carl had to know about Huz.

Zoe had to make sure Carrie Wright wasn't released.

CHAPTER NINETY-FOUR

THE ENTRANCE to Clitheroe Drive was blocked by three patrol cars. Nina walked past, inspecting the few houses on either side of the road.

No sign of any cameras, not that they'd have told her much. Topper had left on foot, according to the call. And they already knew what he looked like.

Half a dozen people were gathered by the cordon stretching across the bottom half of the road. Among them were a middle-aged woman and a teenage boy, both pale with shock.

They'd be the ones who'd called. She'd speak to them later.

First, the house.

She showed her ID to the officer guarding the tape, and he nodded silently and let her through. He looked pale, too.

They knew Huz. He was one of them.

Had been. As she approached the house, the notion buzzed through her mind that maybe there'd been a mistake. Maybe Huz wasn't dead. Maybe it wasn't Huz at all.

The front door was open, the body in the hall. Standing outside, pulling on her forensic suit, Nina could see there hadn't been a mistake.

It was Huz. And he was dead.

Shit.

"You're here," said a quiet voice.

Nina looked up to see Caroline Deane blinking away tears.

"You shouldn't be," Nina told her. "Isn't there anyone else?"

"Who?" Caroline asked.

Apart from the analysts who were confined to the lab, the local CSI team was just the three of them. Stella, Caroline, Huz.

Two of them, now.

"Are you OK?" Nina asked.

Caroline shook her head.

"Can you do this?"

"I've got to, haven't I?"

The two of them were standing over the body now. Close up, it was even worse.

It was Huz, but barely. Impossible to see the wounds, or even work out what he'd been wearing, because there was so much blood.

"The pathologist's on his way," Caroline said, her voice wobbling.

"Good." The sooner the body could be moved, the easier this would become. How could Caroline be expected to examine a crime scene when the dead body of her friend was slap bang in the middle of it?

"And the knife..."

Nina looked up. Caroline was staring at the floor, her

eyes focused on a spot just past the body. The carpet there was – *had been* – grey. Now, it was just a mess. Caroline was swaying. Nina reached out, took her arm, and Caroline shrugged her off.

"No," she said. "Thank you. But I need to do this. The knife."

She pointed in the direction she'd been staring, and Nina followed her gaze and saw it.

He'd left it there. Seven inches, maybe eight. Nina tried to remember the notes she'd flicked through from Neil Colvin's post-mortem. A narrow blade. Thinner than a kitchen knife.

Could it be the same knife?

Caroline was speaking, but Nina hadn't heard what she'd said.

"Sorry, what was that?"

"He's not bothering to hide the traces now," Caroline repeated. "Look."

Nina stepped closer. The knife was streaked with blood.

And in the blood, marks. Smears. The signs of a hand.

Possibly the easiest fingerprints Caroline would ever have to recover, red and silver, stark in the blood of her colleague and friend.

CHAPTER NINETY-FIVE

EVERYTHING WAS MOVING TOO FAST.

Beside Aaron, Tom was on the phone, speaking quietly. The boss paced up and down, stopping occasionally to take a call, make a note, make another call.

What could he do?

His phone rang. Nina.

"Are you there?" he asked.

"Yes." She sounded subdued. Not like the Nina he knew.

"Is it—"

"It's him, Sarge. It's Huz. Pathologist's just arrived. Sarge..."

"What?"

"He left the knife." There was panic in her voice. "Topper left the knife. It's got prints all over it. Like he doesn't care any more."

"OK." He had to keep her calm. "CSI can deal with that. You just..."

You just *what*?

"It's Caroline, Sarge. She's just about coping."

"Do what you can, Nina. Call me if you need help. We'll get through this, OK? We'll fix it."

How were they going to *fix it*? He could hardly bring Huz back to life, could he?

His phone rang again. Control.

"One of yours, I think," said the woman when he answered. Her voice was patient, relaxed. Like this was just a normal day.

"What do you mean?"

"We've had a report of a dropped line from an address on Westmorland Road."

"What's that got to do with me?"

A dropped line meant someone had called the emergency services, then hung up before saying anything. On rare occasions, it meant something. Usually it just meant a mistake or a prank.

"Apparently you visited the house this morning."

Aaron frowned. "I did?"

"Adebola Taiwo," she said, pronouncing the words carefully.

Of course. Westmorland Road. He'd filed his report in the team inbox, but the location would have been recorded centrally. So Adebola had made a call, or started to make a call, and...

Aaron dropped his phone and felt his legs turn numb.
Shit.

He could hear the woman from control saying his name. He ignored her.

"Boss," he said.

DI Finch was tapping on her phone, her face set in concentration.

He stood up.

"Boss," he repeated, louder this time. She looked up.

"I need to go out."

She frowned at him. "Why?"

"I've just had a call." He waved at his phone, on the ground, the voice of the woman from control still audible. "I've had... There's been a dropped line."

He felt sick.

"What's that got to do with us?"

"Adebola Taiwo's house. Topper's friend. I was there this morning."

"OK," she said. She was too calm. "But still—"

"Maybe this is something to do with Topper. Maybe he's been there. Maybe he's there now. I was round there earlier."

"You just said that."

"Before Huz was killed, boss."

He sat down heavily, without meaning to.

Before Huz was killed.

"Look," said the boss, still calm. "It's probably nothing, but it might not be. We'll send Uniform. I'll go and brief the super, OK?"

She patted his arm as she walked out of the team room.

How could she be so calm? It was Topper. He was sure of it. Topper was there, or had been there.

"Sarge?"

Tom was looking at him. Worried. Aaron was standing now, but he didn't remember getting up.

It was Topper. It had to be Topper. There had been...

There had been a pair of boots by the front door. Walking boots. He'd stumbled over them on the way in. Normal. Big, even.

Too big to belong to the diminutive Adebola Taiwo.

And the wire to the shed. Weed, he'd thought.

He walked across the room, ignoring Tom calling after him.

Weed. Because no one could be staying in there, no one could be *living* in there. It was far too small for that.

Far too small. Unless that was precisely what you needed. Unless you wanted to be enclosed. Wanted to be wrapped up tight.

Tried to turn his bunk into a fort.

Behind him, he could hear Tom saying his name. He pushed open the door to the stairway and ran.

CHAPTER NINETY-SIX

"SHE'S EXPECTING YOU." Luke seemed more present than usual. Almost jittery.

Raising her hand to push open the super's door, Zoe could hear voices from inside, or maybe just a single voice. She turned back to Luke.

"Go in. Really."

She entered to see Fiona standing at the window, facing away from her, her phone to her ear.

"Yes, Sir," she heard. "Contingencies in operation. We'll prepare a statement for you."

The super turned, saw Zoe, and pointed at the chair by her desk.

"I understand. We'll... Yes. Yes. We will."

She ended the call and returned to her chair, sinking into it with a sigh.

"ACC?" asked Zoe.

A nod. "He's already heard."

Everyone had already heard. The Hub would be in

shock, half the town, the wider police community. One of their own had been killed.

And Zoe needed to get back downstairs and help catch the man who'd done it.

"What do you need to know?" she asked.

"Is this connected to your investigation? The barn thing?"

"We think it's the same killer."

Fiona nodded. "And PSD? Does this have anything to do with their work?"

"PSD arrested him, Fiona," Zoe said. "They questioned him, would have been charging him. But let's put it this way. He got drawn into criminal activity because he worked for the police. But I don't think that's why he was killed."

"Who did this?"

"Tony Harris," Zoe told her. "Known as Topper. Local dealer, moved—"

"I know who Topper is, Zoe. I thought he was out of the picture."

"Apparently not."

Fiona fixed her with a cold stare. "Until this man is in our custody, Zoe, your sole priority is to find him."

Zoe nodded.

"Good."

It wasn't like there was much else going on. Myron Carter could wait. Hell, Myron Carter could get away with everything, if it came to that.

"I mean it," Fiona continued. "Nothing else matters. I don't care what you have to do. Just find him."

CHAPTER NINETY-SEVEN

THERE WAS no one else here.

Aaron parked four doors from Adebola Taiwo's house and looked around. No other police. Nothing. The sun had broken through the clouds and was bouncing off windows. Across the road, a woman was trying to hold a toddler and unlock her front door at the same time. Further up, a man was inspecting the engine of an ancient Fiat. No other police, no patrol cars, no one in uniform, no one at all.

Why should there be?

He got out of the car and walked towards the house. There was a low brown picket fence around the short path to the front door, with a small gap and hinges where there should have been a gate. He hadn't noticed that when he'd been here earlier.

He hadn't noticed anything.

He glanced up, and stopped. Adebola Taiwo was standing at the wide upstairs window, looking down at him.

Adebola was alive, then. Maybe he'd overreacted. Maybe this was nothing.

"Did you call?" Aaron shouted.

Adebola didn't reply. The window was closed. Had he even heard Aaron call?

Aaron shielded his eyes, looked up again, and saw a knife under Adebola's throat.

He hadn't overreacted. It wasn't nothing.

He stepped back again. He could see an arm, but that was it. Just one of Topper's arms. But it was Topper.

The window opened.

"I betrayed him," shouted Adebola.

"What?"

Aaron heard a sound behind him and turned. The mother had managed to get her door open, and was standing there, watching, her hand on her phone. He gave her a slight nod, then turned back to Adebola.

"I betrayed him." The man was crying. Even from here, Aaron could see fat tears rolling down his cheeks. "I saw him coming in. Earlier."

"Yes?" *Keep him talking.*

"I saw the blood. I lied to you last time. I didn't believe you. But then I saw the blood, and I knew it was true."

"That's OK, Adebola."

But it wasn't OK. Adebola Taiwo had a knife to his throat, and the man holding it had already killed twice. Had already killed that day.

"I told him I wasn't going to lie again."

Adebola gasped, and Aaron saw a thin red line appear on his neck.

"I betrayed him. I have to pay the price," Adebola said.

"Is he making you say this?" Aaron could hear sirens in the distance. How far? He could see the knife digging into Adebola's neck.

This wasn't working.

"I need to talk to Tony Harris," he shouted.

Adebola gave a sob. What had been a trickle of blood was beginning to thicken.

"You've killed people who stole from you, Topper. But this is different. This is your friend. There's no need to do this."

Another voice called down.

"It's over."

Topper.

"No it isn't," Aaron shouted back.

"I won't go back inside. I won't let you take me. So I'm not getting out of this alive, am I?"

What had happened to Tony Harris? He'd always been odd, but just a little. He'd been smart.

"You just need to calm down. How about you talk to me?"

As Aaron watched, Adebola was dragged away from the window, still sobbing. Where his head had been, Topper came into view.

There was a lot of blood on the man.

"What's the point?" he asked. His arm moved. A sudden gasp from Adebola. Aaron closed his eyes and tried to see past all this.

Instead, he saw Huz, alive, his mouth twisted into an apologetic smile after one of his bad jokes. Huz was replaced by Victor Parlick, raising a glass.

Aaron opened his eyes. The sirens were close now.

"You need a hostage," he shouted.

In the window, Topper shrugged, then nodded.

"Fine. You can have me."

"What?" called Topper.

"Let him go. Let me in instead. I'm unarmed. I'll make it easy for you. Just let Adebola go."

The sirens were so close now. Aaron turned to see people standing in the doorway of the house behind him. A little further up, the woman and her child had disappeared.

Good.

Aaron took off his jacket and let it fall to the ground.

He pulled off one shoe, then the other. He stopped and looked up.

Tony Harris was staring down at him. Somewhere out of sight, Adebola was sobbing again.

Aaron began to unbutton his shirt, heard another sound, and looked up again.

Topper was laughing at him.

He returned to his shirt. One more button.

He shrugged off his shirt and dropped it on top of his jacket.

"OK," shouted Harris. "You can come in. Alone. I want you to strip to your underwear and cuff yourself."

Cuff yourself?

Fine. He could do that.

"OK," Aaron shouted back up.

"Do it, then. Do it, and I'll let him go."

CHAPTER NINETY-EIGHT

Zoe entered the team room to find Tom standing, looking worried. There was no sign of Aaron.

"Where's the sarge?" she asked.

"I don't know, boss. He just... it was weird. He took a call. You were there."

Zoe thought back. He'd heard something from control about a dropped line. His reaction had been a little extreme, but that was Aaron right now, wasn't it?

"What happened after that?"

"He just got up and walked out. Ran out. I've tried calling him, but he hasn't answered."

Zoe's phone rang. Inspector Keane. She'd put him off.

"Morris. Things are a little—"

"You need to get down to Westmorland Road, Zoe."

"Why?" she asked. There was a sick feeling in the pit of her stomach.

"I think Aaron could be in trouble."

She was already up and heading out of the room. "What's happened, Morris?"

"I'm getting some weird reports. People saying... Look, has Aaron been OK?"

She pushed open the door to the stairs and kept moving. "Just tell me."

"Fine. Apparently, he's taken off most of his clothes and walked into someone's house, and a moment later someone else has come running out with his throat cut."

Zoe hit the car park at a run. Thirty seconds after Morris Keane had called, she had her keys out and the door to her Mini open. As she headed for the exit an object appeared in front of her and she braked hard.

Tom. He opened the passenger door and jumped in before she could stop him.

She waited, her foot hovering over the gas.

"Tom, I need you to stay."

He shook his head. "If the sarge is in trouble, I'm coming with you."

Fine. No time to argue. She had Morris Keane on the speakers now, but he didn't know any more than he'd already said. Except one extra detail.

"We've had half a dozen calls from that road, Zoe. One of them says Aaron cuffed himself before he went in."

Cuffed himself? What the hell was Aaron doing?

Her phone rang again halfway to Whitehaven. Carl. She answered without taking her eyes off the road.

"I got your message," he said. "Don't worry. We've got no intention of releasing Carrie Wright."

"Carl—" she began.

"We've charged her with the drugs we found at her house, but there's going to be plenty more. She still won't talk, though."

"Carl, listen—"

"I thought she was just braving it out at first, but now I'm not so sure. I think she's scared, Zoe. Maybe she's not the top dog in this pack."

"Please, Carl, listen—"

"Anyway, no chance of Carrie seeing daylight for a while. Unlike your friend Huz, she's going to be on remand until she's tried."

"Stop it, Carl!"

Beside her, Tom sat up.

"What is it?" asked Carl.

"Huz is dead," she said. "And I'm worried Aaron's about to join him."

CHAPTER NINETY-NINE

THE HANDOVER HAD BEEN LESS complicated than Aaron had expected. He'd pushed the front door open, walked upstairs and into what he assumed was the main bedroom.

A bed in the corner. Clothes hanging neatly in an open wardrobe. Tony Harris holding a knife to their owner's throat.

"Lie down," Topper said. He nodded towards the bed.

Aaron lay on the bed.

"Face the wall."

He turned to face the wall. He heard whispering, then movement.

"OK, get up."

Topper was standing in front of him now, dragging him up. He'd done as the man asked. He'd taken off everything except his pants and his socks. He'd walked back to his car, almost naked, the sirens now so close he expected the cars to turn the corner any second. He'd pulled out his cuffs, cuffed himself, and walked back to the house.

And now Adebola was gone, and Aaron was standing by

the window, looking out, just like the doctor had been. With the same knife to his throat.

"Just... Please just stay calm," he said. He wasn't sure if he was talking to himself or Topper.

But Topper did sound calm. Outside the window, Aaron could see three patrol cars. There would be more out of sight. Uniformed officers moving people away. And through it all, Topper somehow sounded calm.

"They tell you what happened to me, inside?" he asked.

"No," Aaron replied. Every time his throat moved, the knife bit a little way into it. If Topper slipped...

Don't think like that. Just keep him talking.

"It destroyed me, DS Keyes. I'd thought I was better than anyone else, you know? Smarter."

"You were," Aaron said. The knife was so close, it came out like a gulp. "You were smart, Tony."

"I was a fucking idiot."

He moved as he said the last word, a tiny motion, probably an involuntary one, that pushed the knife a little further into Aaron's throat.

He'd been afraid before. Now he was terrified.

"You weren't an idiot," he said. "You knew what you were doing. When you..."

How could he put it? He didn't want to make the man even angrier.

"When you went, we were pleased to see the back of you. Because you knew what you were doing."

There was a long silence. The pressure on his neck lessened slightly. Had it worked?

"No, I didn't. I'm an idiot, DS Keyes. That's what prison taught me. A stupid piece of meat being moved around the board by other people. Until they got tired of me, at least."

"What?" asked Aaron. *Keep him talking.* "Who?"

"You know who. Those students. Your mate, Hussein. Carrie Wright."

"You've killed Carrie too?"

Another silence. Through the window, more police. No civilians, now. They'd got them all out of the way.

"I couldn't get to Carrie," Topper said. "She's not around. You lot have her, don't you?"

Aaron said nothing. *Don't make him any angrier.*

"Don't you?" repeated Topper. Aaron felt the knife biting into his neck again, and the trickle of something wet on his shoulder.

Don't look down. Look through the window instead. There was a cordon now. At the edge of his vision, Aaron could see a woman in dark clothes emerging from an unmarked van, her movements swift and economical.

The snipers had arrived. Once they were in position, things could move quickly.

They could move the wrong way, too.

"Yes," he gasped.

"Thought so. You shouldn't have let Hussein go, though."

That hurt. That cut deeper than the knife at his throat.

"You know why I didn't kill myself in there?" asked Topper.

What should he say? Should he guess? What would happen if he guessed wrong?

"I don't know," he replied.

"Revenge."

Revenge. Well, Topper had got that, and some. The people who'd crossed Tony Harris had certainly paid for it. And now it was Aaron's turn.

But he had to try.

"You know, you can survive this," Aaron said.

He felt movement, the knife sliding back and forth against his neck. Topper was shaking his head.

"I'm sorry, DS Keyes. I can't walk away from this. Not even with you as a hostage. We both know that won't work. And I won't go back inside."

Aaron tried not to breathe. Any movement... "So what happens next?" he asked.

"We're going to die. Both of us. That's what happens next."

Aaron closed his eyes again. Saw Huz. Victor Parlick. There was another one, the man who'd died at Lowther Street. Aaron hadn't even been around for that one, had been off work, sick, useless. People died. Good people, bad people. Everyone. Why should he be any different?

In the end, perhaps it was fair.

CHAPTER ONE HUNDRED

ZOE COUNTED six patrol cars on the road, plus a handful of vans from which serious-looking people in serious-looking dark clothing were emerging.

What was going on? Had this turned into an armed siege already?

Uniform were managing the cordon, four of them, and behind it a crowd of perhaps twenty, eager to see what was going on, less eager to listen to instructions and do what was good for them. No one seemed to have a megaphone. No negotiations, yet.

She showed her ID to one of the PCs at the cordon and was waved through, Tom close behind. Good. The snipers weren't in position yet, which meant she still had the chance to see what was happening.

They moved past a handful of innocuous-looking houses. Freshly painted bay windows. A little plastic slide in a front garden. A caravan in a driveway. Scattered among them, more firearms officers, more PCs, other people whose role she couldn't have guessed.

Everyone was looking up.

Zoe stopped outside Adebola Taiwo's house and followed their gaze. There was Aaron, standing at a window. She could only see his upper half, but that, at least, was naked. His hands were in front of him, cuffed.

And there was a knife at his throat.

But it wasn't the knife that worried her most. What had her blinking and trying to control her breathing was the expression on Aaron's face.

She'd expected scared, or brave. She'd expected something. Some emotion. But his face was relaxed, his eyes closed.

He'd given up. There was a man holding a knife to his throat, and he'd simply given up.

Zoe took a breath and turned to Tom.

"Boss, look at him," he said. He'd seen the same thing.

She turned to see a car pulling up at the edge of the cordon. A Fiesta. Out of it burst Nina, running at the cordon, looking up, shouting.

Nina didn't need to see this. Tom didn't. None of them did.

"Go back to the car, Tom," she said.

He looked at her like she was mad.

She turned to intercept Nina, but the DC was through the cordon now, pushing past her, already at the little picket fence that marked the boundary between the pavement and the front garden.

"Stop," Zoe shouted.

Nina stopped. She turned to Zoe and shook her head. She turned back to the house and shouted up.

"Sarge!"

What good was that?

Now Tom was shouting, too. Something unintelligible. This couldn't help. None of it could help.

But Aaron had given up. It couldn't hurt, either. What did they have to lose?

Zoe turned back to the house and started shouting.

CHAPTER ONE HUNDRED ONE

AARON OPENED his eyes and looked down, the slight movement of his head causing the knife to press even closer against his throat.

He was bleeding now. Really bleeding.

He could see them down there. The boss. Nina. Tom. All of them looking up at him and shouting. He couldn't make out the words. He wasn't even sure there were any words.

But it was nice that they were here.

He closed his eyes again. Waited for them to appear. Huz. Victor Parlick.

They didn't appear. Instead, he saw a moment from some night a month, maybe two months ago. Creeping into Annabel's room while she slept. Watching her tiny chest rise and fall. Watching as her eyes opened, as she saw him, started to smile, then fell back to sleep before she could manage it.

Telling Serge about it, seconds later. Seeing the joy in his husband's eyes.

Aaron opened his eyes. People had died. Some of them might have deserved it. Some of them hadn't.

He wasn't going to be one of them.

The window was still open, in front of him. The chaos outside had slowed. Everyone who was supposed to be here was here, everyone in the place they were supposed to be.

He could hear words, from the boss, Tom, Nina. Just one word, from all three of them. His name.

The window.

Ignoring the pressure on his neck, he pushed the top half of his body forward.

He heard a sound from behind him, a grunt of surprise. Topper hadn't expected anything like that. The pressure on his neck eased slightly, and he allowed his body to lean further. As if he were about to throw himself out.

"What the f—" said Topper.

Aaron's head was now nearly a foot in front of Topper's. That was more than enough room for him to snap it back, hard.

Right into Topper's nose.

He had no idea where the knife was, whether he was about to impale himself on it, but he couldn't go back now. He turned.

Topper had dropped the knife. He was holding his bleeding nose in one hand and feeling around on the floor with the other.

In one movement, Aaron was on him. Shouting. Screaming.

There were more noises from below. In the house. Footsteps on the stairs. Voices shouting.

He blocked it all out. He had to beat them to it. He had to do it. No one else. Him.

He glanced down at the cuffs around his wrists, and his bare legs. He resisted the urge to laugh as he spoke.

"Tony Harris," he said. "I'm arresting you on suspicion of murder."

CHAPTER ONE HUNDRED TWO

"WELL DONE, Zoe. But first thing's first. How's Aaron?"

Zoe smiled in relief. You never knew quite what to expect, with Fiona. The super didn't like it when members of Zoe's team got themselves into danger. Zoe wasn't enormously fond of it herself, but she could see why Fiona's reactions weren't always the ones she'd have hoped for.

In the space of a year, Nina had been kidnapped by a crazed killer, Tom had been held at gunpoint, Zoe herself had faced off against another murderer atop a remote fell, and now Aaron...

"Surprisingly well," she replied. "They've patched him up already, and he's expecting to be discharged shortly. I've left Nina and Tom with him, having a go at him for getting himself in trouble, so he's probably desperate to be out of there as soon as he can."

Aaron was already getting enough grief for his decision to go in and risk his life. Fiona didn't need to add to it.

"Good. I'm pleased for you. All of you. It's been a difficult few days, Zoe."

Here it came.

"And the fallout over Huz... Well, I'll be dealing with that for a while. But I hope you know that's not your fault."

Zoe stared at the super. Could the woman read her mind?

They all blamed themselves for Huz. Not just Aaron and Zoe, but Tom and Nina. Carl and Denise Gaskill would be feeling it. She couldn't speak for Branthwaite, but if the man was human, him too.

"Thank you, Fiona," she said. "But I don't think this is all over."

"No?" Fiona raised an eyebrow.

Zoe shook her head. "No. I mean, we've got the killer. And he was acting alone. That's over. But Carrie Wright—"

"Carrie Wright is PSD's problem. Not yours. You did your bit, and you did it successfully."

"I don't believe Carrie's at the top, Fiona. And nor does Carl. The reason she won't talk is because she's protecting someone, or something, and I think she's doing that out of fear, not loyalty."

"Again, Zoe. Not your problem."

How could Fiona be so blind? You couldn't just hand everything over to PSD and pretend it wasn't happening. They'd already discussed what Zoe suspected, that there was a PSD agent undercover in the Hub. Fiona wasn't interested. Did she know?

No. She didn't know, and she didn't want to.

"With respect, Fiona, it is our problem. Because it means there's someone else we need to look out for, someone here. And if Huz was blackmailed into his role, maybe Carrie was too. Someone with that kind of power—"

"Enough, Zoe."

Zoe stopped. The super wasn't smiling.

"Maybe you're right," Fiona said. "And maybe you're not. PSD aren't stupid. They can handle it. And unless Carrie Wright decides to talk, no one can do anything about it."

Zoe opened her mouth to argue. Fiona shook her head. Zoe closed her mouth.

"Meanwhile, you've caught a killer. Why don't you just take the win?"

Maybe Fiona was right. Take the win. Allow herself to celebrate, for once. She stood and was almost out of the room when she stopped and turned.

"Alistair Freeburn," she said.

Fiona was already scanning paperwork, but now she looked up. Nothing tense about her. "What about him?"

Zoe had played this conversation through, plenty of times, and there was no way to put it delicately. She just had to handle it as best she could.

"Why does the man do what you ask him to?"

"I'm sorry?"

It wasn't an apology. It was a question, a challenge.

"When I first came across him," Zoe said, "he was annoying and pompous and as obstructive as you could imagine. And then I mentioned him to you, and now he's like a pussycat. He's still annoying and pompous, but he does what I ask him to. And I can't help wondering—"

"You've been looking for corruption for too long, Zoe. You can't help wondering what sort of hold I've got over Alistair, and whether there's anything untoward about it. Is that right?"

Zoe had handled this badly. She said nothing.

"He's a friend of my husband's, Zoe. They run the local historical re-enactment society together."

"But I met the man who runs the roleplay group with Freeburn. William Enderby."

Fiona nodded. "William Enderby. My husband. Pair of them are utterly ridiculous, with their dressing up and cavorting about the place like children, but they enjoy it, and it doesn't do any harm."

"William Enderby is your husband?"

Zoe had only met the man briefly, during the incident at Freeburn's office a couple of months earlier. He'd seemed perfectly pleasant. Helpful, even. He hadn't mentioned anything about Fiona.

"Ah, yes. You did come across him, didn't you?" Fiona smiled. "And he didn't want to mention me. He claims it's because he didn't want to come across as influencing the investigation, but the truth is, he was embarrassed. And he didn't want to embarrass me. That's all."

That's all? Zoe had spent months worrying about Fiona's relationship with Alistair Freeburn, and it came down to her husband dressing up and re-enacting famous events with the man?

"Thanks, Fiona," she said, shaking her head.

"Zoe." The super was looking serious again. "Don't tell anyone about this, OK?"

Zoe nodded. There were some secrets that were burdens, that dragged her down and had her questioning every decision she made.

This wasn't one of them.

CHAPTER ONE HUNDRED THREE

Tom raised his glass and looked around the table. They were all there, the four of them. Aaron knocking back a double whisky, the boss on her third lemonade of the evening, Nina polishing off something green that looked more like a cleaning product than a drink.

Tom was sticking to lager.

He wasn't sure why they'd picked the Miner's Yard. Only a few hours earlier the sarge had been standing at a window having his throat cut, and now he was getting hammered in a pub notorious for the time Tom and Nina had found a murder victim in the toilets. They were toasting a man who'd lied to them all, who'd used his status within the police to sell drugs. The worst kind of person.

But the sarge had insisted he was fine. The Miner's Yard was comfortable and friendly, even if Tom had to close his eyes every time he walked to the loo. And Huz might have been all that, but he'd sort of been a friend, too. One of the team. They'd all got on with Huz.

This was hard. For Stella and Caroline, it would be even

worse. He'd speak to Caroline. Call her. Just to make sure she was OK. It was the right thing to do.

"My round," said Nina, and got up before anyone could tell her what they wanted. The sarge started to follow, then peeled off for the toilets.

It was just Tom and the boss. And he was already half-drunk.

"You did good work," she told him. "You and Nina. All three of you. You found Topper."

He nodded. None of it would bring Huz back.

"How are things?" she asked.

He shrugged. "Fine."

"You over Harriett Barnes, then?"

He stared at her. It wasn't like the boss to be this direct. Nina, yes, and with a lot less delicacy. But he'd never discussed his personal life with DI Finch. And certainly not his brief relationship with Harriett Barnes.

It was definitely lemonade she was drinking, wasn't it?

"Fine," he said, stammering slightly. She looked around the pub.

Nina was still at the bar. There was no sign of the sarge, and the people at the tables around them were so drunk they could hardly hear each other, much less anyone else.

"I need to ask you something, Tom." The boss was leaning over the table, towards him, her voice low.

He leaned forward to hear her more clearly. "What?"

"How long has she been at the Hub?"

"Who?"

There was a flash of something like annoyance in the boss's eyes. "Harriett Barnes, Tom."

"Oh, right." Maybe he was more than half-drunk. But

this, he remembered. He'd noticed Harriett Barnes the moment she arrived.

"She started about two months before you got here, boss."

The boss nodded, her gaze distant. He sat back, hoping the conversation was over.

Thirty seconds later, she leaned forward again.

"How well do you know her? What's her background?"

Anyone else, he might have decided he'd had enough. Told them if they were so interested in Harriett Barnes, to ask her themselves.

But this was the boss. She didn't start conversations for no reason. Even on a casual night at the pub.

"Raised in Carlisle," he said. "School there. Leeds University, trained in Yorkshire—"

"Harrogate?" she asked.

"Leeds, I think. West Yorkshire, anyway."

"What else can you tell me?"

What else could he tell her? He hardly knew Harriett at all. They hadn't been together long, but still. Had he spent the whole time talking about himself?

He knew men like that. Nina complained about them all the time. He didn't think he was one of them.

"She's got a little rented house on a terrace near the marina. Painted it herself."

"And?"

He shrugged. "She's... well, she's very focused on her work. Being professional, getting the job done as effectively as possible, without any distractions, it's her way of life."

"Forgive me, Tom, I'm not doing this just to bring up painful memories. But that's why your relationship ended, right? She didn't think it would be professional?"

He sat back and nodded. The boss understood. She was

sober, unlike the rest of them. And she wasn't doing this just to bring up painful memories. She wasn't that sort of person.

So why was she doing this?

She was looking around the pub, her eyes flicking between the bar, and the toilets, and the main door, and the ceiling...

She was avoiding eye contact.

"Boss?" he said. She glanced back at him, smiled, then looked away again.

Why had she been asking all those questions? She was his boss. A DI. From Birmingham. She was good at her job – he'd learned more from her in a year than he'd learned in his whole career before then. She had a son who was a student somewhere in Scotland. She lived in Whitehaven with her partner, who also worked for the police, in...

His mouth fell open.

"Boss," he said.

She turned to look at him, and he saw her realise what he'd realised. What she was driving at.

Behind her, the toilet door opened and the sarge emerged, stumbling slightly as the door hit his side on the way out.

"What, Tom?"

"Harriett," he said. "You think she's PSD, don't you?"

CHAPTER ONE HUNDRED FOUR

OF ALL THE places to have this conversation, a crowded pub wasn't the best choice. And Tom was drunk. He couldn't even keep his eyes on her face, kept looking past her at...

Zoe turned. Aaron was making his way back, bumping into tables and apologising with a cheery grin that seemed to be working. No one was shouting at him, at least.

She turned back to Tom. "Not now, Tom. Keep this to yourself, OK?"

He stared at her.

"Tom?"

"Sorry, boss. Yes. Got it. Mum's the word."

He put a finger to his lips. She hoped he didn't get much drunker than he already was. Although Aaron was giving them all a run for their money on that front. She'd never seen the DS in that state.

It wasn't every day you found yourself being held at knifepoint by a murderer.

He stumbled again as he took his seat, and knocked the table, mercifully free of drinks. Nina returned a minute later, with the next round. Tom almost lunged for his beer, and Zoe watched as he gulped down nearly half a pint without a break.

"You thirsty, Tom?" Nina said, nudging her friend. "Didn't think I was up there that long."

Tom nodded blankly and wiped his mouth. Maybe he'd get so drunk, he'd forget they'd ever had this conversation. Zoe turned to Aaron, already putting down his empty glass and gazing into the middle distance.

She had to do something about that.

Aaron had been in a bad way for weeks. Months, maybe. He didn't seem to want to go home at night, and he was always in when she arrived. Tom and Harriett aside – and there were special considerations in play there – it wasn't Zoe's place to dig into her team's private relationships. But if she had to guess, she'd say things weren't going well between him and Serge.

And, of course, he'd spent part of his day being held at knifepoint by a murderer.

She'd only really suggested these drinks because she wanted to keep an eye on him. Now he was drunker than she'd ever seen him, drunker than she'd imagined him capable of being. She wasn't sure it had been such a good idea.

"Want some air, Aaron?" she asked.

His eyes moved towards her, so slowly it was like they were being dragged there by an exhausted pony. "'s OK," he slurred.

"I don't think so. Come on, we'll get some air, the two of us."

With Tom's help, she pulled the DS to his feet and allowed him to lean on her as they made their way to the exit.

Outside, she released him, and he stood with his back to the wall, gently swaying.

"Is everything OK, Aaron?" she said.

He laughed.

"Seriously, Aaron, is there anything I can do?"

He stopped laughing and shrugged.

"No," he said.

"No, there isn't anything I can do?"

"No, everything isn't OK, boss."

She opened her mouth to tell him it was all fine, it would all be fine, he'd work his way through it. But something in his expression left the platitudes stuck in her throat.

"Everything isn't OK," he repeated. "Two people are dead because of me."

"Two people?" she asked, then shook her head. She hadn't meant to say that out loud. And she hadn't needed to, either.

He'd blamed himself for Victor Parlick since the man's body had turned up. It would be just like Aaron to blame himself for Huz, too.

"And the worst thing," he continued, "is that I've turned into a boring arsehole at home, too."

There was a pause.

"Actually," he added, "that probably isn't the worst thing."

He hiccoughed and looked at her expectantly.

She looked back at him. "Have you thought about counselling?"

He laughed again.

"What?" she asked. "Don't rule it out. They've got some brilliant people in—"

"Already booked in, boss. First session next week."

There was something different in his face. Something she hadn't seen for a while. She waited for him to go on.

"I hit a low. You must have seen it."

Zoe nodded.

"When I went into that house I was ready to die."

"You don't—"

He held up a hand, and she fell silent.

"I'm not now, though. I'm not ready to die. I want to get better, boss."

He nodded at her, and she saw it.

For weeks now, he'd been walking around with the air of a man who'd given up. On life, on work, on everything. But now, finally, the look of defeat had left him.

CHAPTER ONE HUNDRED FIVE

"Are you sure they won't mind us going there this late?"

She'd managed to persuade Aaron to go home, and had waited while he was poured into a cab under the disapproving eye of a driver she'd already tipped heavily, just in case.

Nina and Tom were heading somewhere else. It would be a late night, "a big one," as Nina put it, when trying to persuade Zoe to join them, and instead setting her firmly on the side of coming home.

And then Carl called.

"Are you still in town?" he asked.

"Yes. Why?"

"Because I've got the keys to that house again."

"Which house?"

"Hot tub," he replied, and she grinned. Nina and Tom were still waiting for her. She put her hand over the phone and told them she wouldn't be coming, and she expected them in tomorrow morning but would make allowances for hangovers.

"They really won't mind us going there this late?" she asked.

"I think they're quite keen to sell the place, love. When I mentioned we might be seeing it again, they practically begged me to go over there. Estate agent actually drove over to our place to give me the keys on his way home."

No point driving from here. The house was just a few minutes' walk from the centre of town. As she walked away from the Miner's Yard, the sound of laughter and music faded, and soon she found herself alone with her thoughts.

It had been a difficult day. But there were better signs, now. Aaron had looked like he meant it, about turning things around. Zoe hoped Tom wasn't drunk enough to tell Nina about their conversation. She still wasn't sure herself. But the way he'd reacted – it had been Tom who said it, not her. As if the idea was somewhere in his head already, waiting to be unlocked. She smiled to herself, and then her phone rang.

It would be Carl, wondering where she'd got to.

"Nearly with you," she said.

"DI Finch," said a familiar male voice that definitely wasn't Carl's. It took her a moment to place it.

"Ryan?"

"Listen. I know I told you I wasn't interested in speaking to you again."

She rounded the corner onto Scotch Street. "I think your exact words were, 'You'll forgive me if I say fuck off and don't call again.'"

"Yeah," replied Ryan. "Sorry about that. Listen, DI Finch, maybe I was a little hasty."

"You're willing to help?" She could scarcely believe what she was hearing.

"Maybe," he said. "I'm not sure. The thing is, DI Finch, I

could use a favour. What do you know about a woman called
Sinead Conway?"

CHAPTER ONE HUNDRED SIX

IT HAD BEEN A LONG DAY. This early in the academic year, Maryan hoped their problems would be confined to home-sickness, maybe the shock of having to get up and go to a lecture or two. There'd been more than enough time for relationships to start and end, but not enough time for them to become too serious.

But she'd spent all afternoon and most of the evening trying to arrange professional care for a second year who'd decided university was too much for him, but everything outside university was, too. So she'd been dealing with the cash-strapped mental health services, until gone nine, when they'd finally come for him. She was exhausted, but she knew she'd be doing it all over again tomorrow, and the next day, the usual determination to make things just a little better for these young adults coursing through her veins.

She was about to turn the key in her front door when her phone rang, and she sighed. *More work.*

"Hello?" she said.

"Is that Maryan Khalil?"

"Yes." The voice wasn't familiar. Young. Female. A student, probably.

"It's Emma Hudson," said the woman. "You probably don't know—"

"I know who you are, Emma. Where are you? Are you safe?"

There was a laugh. Brief and bitter. Maryan knew the police had found her, then lost her again. They'd got what they needed, a description or a confirmation or whatever it was. And then they'd washed their hands of her.

"Emma? Are you still there?"

"I'm in London."

"What are you doing there?" Emma's family was in the south, somewhere. Not London. "Are you going home?"

"I don't know. That's why I'm calling."

Maryan finally had the door open. She dropped her bag and let her coat fall onto the floor.

"What do you mean? Do you need help? Because—"

"Look," said Emma. "I know I'm going to be kicked out. I've been working with drug dealers. My friend's been murdered, and I was there. I can't get it out of my head. I don't know what to do. I don't even know who to ask."

Maryan gripped her phone tight. She might not be able to fix every problem. But she could still make things a little better.

"I'll tell you what," she said. "How about you ask me?"

ZOE AND CARL trooped back downstairs, excitedly comparing their thoughts about the house, about the bedrooms, the living room, the kitchen, even the garden.

Not the huge art deco bathroom, though. Neither of them would change a thing in there.

"I'm sorry," Zoe said. She pointed to her ringing phone and walked away.

Carl looked at her with a smile of resignation. They'd agreed to this. There would be boundaries. He could do his work in private. She had to be able to do the same.

He probably wouldn't have agreed if he'd known who it was.

She answered, stepped outside, and shut the door.

"David," she said.

"I hear you've had a busy day."

It would have been in the news. Huz's death, Topper's arrest. Hopefully not the fact that Aaron had made that arrest wearing nothing but pants, socks, and his own handcuffs.

"Is this just a casual call?" she asked. Voices drifted up from the chip shop, and further down, a group of young men strode towards the door of the pub. She hated this.

Carl inside, her outside. Secrets. Deceit.

"I'm not doing this for my entertainment, Zoe," Randle shot back. "I've got better fucking things to do with my life than chase a washed-up DI across the country."

He'd been so pleasant since he'd tracked her down. But there it was. The nastiness under the urbane sheen.

"OK." She wouldn't rise to it. "What can I do for you then, David?"

"I've heard about your arrest."

"It was on the news. Everyone's heard about it."

"Not that one. The police officer. The woman."

Zoe took a step back, shocked. She looked around, as if Randle might be there, or someone working for him.

"Zoe?"

"How did you know?" she hissed.

"That doesn't matter. What does matter is that there's no way that woman was running the operation."

This was what she'd thought, herself. What Carl thought. But how did Randle know?

"And there's a pattern here. You'll have seen it yourself, of course."

Patronising bastard. She waited.

"Neither of us has time to play games, Zoe," he said, "so I'll spell it out, shall I? Whatever this operation was, they were stealing drugs from a variety of dealers, but they knew when those dealers would be getting a supply. Which means a single source. Carter."

She pursed her lips. "I know," she said. "We've already been through this."

"And as we discussed last time, when Carter finds out who it is – and that's *when*, not *if* – they'll wish they were only in prison."

"And you think Carrie Wright's working for someone else?"

"I do. And whoever they are, if Carter finds them before you do, they're dead."

"And if we find them first?"

Another pause. Her phone buzzed in her hand, and she checked the display.

A message from a number she didn't recognise. *I changed my mind.*

She frowned.

"If you find them first, Zoe, they might just be your best chance of bringing down Myron Carter," said Randle.

Who was messaging her?

It wasn't Ryan Tobin. She'd told him what she could about Sinead Conway, a local property developer, which wouldn't have been much even if she'd known more than she did. He'd listened patiently, and then he'd hung up.

So who was this? Who had changed their mind? Who had she been talking to about changing their mind?

She closed her eyes and heard the words. Her own words. In her own voice.

I hope you change your mind.

"I'm sorry, David," she said, as her phone buzzed again. "I've got to go."

Another buzz. Another. She made sure the call was dead and pulled up the messages.

An image. A photograph. A whole series of messages, and each one of them had a photograph attached.

"Thank you," she breathed, into the warm night. "Thank you, Olivia."

We hope you enjoyed reading *The Barn*. The story continues in the free novella, *The Liar's Inn*, which you can download for free at rachelmclean.com/liar-book.

Happy reading! Rachel and Joel.

READ A FREE NOVELLA THE LIAR'S INN

For DI Zoe Finch and her partner Carl Whaley, it is supposed to be a day off. A break from murder and corruption, watching the World's Biggest Liar competition, held every year in the western fringes of the Lake District. What could possibly go wrong?

But death is never far from home.

When a woman is found murdered in the dressing room, an innocent day's entertainment takes on darker tone. Professional rivalries and personal feuds that have simmered quietly are suddenly at boiling point. And, as befits the event, nobody seems to be telling the truth.

Can Zoe and her team untangle the web of lies and find the killer? Read *The Liar's Inn* for FREE at rachelmclean. com/liar-book.

READ THE CUMBRIA CRIME SERIES

Buy from book retailers or via the Rachel McLean website.

ALSO BY RACHEL MCLEAN

The DI Zoe Finch Series – buy from book retailers or via the
Rachel McLean website.

The Dorset Crime Series – buy from book retailers or via the
Rachel McLean website.

...and more to come

The Ballard Down Murder, the FREE Dorset Crime prequel

The McBride & Tanner Series – Buy from book retailers or via the Rachel McLean website.

Blood and Money

Death and Poetry

Power and Treachery

Secrets and History

Read the London Cosy Mystery Series by Rachel McLean and Millie Ravensworth – Buy from book retailers or via the Rachel McLean website.

Death at Westminster

Death in the West End

Death at Tower Bridge

Death on the Thames

Death at St Paul's Cathedral

Death at Abbey Road

ALSO BY JOEL HAMES

The Sam Williams Series – Buy now in ebook, paperback and audiobook

Dead North

No One Will Hear

The Cold Years

The Art of Staying Dead

Victims, a Sam Williams novella

Caged, a Sam Williams short